The Fate
of the
Stone

Part 1

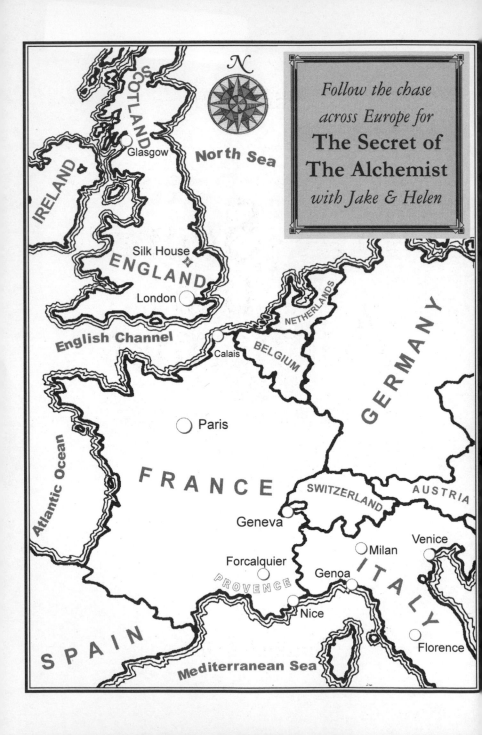

John Ward

The Secret of the Alchemist

a novel of literature and magic

Studio 9 Books

Ordering information:

United States:
Ingram, Baker & Taylor, Bookazine, Koen

Canada:
Jaguar Book Group
100 Armstrong Ave., Georgetown, Ontario L7G 5S4
☎ 905-877-4483, 📠 905-877-4410,
SAN: 118-8801
E-mail: sales@jaguarbookgroup.ca

or from the publisher (special & group orders):
Studio 9 Books / Robert Davies Multimedia Publishing Inc.
Montreal, QC H3H 1A7, Canada
☎ 514-934-5433 📠 514-937-8765
e-mail: mail@rdppub.com

United Kingdom and Europe (except France):
Worldwide Book Distribution
Unit 9, Oakwood Industrial Park
Gatwick Road, Crawley, West Sussex RH10 9AZ
☎ 44-1293-456300 📠 44-1293-536644

France:
Casteilla, S.A.
10 rue Léon Foucault,
78180 Montigny-le-Bretonneux, France
☎ 01-30-14-19-30 📠 01-30-14-19-46

We wish to thank the Sodec (Québec) and the Department of
Canadian Heritage for their generous support
of our publishing program in both French and English.

with grateful thanks to
GALE
who opened the door
&
BOB
who had confidence in me

*I am particularly grateful for the help and support
of my wife Pauline and my children
Kate, Lucy, Fergus and Patrick,
without whom this book
could not have been written.*

I

A friendship made in Hell

Above the great stone gate the legend ran:

lasciate ogni speranza voi ch'entrate

"Abandon all hope ye who enter here," thought Jake Giacometti. Not the most encouraging message. The boy who was on stage now had certainly taken it to heart. He was a tall and gangling youth, who looked as if he was made from some material that had been forcibly stretched while it was still hot, an effect heightened by the fact his costume was too small, and displayed a great deal of his wrists and ankles. He had an unfortunate habit of wringing his hands as he spoke and an expression that went with it that made him seem about to burst into tears. Perhaps he is, thought Jake. He was making a poor enough job of his recital: he stammered and repeated words, leaving huge pauses; the speed and pitch of his voice yawed wildly. From where he stood in the wings, Jake could see one half of the panel of judges, seated at a long table under an enormous banner which proclaimed in bold letters

XXVth Annual International
Dante Alighieri Festival Competition

adding below in smaller type and several languages

made possible by assistance from
the European Regional Development Fund,
Culture and Education Division

Above the banner a gigantic poster showed the striking profile of a man, wearing what might have been a helmet or else one of those hats you contrive out of your scarf in winter; his was a severe, haughty face, sternmouthed, with a long patrician nose and jutting chin that would need only a little exaggeration to turn it into a passing imitation of a nutcracker. Underneath it said:

Dante Alighieri
born 1265 ———— **died 1321**

What am I doing here? Jake asked himself, not for the first time. It was one of that large category of things that had seemed like a good idea at the time: five days in Florence, away from parental supervision, representing Scotland – it was that last bit had clinched it for him, even if the truth was that of all the people in Scotland (or to be more exact, that small part of the Scots-Italian community who had heard of the competition) he was the only one daft enough to actually want to recite mediæval poetry in a foreign language in front of a large audience of strangers.

The stretched boy, all hope abandoned (and a glimpse at the judges showed he had reason there) ploughed relentlessly on. The piece he had chosen was where Dante, at the very start of his guided tour of Hell in the *Divine Comedy*, almost gets no further than the banks of Acheron: as soon as he steps aboard the ferry, his living weight makes it sink lower in the water and Charon, the infernal ferryman, is all for ordering him off until Virgil (Dante's guide) intervenes with all his talk about friends in high places and special permissions.

Jake had begun to wish that Charon had stuck to his guns and insisted on his right to ferry only dead souls – then there would have been no poem, and no need for him to stand anxiously in the wings seven centuries later, waiting to go on. However, he had been on stage often enough before to recognise that he always felt this way at this point, although he could have wished for a more inspirational act to follow: failure could be infectious in this game. He hoped the girl beside him, who was on next, would be better.

He stole a quick glance at her and was surprised to find that she was following the boy's performance with tense concentration, fists clenched, lips forming the words he ought to say, as if she was a coach urging on an unpromising pupil: she certainly seemed to know the passage better than he did. At every blunder she would grit her teeth and shake her head in irritation. She was a strikingly good-looking girl, in a severe sort of way, thought Jake, though not really his type. *As if you had a type*, his scornful inner monitor mocked him. *Who are you kidding, Mr. Man-of-the-World abroad-on-his-own for the first time ever?*

The stretched boy had finished at last: the audience applauded vigorously out of sheer relief, but the judges kept their eyes fixed on the table in front of them. The boy fled the stage at once: he was supposed to wait and welcome on the next competitor, in a show of international amity.

Jake turned to the girl, hoping she would not be upset by the breach: it was little things like this that put you off. He touched her on the shoulder, meaning to wish her well, but she spun round with such a ferocious look that Jake feared for a moment that she was going to slap him. But the sight of his hand, extended in friendship, seemed to change her mind: she looked puzzled, then took it solemnly; only when

Jake whispered "good luck" did she allow herself a small, uncertain smile.

Helen De Havilland went on stage unexpectedly warmed by Jake's well-wishing: spontaneous displays of affection were not what she was accustomed to, especially from a complete stranger – even among people she knew, cool reserve was the norm. It reminded her briefly that things had not always been like that, but it was a thought she had no time to pursue, because now she was in the spotlight, bowing to the judges, and ready to begin:

Nessun maggior dolore che ricordarsi del tempo felice nella miseria … (There is no greater pain than to recall a happy time in wretchedness)

It was a line she had come to think of as her own: she knew exactly what it meant.

In the wings, Jake's anxiety on the girl's behalf subsided as soon as she spoke: her tone was confident, her voice beautifully clear. He recognised the passage as the tale of Paolo and Francesca and smiled knowingly, because now he understood all the erotic nuances of the verse – though only because his Italian teacher had explained them to him, subtle perception not being Jake's strongest suit.

The girl spoke superbly, with genuine feeling, and Jake could almost see them before his eyes, the doomed couple, beautiful Francesca da Rimini and Paolo, her ugly husband's handsome young brother. They are innocently reading a book together – the tale of noble Lancelot, and his illicit love for Guinevere, wife of his King. Each is thinking of the lovers in the story and of their own situation, alone together and so close they are almost touching: then, when the lovers in the story kiss, they chance to look up at the same time, and each sees in the other's face the same thought – the color rises to their cheeks; they "kiss all trembling"; and, as Dante discreetly states it

Quel giorno più non vi leggemmo avante
(We read no more that day)

When Helen finished, there was a moment of hushed calm, then from all around the theatre came cascades of rapturous applause. The judges beamed, then they too stood and applauded. The chief judge, an old white-haired man sporting the colorful sash and ornate silver star of some state honor, gestured Helen across and, leaning over the table, embraced her warmly, kissing her on the cheeks, then shaking both her hands enthusiastically. It was some time before the tumult subsided and Jake was able to take the stage.

As always, his nerves vanished the instant he stepped out. The girl stood facing him, and he focused his attention on her as he crossed to the spotlight. She was radiant now, transfigured, as if the warmth of the audience had got inside her and lit her up: she held her hands out to Jake in welcome and embraced him like a long-lost friend, pressing her cheek close against his so that he could smell the scent of her hair. "Good luck," she whispered, her lips brushing his ear.

Jake spoke his piece like a man inspired: it was as if he had become Ulysses, the great Greek hero, and no longer stood upon a stage, but the deck of his ship, exhorting his crew:

O brothers, who through a hundred thousand dangers have reached the West –

The audience did not exist for him: instead he saw his

loyal companions who had shared so many adventures gather round him once again, all older now, feeling the approach of death; saw how the spark rekindled in their eyes as he told them of his last great scheme, the ultimate adventure, to sail beyond the limits of the world to Heaven itself. Now they sped westward across uncharted oceans; now they saw ahead, hazy with distance, a mountain taller than any they had ever seen; now they were within hailing distance of the ultimate harbor and the crew rejoiced – only for a sudden storm to come and sink them at the last – "as pleased Another."

He's good, thought Helen. She had lingered in the wings, not so much to listen, as to scan the audience, even though she knew it was pointless. Of course he won't be there, she chided herself, but went on looking all the same. That her father would have come all the way from London to watch her was, she knew, not at all likely – for a start, he had no reason to know she was even taking part in the competition. But he might just have phoned The Aunts, her more optimistic side persisted, though that too was highly unlikely, since her guardian Aunts – her mother's older sisters – despised and distrusted her father, whom they regarded (not without cause, she had to admit) as a fortune-hunting confidence trickster.

But he might have phoned about the Collection, she persisted, determined to forge a possible route which might have brought her father there tonight. In his brief time of being married to Helen's mother (now in America, alternating fresh bouts of marriage with attendance at various expensive rehabilitation clinics) he had done a lot to catalogue the numerous family treasures languishing unseen in the bank vaults in Geneva. He had even organised exhibitions, adorning the blank walls and draughty corridors of the dreary châteaux where her family lived in

Swiss seclusion – "mausoleums" was Helen's private name for them.

These displays had been condemned by the family as "irredeemably vulgar" until it became apparent that they earned considerable revenue and enhanced their social cachet, so they allowed Gerald De Havilland to retain a precarious foothold in his daughter's life as an art consultant and exhibition organiser – for The Aunts, unrepentant snobs though they were, knew the value of a good tradesman.

So, reasoned Helen, he might just have phoned The Aunts about the Collection and they might just have told him she was to be in Florence and he might just have come to see her. No he wouldn't, Helen corrected herself, strictly truthful even in her fantasies. Though she loved her father, she was under no illusions about his worthiness as a parent: she knew only too well how feckless and neglectful he could be; but at least he was alive, which was something her Aunts had never been, it seemed to her, just as they had never been young, having been created by some patent process at the age of forty-five out of whalebone and clockwork.

But all the same her father might have been coming to Florence anyway, because there was that man with the shop in the Via Gabriele, not far from here, who was a business associate of his – what was his name? It wasn't Italian – Warlock? No, Orloc, that was it, Victor Orloc – he might have been coming to see him and he might have phoned The Aunts and they might have told him she was here and he might have seen a poster on the way and he might have remembered and –

A sudden burst of applause cut through her thoughts: the boy had finished. Helen abandoned her fantasy and joined in the general acclaim.

*

After the contest, they found themselves together once more, in the long queue of prizewinners trying to wait patiently for the ancient shuffling dignitary to present each in turn with certificates, medals or trophies. They exchanged looks of comic boredom, with much rolling of eyes and grimacing.

When at last they were released into the refreshment hall, it was as if a dam had burst: all the pent-up nervous energy of performance, held back by the protracted awards ceremony, gushed out in a huge surge of emotion. Everyone was a friend, jostling together in little groups, juggling heaped-up plates of food and glasses of drink as they laughed and joked in a multitude of languages.

Even Helen, who had a horror of people her own age and generally held aloof from them, found herself infected with the general mood of gaiety. She recognized the boy beside her as the one who had played Ulysses, and hailed him in courteous Italian:

– *Buona sera, Ulisse, come sta?*

Jake, remembering that Helen had been Francesca da Rimini, replied in kind:

– *Sto bene, grazie, Francesca, e lei? Ha parlato molto bene.*

– *Grazie tanto, anche lei.*

When they got to asking one another's names, Jake said "Giacomo Giacometti" at which Helen's eyes lit up and she launched into a stream of fluent Italian too rapid for him to follow. Jake set aside his plate and glass (he found it a lot easier to speak Italian if his hands were free) and began to explain that he wasn't really Italian at all, but a Scot from Glasgow. He had some difficulty making himself clear, not only because of his limited vocabulary, but also because the noise level around them had risen suddenly: the fun in another part of the hall was becoming boisterous.

All at once he was barged in the back with such force that he went sprawling, and at the same time the crowd seemed to draw away to one side, so that when he sat up he found himself in a large open space. Towering above him was a much older boy, but he seemed less concerned about Jake than something that was happening on the other side of the room.

– To me, to me, Alessandro! he shouted in Italian.

Jake saw that a group across the way were throwing some object to one another, rugby style, while others tried to intercept it, jumping up to block it, or throwing themselves in wild diving tackles. The majority of people had drawn back to a safe distance, happier with the role of spectators, but there were quite a few keen to participate, mostly larger, older boys. The shouts of the boy who had barged into Jake were heeded at last, and from across the room the object came in a high, looping trajectory. The boy stood poised, eyes fixed on it as it dropped.

It was too good an opportunity to miss: Jake rolled to his feet and sprang deftly to intercept. A cheer went up from the watchers. As he caught the object, Jake saw it was a model of Dante's head, presumably someone's prize. The boy he had beaten to it lunged after him, but Jake sidestepped and he went sprawling on his face. Another cheer went up; a large boy planted himself in his path, but Jake shimmied and darted into the space, the head tucked under his arm. Others in the group closed in, intent on bringing him down, but in a movement of fluid grace he dodged between them, then slung the head sideways toward Helen, who was watching uncertainly, not really sure if she approved.

– Hey, Francesca! Catch!

Hardly thinking what she did, she caught it neatly, one-handed, but found herself confronted by the boy who had gone sprawling; she made as if to pass it over his head, and he leaped ponderously upward, arms raised, but Helen had ducked down and dodged aside.

– Hey, Francesca!

Jake had found space again, and she sent the head curving toward him; her ponderous opponent slewed round and lumbered after it, along with several others, all converging on Jake. Things looked bad for him, but he was nimble and elusive, and a shout and a pass brought another onlooker into the game on his side. Helen found herself moving across in support: it would have amazed the games mistress at her school to see snooty Miss De Havilland, who would only ever play individual sports like fencing and tennis, take an active part in an improvised rugby match.

More and more people were drawn into the game by Jake's skilful running and throwing, and at some point it evolved from a simple attempt to keep the head from its original owners to a more coherent effort to carry it to the farther end of the room, as if that were the scoring area.

It was an unequal contest physically, but flair and invention were on Jake's side: he had a genius for wrong-footing his heavier opponents, and he danced and twisted his way among them. His witty style seemed infectious: the head was flicked from hand to hand, now high, now low; it was passed to and fro along the line, and smuggled out of rucks and scrums. Try as they might, their opponents just could not regain possession. Helen ran with the rest, in a wild whirl of enjoyment, adding her own share of nimble running and cleverly disguised passes.

At last a deft manoeuvre brought Jake close to the wall, but a phalanx of hefty opponents looked set to pulverize him. For a moment that seemed to last an age he stood

mixed 05/2003
spi_dj@hotmail.com

poised on the balls of his feet, the head balanced in his hand, as if at a loss; the phalanx converged; there was a collective intake of breath.

– Hey, Ulisse! To me! shouted Helen, and she saw him turn, ducking under a diving opponent's arm, to screw the head out to her; she caught it one-handed in full stride, dodged round a flailing opponent and struck it against the wall, embedding Dante's jutting nose in the plaster. A great cheer went up as she stood, arms upraised in a gesture of triumph, the head of the poet held aloft, looking for all the world like some fierce Amazon who had just decapitated her opponent.

Jake limped over to her, panting with exertion, and she made an elaborate pantomime of presenting him to the crowd, holding his arm up in salute like a boxing referee. The crowd cheered and clapped, and Jake leaned across and kissed her, to renewed cheers, whistles and catcalls.

As the clamor died away, the evening came to an end, as surely as if it had been signalled. People began to drift apart, looking for the exits. An older boy came and retrieved the head from Helen; he ruffled Jake's hair with friendly aggression and said something in Italian which he couldn't quite catch.

– Phew, I could do with some fresh air, said Jake.

Helen felt that her own cheeks must be glowing pink.

– Me too. Look, there's an exit behind that curtain.

Jake, a law-abiding soul at heart, saw that it was a fire exit, marked "for emergency use only", but Helen in her present mood was not one to be troubled by mere technicalities. She felt on top of the world, and flung open the door with the imperious air of a queen emerging from her palace. Jake followed obediently.

Outside, they found themselves on a steel platform, with steps on one side leading down to the street and on the other a vertical ladder going upwards.

– Come on. Let's go onto the roof.

Helen set off before Jake had time to respond. The night felt cool against his cheeks; there was magic in the air. Why not? He shrugged, and toiled upwards.

The sky overhead was brimming with stars. Below them, they could see the city spread out, its prominent landmarks floodlit.

– Look, that's Brunelleschi's dome, said Helen. The tower beside it is Giotto's. That's Arnolfo's tower, on the Signoria – see that very tall thin tower over there? I think that's my favorite building of all time. That's where the Uffizi is – you know, the Art Gallery? There's a corridor runs from there across the top of the Ponte Vecchio. I love Florence.

– It's the first time I've been here.

– Where do you live again?

– In Glasgow. Scotland.

– Tell me about it, commanded Helen.

So Jake did. He was good at describing things, and a natural mimic: Helen could almost see the great horde of the Giacometti clan in front of her, all clamoring round the Sunday dinner, all talking at once.

– I think I'd like that.

– I don't know, it gets pretty loud. No wonder Nonna's deaf, after ninety odd years of listening to it.

– I like noise, declared Helen, surprising herself with this revelation. Noise and bustle and life!

– And playing rugby with Dante's head, added Jake.

Helen gave a rueful laugh.

– I feel a bit guilty about that, actually.

– Come on! It was great fun!

– Yes, but it was – sort of – Oh, you wouldn't understand.

– Try me.

– It was, well, disrespectful.

– Disrespectful!? snorted Jake.

– There, I knew you wouldn't understand, snapped Helen.

– Keep your wig on, said Jake, I mean Dante's hardly going to mind, is he? Not after seven hundred years!

– It isn't that. It's just that he's always been, well, a kind of hero of mine, ever since I was a little girl.

– Unusual sort of hero.

– You think so? Maybe you'd prefer something else then: a hero whose mission is to penetrate an ancient underground city, where all sorts of people are held prisoner and tortured in terrible ways. His only help is from one of the locals, who offers to guide him. They work their way deeper and deeper underground, encountering all sorts of dangers along the way and outwitting these terrible creatures that try to stop them, until finally they come to the frozen center of the city, and there is a huge great monster trapped up to the waist in ice. The only way they can escape is to climb down his body and squeeze through the hole in the ice to the other side. How would that be? More your sort of thing?

– Much more like it. In fact, I'm sure I've seen that film.

– I doubt it, unless it was called "Divine Comedy I : The Inferno." Now she slipped into a rich American accent. "In Hell, everyone can hear you scream! Join all-action hero Dante Alighieri and his trusty sidekick Virgil as they carve their way through the Infernal Regions."

– I'm afraid I only read the bits they set for the competition, confessed Jake. You make it sound really good, though, he conceded.

– I think it's brilliant, said Helen. There's no book like it!

She gave a little laugh.

– I even built a model of the Inferno once. I told my Aunts I was making a doll's house – they're much happier with that kind of thing. I worked on it for ages. It had all the different circles of Hell, complete with the characters, all cut out of cardboard, and a little Dante and Virgil. I even had a little cut-out me: I used to make believe I had wandered into Hell and got lost, and Dante would come and rescue me.

She paused, as if the recollection had stirred some sadness.

– When I was younger, of course, she added hastily.

She fell silent, and Jake sensed she was embarrassed to catch herself blurting out these childhood confidences. They sat like two new children in a quiet corner of the playground, surprised by their own boldness in talking to one another. Then across the rooftops came the distant rattle of a night train and the poignant melancholy bray of its two-tone horn.

– That sound always gives me the shivers, said Jake.

– Wish my dad could've been here, said Helen reflectively.

– Was he supposed to be?

She looked round, as if surprised to find Jake still there.

– Not really. It was just an idea I had, that he might come. Come on, she said briskly, It's too cold to be sitting up here.

2

An artist at work

Helen's fantasy about her father had been, by chance, uncannily accurate. Although she was right in her eventual surmise that he had not been in the audience, Gerald De Havilland was indeed in Florence, and at just about the time when she was thinking it, in Victor Orloc's shop. What was more, not only had he phoned The Aunts, he had been to see them in person – something almost unprecedented since the separation. And it had been about the art collection, or rather a particular painting in it, which was now (although The Aunts did not know this) heading across the border into Italy, concealed in an antique writing desk.

The concealment (the desk had a number of secret compartments) was almost certainly unnecessary. De Havilland could probably have taken the article across the border openly himself, but a childish love of subterfuge combined with the fact that he did not entirely trust the people he was dealing with had made him opt for the clandestine route. He had known Victor Orloc long enough to be sure he could not trust him, and he trusted the man he · was representing in this matter even less. That man was Aurelian Pounce. De Havilland had never met him, but knew something of his reputation. Ostensibly an art dealer, he was reputed to dabble in black magic. From the little he knew of it, De Havilland reckoned that such people were of two sorts: harmless cranks, who had a certain amusement value when they were not overwhelmingly boring, and unpleasant fanatics, who were best steered well clear of. Pounce was one of the latter. He was certainly not a man to cross.

One of the prime requirements of being a con man (perhaps even the cause of someone's becoming a con man in the first place) is a capacity for boundless optimism. No matter what the odds, the con man always believes that somehow *he* will get away with it, even if no one else would; and so often, that is all it requires. Sheer cheek carries it off: no one is willing to believe that anyone would take such a risk, so they do nothing to guard against it, do not even entertain the possibility. Thus it was that Gerald De Havilland, despite his client's fearsome reputation, had already begun to consider double-crossing Aurelian Pounce.

It was not any certain knowledge about the article in question, but only his trader's instinct that had prompted him. He was always wary when someone offered at first bid a more-than-fair price to obtain any article. If the client was willing to pay that much, how much more must it be worth?

The object was certainly worth a great deal more on the open market than Pounce was offering for it, but then his chances of reselling it openly were nil. So there must be something else about it that made it valuable, or more probably some*one* else – another buyer again behind Pounce, one of those fanatical millionaire collectors who simply must have the thing they have set their hearts on, no matter what it cost. And if that was the case, why bother with Pounce at all? It was the oldest adage in the trader's book: cut out the middleman. The only problem would be discovering the identity of the ultimate buyer, but to an eternal optimist like Gerald De Havilland, that was simply a challenge, not an obstacle.

The interior of Victor Orloc's shop was cast in gloom, a
fit setting for the shadowy business to be transacted there.
The only light came from an antique table lamp, heavily
shaded so that the glow it emitted seemed to fall nowhere
useful, serving only to illuminate parts of all sorts of things,
but nothing in its entirety. The sinuous curves of bronze
statues gleamed; an angular slice of hanging rug stood out
in brilliant color; the moon face of an antique clock loomed
eerily out of the surrounding dark. Although it could only
be an illusion, for the light was static and there was no
current of air in the room, there was nonetheless a
persistent impression that the shadows round the table
where the two men sat moved and shifted like restless
watchers.

My guilty conscience, thought Gerald De Havilland,
whose Catholic childhood, long submerged by the
disappointments of adult life, was apt to resurface at
awkward moments. He looked with an uneasy smile at the
man across from him. The light caught his thick bottle-glass
spectacles, making him look as if he had huge discs of light
for eyes, which combined with his elongated and angular
figure gave him the aspect of a giant insect.

– A favor, Victor, before we get to business.

– A favor?

The dry whisper was like an echo.

– I have a writing desk – nice old thing, had it for
years, not worth much – always meant to sort out some
missing inlay. Wondered if you might see to it?

– Certainly. You have it with you?

His inflection suggested some slight surprise that a man
should bring a writing desk all the way from London for a
minor repair.

– Having it sent down from Switzerland as a matter of
fact. Picked it up while I was attending to that – er – other

business. Should be here tomorrow. Thought it might make a nice present for my daughter if I had it tidied up.

– A present you say? Is there any rush? It's just that the workshop is quite full at the moment, and Pierluigi is agitating for a holiday.

The dry rustle and even tone of the voice robbed it of any human quality: it might have been an early phonograph recording.

– No, there's no hurry. Her birthday's ages yet.

– How very thoughtful of you to think so far ahead.

– Quite.

This constant harping on what he had hoped would be a minor matter irked him; perhaps what he had in mind was not such a good idea after all.

– But you didn't come here to discuss old writing desks. Did you get it?

– In a manner of speaking.

The glasses tilted: for a moment the eyes behind them were visible, grotesquely magnified.

– What does that mean? Either you've got it or you've not.

– Not so hasty, Victor old chap. You've no idea the trouble I've had even to get this far. I'm about as welcome as a glass of poison to the old biddies up there. Dam' near gave me the bum's rush before I had a chance to open my mouth. That's where the business of the writing desk came from, if you must know.

Embroidering a story as he went along was one of his specialities.

– I've managed to get the item out of the château, but only on the pretext that it needs attention from an expert. Even then the old buzzards wouldn't let me take it with me. They insisted on sending it to a bank in town, "to be called for."

– So how does that help us? Seems you've made something of a pig's ear of this, Gerald. You told me it would be simple.

– And so it will, so it will, Victor. All I need is a set of *bona fides* to present at the bank in the person of a fictitious art expert and presto! they will hand it over to me.

Orloc gave a weary sigh, as if he had suddenly seen where all this was leading.

– And these *bona fides* will cost extra, I suppose?

De Havilland looked hurt. Inwardly, he was delighted; he had always taken an almost childish pleasure in weaving his fictions, and this one was going particularly well.

– Victor, Victor! How could you? Anyone would think you suspected me of making this more complicated than it need be, in order to wring more money out of your client!

– The idea had crossed my mind, said Orloc heavily.

– Well, I'll tell you what, Victor. The *bona fides* will cost money, there's no doubt about that, although I should be able to call in a favor or two and get them cheaper than anyone else might – but to show my own good faith, Victor, I shall bear that cost myself – regardless. Of course, if your client did feel disposed to compensate me for the extra trouble I have taken on his behalf, I'll not say I would refuse it; but if not, well, I make him a free gift of it. You're quite right to say it wasn't in the original bargain, Victor, and Gerald De Havilland is a man of his word.

He beamed on him, radiating a generosity which, at that moment, he had convinced himself was perfectly genuine – if the story had been true at all, that is how he *would* have acted. He had a weakness for the noble gesture, in stories if not in life.

– I'm sure my client will be happy to recompense you for any *genuine* expense you have been put to on his behalf – *when* he has the goods.

– Of course, but you do understand it will take a little longer than we originally thought.

–Than *you* originally *said*, Gerald. How much longer?

That was the question. As so often, he appreciated the true artistry of his fabrication only in reflection. He saw now that his brilliantly improvised fiction – for he had invented it all since coming into the shop, without the least forethought – had not only bought him time to identify the mystery man behind Pounce, but if he was unable to do so, it still left him the option of selling to Pounce at the original price. He really had to work quite hard to keep the grin off his face, and put the effort into building up a pucker of frowns, as if making a complex mental calculation.

– Well, he said at length, studying a point in the air above Orloc's head, let me see. There's at least two people I have to see who could do the job: that's a question of who comes through cheaper. Then there's the job itself: the papers are straightforward enough, but there's references to set up too in case they check them out – they generally do these days –

– How long, roughly? demanded Orloc impatiently. A week? Two weeks? Longer?

– Oh, two weeks at the outside, Victor – ten days would be my guess. Less, with a fair wind.

He knew of old that there was no harm in making an optimistic initial estimate – you could always extend it for "unforeseen circumstances." People expected it: no one took a first estimate seriously in this game.

– Yes, ten days should see it done and dusted, Victor. That suit your client, do you think?

– It's going to have to, isn't it?

Time for a little righteous indignation.

– Look here, I think you're forgetting what I'm actually doing here – it's my neck on the line, you know. As it is, I doubt if I'll be able to show my face in Switzerland again. Had you thought of that? My daughter *lives* there, for God's sake!

Mr. Orloc was most apologetic. He had not thought of that. Of course, until that moment, neither had Gerald De Havilland.

– Well, he said huffily, no one likes their efforts to go unappreciated. Your client is not the only one paying a price for this transaction, you know.

Orloc was now at pains to mollify him. He made soothing noises, and from somewhere underneath the table produced a bottle of brandy and two glasses.

– I see now why you made such a fuss about that writing desk. I'll see to it myself if you like.

Another bonus of his handiwork! It had never occurred to him that the desk must now be viewed as the parting gift of a self-exiled father to his daughter. Like any true artist, he could admire his own work, because he knew how little he was consciously responsible for its complex brilliance – it was a gift, truly a gift. He raised the glass to his lips.

– Most excellent brandy, Victor. Quite up to your usual exacting standard.

Although he was now anxious to be on his way, Gerald De Havilland forced himself to linger. The habit of deception was ingrained in him: he hated to think that his outward actions gave any clue to his real intentions. He had allowed a generous margin to get back to his hotel, slip out, and catch the train; he could cut a fair slice off it if need be. He would far rather catch the train by the skin of his teeth than give Orloc the least indication that he was eager to be gone.

Fortunately, Orloc seemed to have no desire to prolong the meeting. He downed his brandy with unseemly speed and pointedly returned the bottle to its place of concealment. Perversely, De Havilland sipped his glass with exaggerated deliberation.

– Really, Victor, I am surprised at you. A man in your business should have more respect for antiquity. A fine old vintage like this should be savored, not tossed down like potato vodka!

– You must excuse me, Gerald, I have early business tomorrow.

– Shame you have to chase me. We could have made a night of it.

He drained his glass, smacking his lips with relish.

– Still, another time, Victor?

– Another time, Gerald, as you say.

Orloc shepherded him to the door through the furniture-crowded shop.

– My respects to your client, and my apology for the delay.

– I will be sure to convey them.

Orloc bundled him out the door, shooting the bolts home as soon as it was closed, as if he feared his guest would try to force his way back in. De Havilland stood for a moment feigning dismay at this early conclusion to the evening's entertainment, then went on his leisurely way, grinning broadly at his own cleverness. Once around the corner he was inclined to hurry his pace, but at that very moment a taxi appeared, plying for hire. Fortune was indeed smiling on him tonight.

In the back of the cab, he reflected on the evening's work. It had gone better than he had dared hope. He had bought himself a fortnight at least, without jeopardising his original arrangement – and the story of the bank vault offered potential for all manner of further delay if necessary. Not that it should be necessary, if things continued to go as well as they had done tonight. He turned his mind to Pounce, and the question of who might be his principal.

He had been careful in his conversation with Orloc to avoid any hint that he knew his client's name. There was no specific reason for doing so, but he had found it a good general rule never to surrender information needlessly. His knowledge that Pounce was behind the scheme had come to him entirely by accident, from an unlikely source: his daughter's guardians.

His initial reception in Switzerland had been so frosty that he had almost given up there and then. No, Helen was not at home. Neither was she at school. Really, if he took a more consistent interest in his daughter's welfare instead of shooting in and out of her life like a – a comet, he would know these things. As a matter of fact she was in Florence, at the Dante Festival (As he recalled this in the taxi, the thought that his daughter was therefore very close at hand did occur to him, but only briefly. As it happened, she was just then playing a game of rugby with a resin model of the Florentine poet's head). It was only when he had mentioned the item that interested him that, strangely enough, the atmosphere had thawed and he had discovered that there was someone whom The Aunts loathed even more than him.

That! – how curious that he should ask about that particular article! That vile man, what was his name? had talked his way in here – the butler really should have known better – and asked if he might see it. Of course they had refused. But that was not the end of it! The unspeakable creature – to take such a liberty, with a girl of Helen's age! She had been really quite upset.

So, to his credit, had her father been on hearing this; although he also saw the advantage in establishing some common ground with The Aunts. It seemed that the man

Pounce, – yes, that was his name, he had left his card but they had thrown it on the fire – Aurelian Pounce, a ridiculous name, what sort of person had a name like that? Anyway, he had quite unwarrantably been left to his own devices while he was announced – that butler really should be sacked, but trained staff were so hard to come by these days – and had taken the liberty of wandering about the house, looking – so he said – at the paintings.

He had represented himself as an *art dealer* (the lowest form of life, like you, their pointed emphasis made clear) and had somehow bumped into Helen and engaged her in conversation. No, that was bad enough of course, but that was the least of it: on the pretext of asking her to study some detail of a painting he could not make out – eyesight was bad, he claimed – he had waited until she had leaned forward and incredibly, had snipped off a lock of her hair!

Gerald De Havilland, who had steeled himself to expect some more flagrant assault, was hard put to it not to laugh. He thought he knew his daughter well enough to suppose that she had not borne the affront meekly, but for the benefit of The Aunts he had composed his features in a fair semblance of disgust. The opportunist in him was quick to seize the moral high ground: who were they to lecture him on parental responsibility, when such a thing had happened under their very own roof? Would he not be entirely justified in calling into question their competence as guardians? He might not be able to offer his daughter the trappings of wealth, but he did think he could at least ensure that she was safe from molestation.

After which they had been putty in his hands. He needed to verify the authenticity of the article? There was some question that it might be a copy? He did not seriously entertain it, but all the same it was better to nip these things in the bud. He would need to remove it for a couple of days, three or four at most, but of course if they did not trust him he could arrange – not at all, not at all, they were very much obliged, he could take it with him that very day – was there anything else? What, that old writing desk? Why of course, it was a favorite of Helen's; but if she was away, and the inlay could be restored – which would of course enhance the value – Why, certainly!

They had parted on most cordial terms.

The taxi drew up outside the hotel. Bidding the driver to wait, he hurried in, retrieved his key, and going to his room recovered from beneath his bed a large canvas bag.

Old habits died hard: on the way out, vividly conscious of the approaching departure time of the train for Venice, he lingered nonetheless in casual conversation with the youthful night porter. Yes, he was going out again, he was not certain when he would be back – or even whether! (This with a wink, as of one man of the world to another.) But he was sure, if anyone came enquiring for him (here he folded the night porter's hand over a wad of notes) that the word would be given out that he was safely tucked up in bed, and not to be disturbed. The night porter smiled, and nodded in complicity. Gerald De Havilland sauntered out, pausing at the door to give his new-made friend a mock salute.

He made the train with half a minute to spare. His breathing and his heartbeat had not yet dropped to normal when the engine sent its melancholy two-tone howl across the sleeping city to disturb the reflections of two young people sitting on a distant rooftop.

******

An unpleasant interlude

In a shop full of polished surfaces, wood and mirrorglass, Aurelian Pounce on ballet dancer's feet shod in shining patent leather moves daintily among antique furniture and *objets d'art*, attending to an elegant female customer. His hands flutter like butterflies over the polished inlaid tabletops, dance about the sinuous bronze figures, hover round the lady's shoulders to relieve her of her cashmere shawl. And all the while his high melodious voice flutes pleasantly, discoursing of matters trivial and profound, gossip and high art, the oppressive heat and the vagaries of the antique market.

He is a man of curious contrasts: thickset and barrelchested, he moves with a feline grace. His massive head with its sleek mane of wellgroomed grey hair sprouts from bull's shoulders with no apparent intervening neck; his truculent squarejawed face is all rugged masculinity, even to the imperfection of his pitted cheeks, yet his light voice is suave, caressing, feminine; and those butterfly hands for all their delicacy of motion are like the rest of him square and strong, their backs notably hairy.

Below in the kitchen the young gypsy woman and her little girl sit warily in the warmth and apparent kindness, wanting to wolf the bread and drink the hot soup greedily, but constrained by the strangeness and opulence of their surroundings. They wonder at so many marvels in one day: the sleek black motor car with windows like mirrors drawing to a halt just where they sat begging on the station steps; the tall driver in his dark uniform that rather frightened them in this foreign land with so many different kinds of policemen; the very broad, rich-looking gentleman smelling of cologne who emerged from the back, and came and talked to them in their own language, giving them money and telling them to wait for the car again at four o'clock. No, not here but round the corner in that little street where it was quieter; and now this, hot soup and bread in the kitchen of a big house with a driveway longer than a village street. Whatever next?

Upstairs Mr. Pounce has shooed away his customer with the cashmere shawl so deftly she is unaware of it. As the shop door closes behind her, another lady emerges from the shadows at the back of the shop, tall and thin and rather older than she'd like to be, for her jet-black hair is surely dyed and her face has that tight drawn look that not even the most skilful cosmetic surgery can avoid. He calls her "Countess."

The Countess is not in the market for Pounce's usual wares: for it must be said that he does not confine himself solely to antique objects, nor the arts of painting and sculpture only; his province extends to ancient knowledge, of a secret and forbidden sort, and the practice of arts sinister, occult and dark. In his dealings with the Countess he drops much of his fluttering affectation; between the two of them there is a steely directness, as of people who know and understand one another only too well. Though eager and impatient the Countess holds herself in check: Aurelian Pounce is not a servant, but a partner – she hopes; but she fears he is already more than that.

– And so, the preparations are in hand?

– They are complete, my dear Countess; I have procured the final ingredient this very afternoon.

– Am I to have my little servant then, to fetch and carry me what I please, to watch others unseen, to pry into secret places?

The eagerness on her face transforms her a moment into a grotesque caricature of the greedy schoolgirl she once was, many decades past.

– You shall have her.

– A little girl? But how delicious!

– However, I must make use of her first. There is something I must look into.

At this, the Countess's look again recalls the schoolgirl, but this time when she has been told a promised entertainment has been cancelled.

– Now, no sulks, Countess! You shall have your servant – think on that.

The Countess thinks on it: her eager look returns.

The young gypsy woman has just finished her bread and soup when she is startled by the sudden appearance of the very broad gentleman she saw before and a tall dark scrawny woman who has eyes only for her little girl. So openly greedy is her look that the mother instinctively moves to shield her child; but the gentleman speaks to her kindly in her native tongue, in such a pleasant voice; he explains that the scrawny woman – he calls her "Contessa" – is a very wealthy person, very learned – a *professoressa* also – who is studying all the peoples of Europe. She is especially interested in travelling people like herself, the true Romanies, the last pureblooded people in Europe. She has a passion for photography and is making a big book with many pictures, and she would be willing to pay to take some pictures of the gypsy and her little girl.

His manner suggests that here is a mad old lady with more money than sense, so where is the harm in taking some of it from her? Which is an argument the young gypsy woman can readily understand. And he produces a wad of notes, American dollars, more money than the young gypsy woman has ever seen. It will not take long, he says, but perhaps the little girl should get tidied up first? And while that is happening, they can have a drink to her good fortune. He smiles at her, then rolls his eyes archly, out of sight of the stern-faced scrawny baroness. The young gypsy woman laughs, looking even younger as she does so. Go on, she tells her child, this mad old hag will give us lots of money to have our picture taken; you go with her now and get cleaned up, while I speak to the kind gentleman.

It is a sweet, heady wine, quite unlike anything the young gypsy woman has ever tasted; she can feel it going straight to her head. Perhaps she ought not to let the gentleman refill her glass, but on a day of wonders such as this, why should she hold back?

– To Fortune! says the broad gentleman, folding her hand round the wad of notes.

– To For ... the young gypsy woman replies, but cannot complete what she is saying, because something has gone wrong with the room: the walls are all rushing away from her and she is falling, falling into an abyss of light.

The tall chauffeur enters, and pointing at the woman sprawled across the table, mimes the action of strangulation. Pounce shakes his head; uncorking a bottle of spirits, he hands it to the other man, who pulls the woman's head back by the hair, opens her mouth, and roughly pours the liquor into her throat. She coughs and gags but does not wake. The chauffeur takes the wad of money and offers it to Pounce; again he shakes his head, indicating that he should stow it in the young gypsy woman's pocket. This he does, with an unconcealed air of puzzlement. Then he hefts the unconscious woman by her armpits and drags her out the kitchen door, which Pounce obligingly holds open for him.

Distantly, along the corridor, the little girl calls plaintively.

3
A Venetian fishing expedition

Like many other romantic improvisations, Gerald De Havilland's late-night dash to Venice turned out to be completely unnecessary. He could easily have waited until morning, and still arrived ahead of the lorry he had been hoping to meet, since it would not be in until four in the afternoon at the earliest, as the grizzled little man in the *zona artigianale* in Mestre took pleasure in telling him. It seemed that Gianluca, the driver, had a woman in Bergamo: he never came that route without a stopover.

In a moment of exasperation, Gerald De Havilland wondered why he had contrived the whole silly scheme in the first place: like so many things, it had seemed a good idea at the time. The romance of it had been a major factor, he had to concede, and his constant obsession with obscuring his movements; but it was not without its practical advantages: no need to lug the article about himself, or worry about a secure place to keep it. But why he had insisted on picking it up in Mestre instead of arranging to have it forwarded he could not think. Still, he was not one to dwell on his mistakes. There might be few worse places than Mestre to spend a day of enforced idleness, but at the other end of the *Ponte della Libertà* was one of the most beautiful and fascinating cities in the world: Venice.

Venice, la Serenissima: a fantasy city in the middle of

the sea, built, ultimately, on quicksand: a city of marvellous contradictions, a Byzantine jewel in a classical setting; once, as the Serene Republic, one of the most powerful and successful business corporations in the world. Even now, in the long melancholy Autumn of its decline, a city beautiful beyond compare.

His spirits rose as he emerged from his squalid surroundings to glimpse it first where it lay glittering across the lagoon, part-wreathed in the still-dispersing morning mist, a city whose colors seemed half-dissolved in the rising light of day.

Then with a smile he remembered that Venice was where Baldassare Buonconte had his little gallery, and Baldassare Buonconte knew Aurelian Pounce. It had not been such a bad idea to come here after all, he reflected, whistling as he walked; in fact, he could scarcely have planned it better.

He found Baldassare Buonconte unchanged in the years since he had seen him: a big man with a florid complexion and a wheezing chest, whose light blue eyes, round face and hairless head gave him the look of a giant baby; immaculately dressed to match the fastidiously neat interior of his gallery; urbane in manner, if a little melancholy.

– Ah, Gerald, how good to see you! How are things? Here it is the same as always – only not so good. Venice has been dying for over three hundred years ... I only hope she will outlast me. A close-run race, I think, he added, striking his massive chest with his hand and producing a light, hoarse cough. No, Gerald my friend, things are not so good as once they were. I wonder why I keep going at all. Every year it seems the tourists are less cultured, more fearful of parting with their money – "but is he a *well known* artist?" – always that: unless the name is famous, they will not buy. No taste of their own, of course, that is the problem. Ach! Let us have coffee and a little something.

At a nearby café they sat out on the pavement watching the play of light reflected from the canal onto the façades of the buildings. After much talk of this and that, De Havilland inserted the name of Pounce into the conversation. Buonconte's response was to extend his hand downward, middle fingers curled in and held by the thumb, index and little finger pointing to the ground: the traditional sign to ward off the *malocchio* or evil eye. Although it was done with a smile, De Havilland sensed that it was not meant entirely in jest.

– Now that is a strange one, Gerald. No one seems to know where he comes from. Some say Hungary, but the Hungarians say Romania. Others again say he is English. But I never heard any claim him for one of their own. He has something of a reputation as a – how do you call it? – a witch.

De Havilland laughed.

– Witches are generally held to be female, Baldassare, with pointed hats and riding broomsticks. He's not a transvestite, is he?

– No laughing matter, Gerald. *Uno Stregone,* what is that again? Ah, a sorcerer, a wizard. A practitioner of the Black Arts. You may laugh, Gerald, but there is a lot more of that goes on than people think. It has always been a popular pastime of the rich, believe me. Why, close to this very place I think I could show you one, two, even three highly respectable people, all of whom are clients of Mr. Aurelian Pounce – and it is not his services as an art dealer I am talking about.

– And does he make a strict division between his art-buying clients and his clients for – other wares?

He had hoped to make the question sound casual, but Buonconte was a shrewd businessman.

– Now there, Gerald, it seems you touch at last on whatever it is has brought you all this way to Venice – or are you going to tell me this is purely a social call and that you are here on your holidays?

– There is no hiding anything from you, Baldassare. It happened that in a roundabout way I heard Pounce was interested in obtaining a certain item that is in my wife's family. It has what I suppose you might call occult associations, so I did wonder if he wanted it for a client or for himself. That is all.

– That is all! Indeed, I am sure that *is* all, Gerald my friend. Let me give you a bit of advice here. It would not be a good idea to think of going behind Pounce's back to try and deal directly with his client. He is not a man who would take kindly to that – what man would? But I mean that this man particularly would not take it well.

Gerald De Havilland, a little nettled at Buonconte's perspicacity, had recourse to mockery:

– Why, Baldassare, if I did not know you better, I'd say you were a little afraid of our Mr. Pounce.

– Sometimes it is wise to be a little afraid, Gerald. What is your English saying, about curiosity and cats? Here too it might be fatal I think.

– We also say that cats have nine lives, Baldassare.

– Meaning?

– That in my case if Pounce wants to skin me, then he'll have to catch me first.

– Ah, ever the lighthearted optimist – you English, you are all boys at heart.

– So just a name or two, Baldassare, to set me on my way. I'm sure I could find out some other way, so there's no reason it should come back to you.

Buonconte regarded him gravely, stroking his chin.

– This item – it is valuable?

– On the open market, certainly.

– Big money?

– Not millions. Half a million, maybe. Three-quarters with the right promotion.

– Dollars?

– Pounds.

Buonconte thought some more.

– Of course for an occultist it may have some value beyond its artistic worth.

– It might.

– Girolamo Griffolino in Arezzo and Contessa Regina D'Ambrosio in Milan. One is an art collector with an interest in the occult, the other an occultist with an interest in art. Both are certainly wealthy enough. But tread carefully, my dear friend, and remember that you did not hear their names from me.

– Names? What names?

Gerald took his leave, smiling. Buonconte watched him until he was lost in the crowd, another casual stroller in the summer heat, jacket slung over his shoulder. He liked the man – his boyish charm, his optimism, his Englishness, his naivety. However, these matters were seldom straightforward, and in this case he had other, more important loyalties to consider. He returned to his gallery and quickly dialed a familiar number, shaking his head regretfully at the wickedness of the world and the duplicity in men's hearts. After a single ring the voice he knew so well put itself at his service.

– Aurelian, how are you? Baldassare here. I've just learned something you ought to know.

Gerald De Havilland, well pleased with his progress, bought himself an ice cream and went to savor the Byzantine splendors of the Piazza San Marco until it was time to return to Mestre to meet Gianluca with his van.

Over coffee and cake in Florian's he fell to revising his plans. His original idea had been to keep the article concealed in the desk until the time came to hand it over to Pounce: with his love of theatricality he saw himself turning up at Orloc's shop, no evidence of having the item about him, enjoying the looks of consternation on the faces of the two men. "Where is it?" they would ask; "where it has been all the time," he would respond with a smile, "right here in Victor's shop, safely under lock and key." They would stare at him open-mouthed, wondering if perhaps he had gone mad; then with a flourish he would walk over to the desk, activate the hidden spring and slide the top aside to reveal what was concealed within.

He smiled, picturing it to himself – it would be an excellent scene; or would *have been* an excellent scene, he corrected himself – for he did not now intend to play it. There was no question now of storing the article on Orloc's premises when he might need to lay hands on it quickly and without interference. If Buonconte's hints put him on the right track, then his aim would be to conclude the business at once, hand over the goods and clear out to London (or wherever, he thought, calculating how much a direct deal might bring him) before Pounce was even aware of any double-dealing. He might even spin out the Swiss bank saga a little further, to give himself more time to cover his escape.

The present problem was where to put the goods in the meantime. It would have to be somewhere at once convenient, discreet and secure. Convenient, discreet, secure: something in the combination of words provided a trigger, and he smiled broadly, shaking his head in simple wonderment. Of course! The solution was at hand – it was as if his instinct had led him to the very spot and was just

waiting for his conscious mind to realise it. He had to laugh
aloud (which startled people at the next table) when he saw
how very convenient after all coming here had turned out
to be. The Kingdom of Heaven, that was the place to go.

There can be few less appropriate names than that of
the *Regno del Cielo* glassworks in Murano. It is a narrow,
dark place tucked away behind the church of *San Pietro
Martire*. More than one person has made the joke that if this
is the Kingdom of Heaven – for that is what the name
means – then it is little wonder that so few enter it. It has
been there from the beginning. "One cannot but wonder,"
one eighteenth century traveller remarked, "at the long
survival of a producer of such indifferent glass." Certainly,
if its survival had depended on the products of its factory,
it would have disappeared long ago. But the *Regno del Cielo*
provides another kind of service, one that ultimately
explains the complicated joke of its inappropriate name.

If you squeeze through the narrow doorway, you find
yourself in a tiny room: it is a characteristic of the building
that everything in it (doors, rooms, staircases and
courtyards) seems to have been cut in half. Your way is
barred by a counter, behind which are two doorways and a
man. The doorway on the right leads to a little half-
courtyard, where the glass factory is. The one on the left,
ancient and iron studded, has nothing but a corridor behind
it, a corridor lined from ceiling to floor with what looks at
first like dark wood panelling but turns out, on closer
inspection, to be a multitude of doors: the entire wall is
made up of cabinets. The man who sits between the doors is
the latest reincarnation of Fabrizio Favilla, who five
hundred years ago realised that there was more money to
be had from keeping secrets than from making glass, and in
doing so acquired the nickname San Pietro, which his
descendants have borne ever since.

St. Peter, of course, is the keeper of the keys, the keys of the Kingdom of Heaven. Fabrizio Favilla kept keys also, in time many hundreds of them: the keys of the doors in the corridor of cabinets. These cabinets in their day have housed many secrets: some precious in themselves (jewels, paintings, chests of money), some precious only to those affected by them (compromising letters, incriminating documents, and later, altered wills) but always anonymously and with great discretion.

Possession of either of the keys to a cabinet (each has two, handed over when the deposit is made and paid for) is the warrant to open it: no questions are asked, no names given, no papers signed. If someone turns up with the second key after the goods have been collected, too bad. He is shown the other key and told the cabinet is empty. No conversation is entered into. At one time the keys themselves were like currency: more than one young rake, cleaned out at the gambling tables, would make a last desperate stake of the keys to one of Sanpietro's cabinets – and such was the value of the secrets known to be stored there that it was seldom refused.

From being a keeper of keys, Fabrizio Favilla came to be known as St. Peter; from being in the charge of St Peter, his glassworks came to be called the Kingdom of Heaven. It was there, late in the afternoon, that Gerald De Havilland headed – by his usual devious route – after removing the article from its concealment in Helen's old writing desk. Having rendezvoused with the amorous Gianluca in Mestre, he had hired a van and transferred the desk into it, driving a short way to a secluded spot before transferring the goods to the large canvas bag which now nestled beside him as he sat in the puttering motorboat nosing its way across the glittering waters of the Venice lagoon.

Unexpectedly, he found himself troubled by pangs of

conscience. Not at all to do with double-crossing Pounce: it was about his daughter Helen. Handling beautiful or curious objects had always affected him powerfully: it was perhaps what had led him into the art trade. The feel of an object in his hand called up associations in his mind so vivid as to be almost real: running an antique necklace through his fingers conjured the thought of the beautiful throats it had once encircled; the smell and touch of a fine old piece of furniture evoked the long dead households where it had once belonged. So, in handling the old writing desk to open the largest of its secret compartments (it had several) he was reminded vividly and poignantly of showing the same compartments to his daughter as a child. How she loved that old desk!

The statement he had made so glibly to Orloc about not being able to show his face in Switzerland again now hit home with real force; the idea of being cut off from contact with Helen, which he had used so lightly as a counter in the game he was playing, now acquired its proper weight. It was curious that he could be so much estranged from her yet be so moved at the thought of being cut off from her completely. The truth was that although he loved his daughter, the thought of her made him feel rather helpless. She was so self-contained, self-confident, self-reliant; that's it, he thought – she makes me feel redundant. What can I do for her that she can't do herself? She had all the poise and assurance of the very rich, and her education was formidable. With a sigh, he realised that in a very few years she would have turned into a junior version of her Aunts, wanting for nothing and needing no one.

If only to prevent that, he really should make an effort to see more of her, perhaps rebuild the relationship they had had when she was younger. She had a good eye, a fine taste in art: once they had shared a lot of pleasures together, hunting round antique shops and auctions. He smiled at the recollection. The sphinx! He had forgotten that. It had become their code word for something to be kept secret from The Aunts. He used to encourage Helen to make speculative purchases, which he would then sell on elsewhere and give her a share of the profits.

The Aunts frowned on this exploitation of his daughter's funds, which they saw as motivated purely by self interest. All right, he did make something out of it himself, but it was an education for Helen, and she enjoyed it. She also enjoyed the complicity of keeping the knowledge of their purchases from The Aunts who would quiz them on their return about what had been bought and how much had been spent. If they steered too close to something, he would somehow contrive to introduce the word "sphinx" to warn her off: the easiest method, and one of the funniest, had been to incorporate it in a sneeze. He laughed aloud at the recollection.

– Sphinx! he exploded into his handkerchief.

– *Gesundheit!* said a German tourist next to him.

He could make a start by contacting her in Florence. He took out his cell phone and punched in Helen's number: assorted bleeps and noises resolved themselves into the statement that the number was unobtainable. After some cursing, a search of his wallet turned out the card on which he had scribbled, at The Aunts' behest, the address and phone number of the hotel where she was staying.

Having eased his conscience by leaving a message to meet for lunch the next day, he set off in search of the Kingdom of Heaven. A pair of cats padded after him through the sunstruck streets, winding their scrawny bodies in and out of his legs, but declined to accompany him through the narrow slit that was the mouth of the dank *Calle delle Chiavi* –

the alleyway of the keys – at the end of which Signor
Sanpietro (a grizzled dwarf of a man) received him
taciturnly. Sanpietro spoke only to name a price before
relieving him of the canvas bag and the money and giving
him in exchange a pair of incongruously modern-looking
keys. Each was stamped with a number and bore a small tag
reading "property of S. Sanpietro, Regno del Cielo
Glassworks, Calle delle Chiavi, Murano."

When he got back to the van – rather later than he
planned – his first act was to detach the tag from one of the
keys and throw it in a wastepaper bin. After all, he knew
what the key was for; there was no reason why anyone else
should. Once attached to his key ring, it blended
inconspicuously with the rest. The second key was
something of a nuisance.

He would have thrown that away too, but his fertile
imagination contrived all too readily ingenious tales of how
someone might by chance retrieve it. Keeping it on his
keyring seemed pointless – there was no sense having a
spare that you lost at the same time as the original. Keeping
it separate, without its tag, just increased the likelihood of
mislaying it. At length he hit on the idea of hiding it in the
desk. He opened another of the secret compartments, a tiny
one this time, and was rewarded by the poignant discovery
of a barley-sugar sweet and a silver threepenny bit:
treasures his daughter must have stored there. He removed
the sweet, and placed the key, tag and all, beside the coin.

He was glad of the sweet a short time later when he
found himself snarled up in the evening rush hour, with the
prospect of a long drive to Florence made longer still.

4
The morning after

The magic of the night before seldom lasts till morning. At about the time her father was in Mestre, finding that his late night journey had not been really necessary, Helen De Havilland woke to similar feelings about her own excursions of the night before. Had it really been necessary to go charging about like that making a complete exhibition of herself in a hall full of people? Playing rugby, for God's sake! And what had possessed her to go up on the roof with that boy? The way she had chattered on – baring her soul to a complete stranger! What had got into her? It was as if the euphoria of the competition had been a kind of drunkenness that had made her do all sorts of mad, uncharacteristic things, and now came the hangover. With each fresh recollection of what she had done and said she buried her head in the pillow and groaned.

Her prim and proper self was very much back in control as she made her way down to breakfast half an hour later. She sat deliberately alone and apart in the dining room, daring anyone to come near her.

Jake did just notice the girl he had been up on the roof with the night before coming down late to breakfast, looking very severe with her hair tied back and a stern expression on her face. He tried a smiled "hello" but got no response. Oh well, he thought, and then he turned his mind to the prospect of the guided tour of Florence: he was looking forward to that. He joined the excited bustle of people moving into the foyer, and was surprised to hear his name called:

   – Giacomo Giacometti! Giacomo Giacometti!

   Giacomo Giacometti, thought Helen, hearing the call. *That* was his name: only he called himself Jake. He wasn't Italian at all: he was from Scotland. She wondered what impulse had driven her to talk to him like that. They really had nothing in common. Her mind turned to other things. This was the last day of the festival: tomorrow they would be going home. She really did not fancy going back to the Swiss mausoleum. She wanted to stay on in Florence. Perhaps cousin Laura would put her up. Cousin Laura was a bit of a pain, but she had a nice flat. The Aunts would not really mind, although they would pretend to be offended that she preferred Cousin Laura's company to theirs. They too thought her a bit of a pain.

   Never one to linger once she had made up her mind, she took out her phone, only to find it completely dead. Why, she demanded of no one in particular, did this always happen to her? Other people seemed to use mobile phones with impunity. Hers, however, never seemed to work when she really needed it. Now in a thoroughly foul mood, she went through to the lounge to read.

   Jake put down the telephone he had been called to answer with a mixture of anger and indignation. The indignation was directed at his parents, and every other authority up to and including God that had the power to intervene arbitrarily in his life and stand it on its head. The anger was mainly at himself: why hadn't he said something? Why hadn't he spoken out? He had *plans* for the rest of the summer: there was that football tournament, and he was going to go cycling in Argyll with his friends, and there was that drama production that he was 99% certain (Dougie Mackinnon who was a pal of her brother had *sworn* to him) that Claire Louise Foley was going to go in for. So why, having lasted for 106 years, had Great-great-uncle Giro chosen to shuffle off this mortal coil at this particularly inconvenient moment? The funeral would be *huge*: Giacomettis from every corner of the world – not only Scotland, but America and Australia too – would feel bound to come. The whole business would probably last for a month, long enough to ruin his plans.

The trouble was he could see the logic. When his father said "We'll all be coming over anyway so you might as well stay there" he had answered "Right enough." He should have said "don't leave me alone in this foreign city where I have never been before in my life." When his father said "Phone your cousin Gianni in Naples and tell him you'll be coming to stay" he should have said "Who is he? I have so many cousins that I can't remember them from one day to the next; what do you mean I had a great time playing football with him when he was over three summers ago?" But in the end he had simply nodded and replied "Yes, Dad." When his father had said "You'll be all right getting the train, won't you? I don't think you have to change at Rome, but you better check" he had not screamed "Look Dad, this is Jake! I once got lost in *Motherwell*, for God's sake!" nor had he added "I meant to tell you, but I skipped a lot of those language lessons on Saturday morning at the Italian Circle and went to eat ice cream at cousin Ricci's instead."

Then when his father had concluded by asking – no, by *saying* "You'll be all right, won't you? After all, your brother

Ben wasn't that much older when he went all the way to India by himself" he had meekly said "Of course I will" instead of yelling down the mouthpiece "look Dad, do you seriously want me to travel with next to no Italian on a train to the No2 gangster capital of the universe? I mean, wouldn't you prefer me to go to Sicily? And aren't you forgetting that brother Ben is the oldest in the family, and *expected* to do things like that, and besides looked and acted like a full grown man from about the age of 12? He had to shave in primary school, for God's sake!" It was no use. When his sense of manhood, his grownupness, had been appealed to, he had nodded meekly and said "No problem Dad – what's the address? And the phone number is?"

He sloped into the lounge feeling distinctly sorry for himself. His spirits were raised a little, however, by the sight of that girl he had been talking to last night – what was her name? What he felt in need of, just at the moment, was a big sister to confide his troubles to; and this girl – Helen, *that* was her name – struck him as the closest he was going to get at short notice. Jake had two sisters, both older than he was, with a brother between them and him. Some sort of genetic throwback had transformed this brother at puberty into an archetypal Italian male: he baited his sisters ceaselessly with his macho swagger. The principal beneficiary of this had been Jake himself, who in his unselfconscious boyhood had become a great favorite of theirs. True, the relationship had operated largely in their favor (as when they had regaled him at tedious length with details of the faithlessness of their male companions) but he had received tangible benefits (as on the death of his newts). It was, therefore, with an experienced eye that he approached Miss Helen De Havilland, absorbed in her book in the lounge of the Hotel Excelsior.

There are few things more annoying when you are reading than to have someone plant himself not directly in your line of sight but a little to one side, so that you are aware of his presence on the edge of sight. Some instinct makes you want to look up, to confirm this vaguely sensed intrusion; equally you do not want to take your attention from your book. It is already too late, of course: your attention has been taken away. But at least if the person stays still, you will be able to resume reading without *too* much difficulty. But of course the person does not stay still. He makes repeatedly some movement just large enough to register with you and once more distract your attention. You could shift your position, turning away your head, but you are comfortable here, and the light is just right, and besides you don't want to yield, don't see why you should have to – you were here first.

– Go *away*! Can't you see I'm reading?

– I'm not stopping you.

Excellent, thought Jake. Communication opened already. He had known his sister to last nearly twenty minutes before a word came out.

– Yes you are, as a matter of fact. Can't you go and sit somewhere else? I thought you had gone on the tour with the rest.

– So did I, only then I got this phone call. From home.

Well lucky you, thought Helen. I wish someone would phone me from home sometime.

– My uncle's dead.

No response. Perhaps too bold a stroke. Or the wrong relative – people never know if uncles are near or far.

– Well, my great-great-uncle actually.

Still no response. What was this girl made of?

– He was 106.

– So?

At last!

– So his funeral will be massive. Giacomettis from all over the world will come to lay him to rest. So instead of going home I have to stay here and wait for them all to arrive.

– So what's the big deal? I was thinking of staying on myself as a matter of fact.

– Well no, it's worse than that. I have to stay here, by myself, and find my way to Naples!

– Ah, the poor little boy! Does he have to go all the way to Naples then all by himself?

This was good – mockery was undoubtedly good: it showed an underlying concern and even sympathy.

– It's all right for you to talk, you're used to travelling. Besides, (here he made a rapid calculation – what age was she? – sixteen probably) you must be about eighteen *and* you speak great Italian.

Helen snorted, but she was flattered all the same.

– I hate to spoil your illusions of pursuing older women, but I'll be fifteen in October.

– No kidding? What date?

– The 27th.

– Same as me. We could be twins!

– What a perfectly revolting idea.

However, like most people, she attached significance to coincidences, especially relating to birthdays. Besides, she had by now lost interest in her book, and felt in need of a little exercise.

– Look, if you really want to see Florence, I can show you around. We can even stop off at the station and buy your ticket to Naples, if you like.

A result, thought Jake, a definite result. He would

scarcely have hoped for more from his own sister.

Helen would have made a good tour guide. She knew her subject, having been trained in a rigorous school: several of The Aunts had at various times taken it on themselves to introduce her to the delights of Florence. Her presentation to Jake was to a large extent a skilful caricature of their efforts. She too was an excellent mimic, and invigorated by the sunshine and her genuine love of the city, she produced a bravura performance quite the equal of Jake's evocation of his family life the night before. Jake knew well how to be a good audience, although on this occasion it was not a difficult task. They saw the sights, ate ice cream, bought Jake's ticket, rehearsed his lines for phoning cousin Gianni from Naples station. Then they hung over the parapet of the Ponte Vecchio, watching the fish hold themselves stationary in the current beneath the old bridge.

– Do you think Dante ever did this? Jake asked.

– It all depends how *vecchio* this *ponte* is.

Jake laughed.

– Thanks for doing all this, Helen, showing me round, buying the ticket and all that. I mean, I know it's no big deal to you, but I really was dreading it. I'm always convinced that I'm waiting at the wrong bus stop, or that I've got on the wrong train – and that's only in Scotland! But I think I should make it to Naples okay, and I'm sure from there there'll be loads of cousins eager to fold me in the bosom of the family.

Helen felt a momentary twinge of envy to hear him speak so casually of something she had never known. He must have picked up something of her unease.

– What'll you do? Will you stay on here?

– For a bit, if I can reach cousin Laura.

– Then what?

– Oh, go home I suppose – back to the gay social whirl. Let's not talk about that, it bores me just to think about it.

– What would you really like to do? Now, I mean?

The question startled her; no one else had ever taken the trouble to ask her that. What did she really want? She furrowed her brow, watching the fish.

– I'd like my Dad to phone, and ask me out to lunch tomorrow. Only that's not going to happen.

– Why not? Don't be so pessimistic!

– Well, my phone's broken for one thing, and besides, it's just not something he would do, not really. Come on, it's time we were getting back.

The magic, so briefly restored, vanished again like a soap bubble bursting. They trudged grumpily back to the hotel, aware only that the day was hot, their feet were sore, their throats dry and their stomachs empty.

When they entered the foyer, it was tacitly understood that they were going their separate ways. Helen had already accelerated towards the lift when she heard her name called. She stiffened in annoyance: she had already begun to anticipate the refreshing shower she promised herself as soon as she reached her room. What was it now? Honestly, you take pity on people for a few hours and they want the rest of your life! What was the fool pointing at?

– Helen, is that you?

– No, it's a bloody noticeboard. I'm over here.

– Oh, ha ha! It says "Helen De Havilland – telephone message at reception."

Her heart leaped – it couldn't be!

But it was.

Jake had been shrewd enough not to disappear, and was among the first to benefit from Helen's incandescent smile. The girl at the reception desk, two porters and a waiter were also irradiated.

– Bad news then?

She laughed.

– You were right, he did phone!

Jake felt absurdly flattered and pleased with himself, as if he had actually somehow brought this about.

– See, I told you not to be pessimistic. And are you going to lunch?

– At the Gallo Nero at half past twelve.

– Well, that's great. I'm really pleased for you. See – sometimes wishes do come true.

Helen, delighted beyond words, grabbed hold of him and together they executed a little dance that took her to the lift, where she curtsied solemnly.

– I thank you, kind Sir.

– My pleasure, dear lady.

Jake bowed. The waiters applauded. The lift came.

5
A little night visitor

Gerald De Havilland was even later arriving in Florence than he had expected. As if the traffic had not been bad enough, he had found himself caught up in a disturbing incident at a transport café. He had just settled in what he thought was a quiet table in an obscure corner when he realised that there was someone at the table next to his, in the corner, slumped against the wall and snoring intermittently. The reek of drink from that direction suggested the slumber was alcohol induced. Peering closer, he saw that it was a young woman, a gypsy by the look of her.

Just as he was considering whether to move to another table, she woke with a start and looked about her with every evidence of bewilderment. She seemed to be searching for something, with increasing desperation. She looked around wildly, then began to crawl about the floor, moaning and talking to herself in some incomprehensible tongue. Her head appeared suddenly and alarmingly on the other side of Gerald De Havilland's table. She asked what was obviously, from its tone, a question, but in a language he could not make out. She repeated the question again, eyes wide with horror and incomprehension that he could not or would not understand; then she began to scream, pointing at him and jabbering, pulling at her hair and clothes.

The commotion brought the proprietor of the café, who made a rapid assessment of the situation. Seizing the gypsy woman, he bundled her roughly away, accompanying the action with a rapid commentary of harsh words, in which the word "Polizia" figured frequently. He pushed her out at the door, but she was not to be got rid of so easily. After a moment or two of calm, she burst into the café like a furious whirlwind, yelling and shouting, and went straight for the proprietor. He, however, was clearly accustomed to incidents of this sort: he sidestepped neatly with a speed that belied his bulk, and felled the woman with a heavy blow to the side of the head; she went down like a sack of potatoes. He shouted to someone in the back shop to phone the police, while he, paradoxically, set about reviving the woman he had just rendered unconscious.

The police patrol must have been near at hand, because they appeared right away. The proprietor – perhaps in attempt to distract from his own excessive use of force – directed them towards De Havilland. One of them ambled over, while the other attended to the now groggy gypsy. Gerald De Havilland gave a straightforward account of what he had seen, emphasising the woman's evident distress and the fact that she seemed to have lost something. Fearing to become entangled further, he said little about the proprietor's part beyond the fact that he had "removed" her. The patrolman's questioning was brief, his notes perfunctory: it was clear that he did not attach much importance to the matter. When he had finished, De Havilland asked if he might go, and the patrolman assented. He followed him back across to where his colleague was interviewing the gypsy. She seemed calmer now, perhaps still dazed, perhaps cowed by the police uniforms.

As he tried to slip past, a further distressing incident occurred. The policeman must have been asking the woman for some form of identification; she was searching her pockets, and suddenly fished out a wad of dollar bills. De Havilland smiled ruefully – here was the explanation of the cause of her distress. He only hoped that, having found it again, she managed to convince the police that she was entitled to have it in the first place; it was clearly a pretty substantial sum. He had expected rejoicing, but instead the woman thrust the wad of bills from her as if it was a live snake she had taken from her pocket. Her eyes bulged in her head: she said again the word that she had addressed to him, and looked round her at the faces staring at her uncomprehending. Then something seemed to click, and she collected herself with an effort. Forming the words with difficulty, she said in heavily accented Italian:

– My child, they have stolen my child!

De Havilland looked to the police officers, but saw no upsurge of sympathy, only an exchange of nods and glances, as if to say "we know what's going on here." He was sufficiently struck by this lack of reaction to ask the officer who had questioned him what seemed to be the problem. The officer shrugged, and rolled his eyes, accompanying him outside. He was an older man; he did not look unkind.

– These gypsies! he said. She has sold her child.

– *Sold* it? She said the child had been taken!

– Yes, she is sorry now that she is sober. But that's what they do, get them drunk and offer them money for their children.

– Who does this?

– Racketeers. Adoption is getting more difficult, all over Europe. Couples who are aching for a child will go to any lengths. These people, these racketeers, they prey on that: the rich and desperate on one side, the poor and desperate on the other. An old story, I am afraid.

– Will you be able to do anything? I mean to get the child back?

He gave a look that suggested the question was not an intelligent one.

– We will go through the formalities, of course. The woman will probably be deported.

– For having her child stolen?

– For selling it. You saw the money – she didn't get that begging on the street. As for the child, it is probably out of the country by now. This is an international racket we're talking about. Still, if there's any consolation, the child is almost certainly better off.

He clapped De Havilland on the shoulder, offered him a cigarette. He declined, and went on his way.

When he eventually arrived in Florence he found Victor Orloc little inclined to hear explanations.

– I had begun to think you were not coming.

– I told you Victor, if I start a thing I see it through.

Orloc made a noise which suggested that he had his own view on that.

Together they manhandled the desk into the cluttered, ill lit shop.

– Have you made any progress on your *bona fides*?

– Yes indeed, very promising. My first contact gave me a price that the other will find it difficult to match. But I'd still better try him, in case he can do it quicker. It should be settled tomorrow.

– My client is not pleased. I spoke to him this afternoon. He smells a rat.

– Well I hope you stood up for me, Victor!

– I told him only what you said, but he was not happy. For your own sake, Gerald, I would suggest you get a move on. My client is not a patient man. If he thinks you are dragging your feet, holding out for a better price ... he will take steps.

It may have been only a trick of the light, but it seemed to Gerald De Havilland that Orloc shuddered a little.

– Don't you worry Victor, I'll deliver the goods. Man of my word, I told you.

– It is not me you have to convince, Gerald. Please remember that.

De Havilland took his leave in the shadowed room. Orloc peered after him, looking more than ever like a giant insect with his shining disc like eyes. He drove the van wearily back to the hotel. He could drop it off at the hire depot in the morning. What he needed now, above all else, was a good night's sleep.

The uneasiness came on him as soon as he reached his floor of the hotel. The lights had been turned down, so that only the emergency lighting offered its soft, minimal glow at intervals between dark pools of shadow. As he made toward his door, he thought he saw something moving a little way ahead of him, in the area midway between two lights where the darkness was deepest. It was nothing definite: could easily have been what he told himself it was, his eyes adjusting to the dimness and creating an illusion of movement. Or was it perhaps a cat? A big one if it was. He drew level with the spot and saw that of course there was nothing there. Then looking up he thought he caught it again, this time between the next two lights.

Which shows it's an illusion, he told himself – always at the same distance from the eye. Even so he was not entirely reassured. As he fumbled with his key at the lock, the darkness deepened; the lights had dimmed almost to nothing. The unpleasant idea entered his mind that something was crouching beside him in the dark, keeping just out of sight. He felt fear rise in his throat. He dispelled it with a cough and a brisk and businesslike turning of the handle.

He purposely resisted the temptation to open the door to the minimum, slip through and slam it shut behind his back as soon as he was in. Instead he opened it slowly and deliberately and held it a moment before stepping over the threshold. Behind him, the lights blinked and came up again. See? he rebuked himself. Nothing more than a dodgy junction box. He shut the door, stepping awkwardly as he did so, just as if a cat had slipped in with him, winding its way between his legs. He reached for the light but the switch simply clicked, leaving the room lit only by the faint light from the window.

Damnation! At least there was a light by the bed, and if that didn't work then by Christ he would have that night porter rouse the manager to damn well fix it himself while he stood over him. He found that the sudden spurt of anger served to get him to the bedside without dwelling on anything else, and he was so relieved when the light did come on that he laughed aloud. It's been a long day, he thought, and the old eyes are not what they used to be. Or the old nerves either, if it comes to that. A visit to the minibar was definitely called for.

He opened the little fridge, ignoring the stubby bottles of *Nastro Azzuro* beer. Something a little stronger, if you don't mind: whisky and dry ginger ale, that should do it. He eased off his shoes and socks, flung his jacket on a chair, loosened the neck of his shirt. Drink in hand, he padded back over to the bed. *Was* that something, over in that dark corner? Don't start that again! He stretched out on the bed, taking generous sips. Be finished this in no time – should've brought another one across. Damn bottles too small, encourage you to drink more, then you find your bill has spiralled. Still, to hell with poverty!

He set the remains of the drink on the bedside table and went back for fresh supplies. He returned with all the spirits and all the mixers, making a point of not looking toward the dark corner of the room. You'll regret this in the morning, he told himself as he mixed a gin and tonic to follow the whisky.

However, the short term effect was what he hoped for: his body relaxed, his mind slowed, and a heavy drowsiness crept up on him. His last conscious act was to reach across and switch off the light.

As a child, he had been visited by the nightmare of being fixed to the bed, unable to move. It was not that he was tied or held in any way – it was simply that his body would not obey him. The effort to raise even his little finger was beyond him; he knew he should be able to do these things easily, but he seemed to have forgotten how.

He had the same experience now: he dreamt that he had opened his eyes to find the room curiously illuminated by a soft blue light. The source of it seemed to be the distant corner of his room, but when he tried to raise his head to see better, he found he could not. Nor could he move his arms and legs: he seemed to be paralysed. The source of light was coming closer: it was at the foot of the bed now, but although he could move his eyes he found, absurdly, that his own face was in the way: the effect was of trying to look at your feet with your head tilted back.

Up to this point, he had felt wonder and curiosity rather than fear, but now what was definitely a hand was laid on his naked foot. He wanted to cry out, but was unable to. The hand (it seemed a small one) took a firm grip of his foot. There then followed a sound and a sensation that he had difficulty identifying at first, until he realised incredulously that it was his toenails being cut. The bizarreness of the realization drove fear from his mind: what on earth was going on? The hand released his foot and the blueness moved up the side of the bed, and at last he could see.

A young child stood at his head, a girl no older than five or six. Everything about her (skin, clothes, hair) was covered in a blue sheen that was slightly luminous. Her face was without expression, her eyes downcast, lids drooping almost shut. She might have been sleepwalking. There was something infinitely pathetic about the way she stood so still and undemanding. Then she raised her hand, and he saw that she had a pair of nail scissors. He watched fascinated as she stretched her other hand toward him (still without raising her eyes) and felt for a lock of his hair. Her cool small fingers brushed his temple. They took the lock tenderly, stretching it taut, then snip! the scissors severed it. What did that remind him of, the taking of a lock of hair? He looked at the closed, expressionless little face in wonder.

All at once the lids opened and he recoiled in horror. The eyes that looked at him were large and dark and horribly malign. He knew with certainty that they were not the eyes of the little girl at all but someone else's looking out from her head. The shock roused him, breaking the spell of his paralysis, and he flung up a hand to shield himself from the dreadful gaze.

He woke with a thudding heart, his breath coming in labored gasps. The room was in darkness. The afterimage of the horrible eyes stayed with him – the eyes only, not the little girl – and he scrabbled for the light. He sat up, panting, his hands pressed to his cheeks, shaking his head to free it from the nightmare.

Those eyes! Ugh!

He took off the rest of his clothes and climbed into bed properly, lying with the light on until he passed eventually into a deep and dreamless slumber.

Morning brought no recollection of the incident. It was only in shaving that he was struck by a jagged irregularity in his hair, and moved by a dread that was not yet fully conscious, bent to examine his foot and saw that three of the toenails were neatly cut.

His mind reeled. He sat down heavily on the toilet, staring absurdly at his own foot, his hand fingering his hair. A wave of panic swept over him, as he recalled the awful eyes gazing out of the little girl's expressionless face. Something he had known only as a detail of stories all at once came close up and horribly real: hair and nail clippings, parts of the living body, were used in black magic to gain power over the person they were taken from. He found he was shaking. Something told him that the malevolent eyes that had looked out at him belonged to Aurelian Pounce.

To say the incident had unnerved him was an understatement: he was a hair's breadth from panic. He enjoyed tales of the supernatural and the occult. It was an indulgence in safe fear, because he knew at bottom that it was all just a story; he could shut up the book and the horror with it, until the next time he wanted a dose of pleasurable fright. Now that these things had emerged into his own life, he was appalled and terrified. He did not even attempt to offer a rational explanation. Baldassare Buonconte's warning, Orloc's hints, what he knew himself of Pounce from other sources: all these combined to convince him that something awful was after him, and his overwhelming impulse was to flee. If he could get to London, to home territory, none of this would seem so bad. He also had some confused notion, dredged up from somewhere, of putting running water between himself and his pursuers.

His mind could not stay concentrated on one thing for more than a moment. There seemed to be so much to consider, and yet there was no time, because he must get away. The transaction could wait – the item was safe enough where it was. There was nothing to stop him going at once, by the quickest way. In the midst of his racing thoughts, the recollection of his daughter and the luncheon appointment he had made came to mind. Damn! Still, he could phone her from somewhere. It wouldn't be the first time he had let her down, he admitted ruefully. Perhaps it would be better if he sent a note.

The recollection of the second key came back to him. Why on earth had he put it there? Suddenly, from being safe in a place where no one would think to look, it seemed glaringly vulnerable to discovery. All it would take was the merest curiosity on Orloc's part about the desk. He was bound to have seen others like it, he was in the trade after all. And if he increased that curiosity by making a run for it – far from being safe, it now seemed to his hectic mind that the second key was bound to be discovered.

The idea he clung to was that it was still possible to make everything all right: the item could be returned to the collection (The Aunts need never know that he had intended to steal it) and he himself could return to London. Everything would be back where it started, as if it had never happened, and this nightmare would cease. He would have disentangled himself from the horrible world of

Aurelian Pounce and he would never, *never* go anywhere even remotely near him again.

The notion that Orloc might find the second key and so retrieve the goods was like a spanner inserted in the whirling machinery of his disordered thoughts: unless he could do something about that, he was paralyzed. He would just have to go back to Venice first, to Murano, and retrieve it himself. For two seconds, that seemed like an excellent idea. Then the thought that Pounce clearly knew where he stayed and would therefore be watching him intervened.

No, he would have to get away first, concentrate on getting himself clear, and then he could double back and pick up the painting; he would just have to hope that in the meantime Orloc did not become too curious about the desk. Unless ... In one of those moments of illumination that seemed to come to him in times of crisis, he saw all at once another way: saw the desk where he had left it, in the clutter of Orloc's shop; saw someone examine it casually, as any customer might; but someone who, as soon as Orloc's attention was distracted, deftly operated the hidden spring to release the compartment and retrieve the key. The same someone who, with equal ease, could travel unsuspected to Murano and retrieve the goods. Someone to whom he could send a message which, even if he was watched, would probably pass unobserved; a message which could be set out in such a way that it would look unremarkable to prying eyes, yet still be understood by the person it was intended for.

Able to focus his mind on something at last, he settled to the task of composing it.

6

Daylight robbery

Jake had not long settled in the hotel lounge when he heard Helen's name paged. He had seen her at breakfast earlier that morning, and then she had dashed off to town to do some shopping. She had returned laden with packages and dashed up to her room to reappear a few minutes later, looking radiant in a new outfit. She was bubbling with delight: the transformation was extraordinary.

– Great outfit, said Jake.

Helen beamed.

– This is for you.

She thrust a small but heavy package into his hand. Unwrapping it, he found a little bronze boar, beautifully detailed, its surface like shiny brass where it had been rubbed but with green verdigris in the indentations.

– Is this because I'm a little bore?

She laughed.

– It's the *porcellino*, silly! Don't you remember I showed him to you yesterday, in the Mercato Nuovo? You stroke his nose for luck.

She reached out and ran her fingertip down the length of Jake's nose, resting it a moment on the end.

– Wish me luck, Jake.

– Good luck, Helen. And thanks!

He shouted to her back as she went bounding away,

taking the steps in front of the hotel two at a time.

I suppose I should go and tell them where she is, Jake thought when he heard Helen paged. Making his way across the foyer, he was hailed by one of the porters. He recognized him as one of the witnesses to their impromptu dance of the night before. He had a parcel in his hand.

– Your lady friend, Signor – she is with you?

– No, but I know where she is. She's having lunch with her father at the Gallo Nero.

– This parcel came for her: the boy who brought it said it was urgent.

– I could take it, if you like.

– Would you, Signor? That would be most kind. My legs, alas, are too old for chasing after young ladies. But you have your health and your strength!

– No problem, said Jake, going jauntily out the door.

There was one slight problem, however, which occurred to him halfway down the street: he had really no idea where the Gallo Nero was. However, he was a man with a mission, not to be deflected. After picking three tourists on the trot, he opted for the safer bet of asking in shops, and was at length successful. However, it was some considerable time after he had set out that he eventually stumbled from the bright sunlit street into the cool subterranean gloom of the Gallo Nero, which occupied what must once have been a cellar, below street level.

Helen sat alone at a table directly opposite the door and as he entered he saw her face take on that eager look with which, he realized in a moment of painful insight, she must have greeted everyone who had entered as he did, pausing in the doorway to let his eyes adjust, a silhouette against the brightness outside. Then when he stepped forward and she saw who he was – or rather, who he was not – her face crumpled in misery. Her eyes seemed enormous, disbelieving; her mouth contracted into a tight line; the tip of her chin wobbled slightly.

"Always carry a clean handkerchief" was an injunction of his mother's which Jake followed faithfully, though it had never proved particularly useful until now; but now he was glad to be able to plunge his hand in his pocket and offer, instead of words, a crisp expanse of fresh linen. A hovering waiter, clearly identifying him as the late arrival which was the cause of the young lady's distress, closed to secure an order before a scene ensued and the chance was lost.

"Food is a great restorative" was another family maxim, this time his father's – he was the owner of Garibaldi's, one of the top restaurants in Glasgow. Right now, Helen, half buried in the handkerchief, looked much in need of restoration. Feeling (for once) the master of the situation in a setting familiar to him from earliest childhood, he took the proffered menu, perused it with an expert eye, and made a rapid order for them both. The waiter, impressed by this brisk decisiveness, scuttled off.

Helen had emerged from the handkerchief and now sat with her head between her hands, the picture of dejection. Her mouth made a few attempts to shape words, but she seemed unable to speak. Jake had never seen anyone look so wretched. He produced the parcel.

– This came for you, just after you left. I tried to catch you up but I'm afraid I got a bit lost.

She stared at him, big-eyed, uncomprehending.

– He didn't come! she wailed, resorting noisily to the handkerchief.

Jake, unable to think of anything to say, just sat through the symphony of sobs and snuffles. All at once she stopped, inhaled slowly through her nose and let out a sigh.

She dabbed each eye with the handkerchief, then said, matter-of-factly:

– I don't know why I'm making such a fuss. It's not as if it was the first time.

She shook her head, as if to shake off the last of her distress. It was an impressive piece of self mastery: utterly abject a moment before, she now looked at him with eyebrows raised and mouth pursed in a wry smile, an expression that seemed the facial equivalent of a shrug. She snorted through her nose.

– What did you say this was?

– It came for you not long after you had left. I told the porter I knew where you were, so he let me take it.

The waiter appeared with two plates of food.

– I better go and clean myself up. I must look a sight.

She slipped away, taking the parcel with her. Jake wondered if going to the toilet was just a pretext to allow her to open whatever it was in private. She returned shortly after, much improved in appearance, but wearing a puzzled expression.

– What is it?

– It's a catalogue my Dad made of all the various paintings in the mausoleums, once he'd persuaded The Aunts to let him hang them.

– Is it a present?

– I hardly think so. I've already got one, and this one's a bit dog-eared.

– No message with it?

– Only this.

She handed him a business card. "V. Orloc, Antiche" it read, with a Florence address, phone and fax numbers, all in green on a cream background and surrounded by an odd shaped decoration that might have been a stylised leather belt.

– Look on the back.

On the back there was a curious drawing, clumsily drawn, as if in great haste or with a shaky hand. A creature, just recognizable as the Sphinx, had a speech balloon emerging from its mouth; but the artist had made the classic blunder of drawing the balloon before he wrote the message, which consequently spilled out over the lines. The writing had a peculiar look. Where the Sphinx was shaky, this seemed to have been done with an almost rigid hand: the letters were awkward and angular; the lines dug into the card.

Jake read it with difficulty:

Sorry Lunch. Had to go. Key to N° 59 is where you put barley sugar & silver 3d. Please fetch.
Sorry again, Dad. XXX

He looked to Helen for enlightenment, but she looked as baffled as he was.

– What's it mean?

– I've no idea.

– Is 59 an address or something?

– I don't know: Dad has a flat in London, but it isn't N° 59. None of the mausoleums has a number.

– What's all this about barley sugar and silver 3-D?

Helen looked at him blankly, palms turned outward.

– Och well, let's eat. It's getting cold.

They ate steadily and in silence. The food disappeared rapidly. When it was done, they ordered ice cream.

– Any thoughts?

– Only that Dad must be in trouble of some sort. The writing looks so strange, then there's the Sphinx. It's a code we used to have, for something that was meant to be kept secret.

Jake thought for a bit.

– How did your Dad know you were here? I mean, here in Florence. Did you tell him?

– No, he must have got it from The Aunts.

– Well phone them then. They might be able to tell you something.

– I doubt it, but it might be worth a try.

They finished their ice cream and hurried to the hotel.

Helen returned from the phone call looking considerably excited: it clearly had been worth a try.

– Any joy?

– Sort of. Dad was there not so long ago, and said he was going to Florence. Then he asked them about something in the collection, and – this is the strange bit – he asked if he could take my desk to have the inlay repaired.

This was evidently significant, but Jake could not see why.

– You have inlay on your school desk?

– It's not a school desk, silly, it's an antique writing desk. Dad bought it for me as a present. It's great, you should see it. It has lots of secret compartments.

The expression on Jake's face made it clear that he was still all at sea.

– That's what I remembered: something I put in one of the secret compartments, ages ago – a sweet and a silver threepenny bit!

Light was beginning to dawn.

– So the key to No 59 – wherever that is – is in the desk?

– In the same compartment where I put the barley sugar and the threepenny bit!

– But where's the desk?

– I think I know that too. It'll be in Victor Orloc's shop. That's why he sent the card.

– So are you going to go and ask for it then?

– I don't think it can be as straightforward as that: there is the Sphinx, remember. Something's supposed to be kept secret.

– Couldn't it just be another clue to the secret compartment?

– I don't think so: we only ever used it to signal something we weren't meant to talk about in front of The Aunts. *Asphinx*!

– Bless you!

– That's what we used to do. It meant "keep quiet about that, change the subject."

– So you're just going to walk into this Mr. Orloc's shop, spring the secret compartment, and walk out again with the key to no 59, wherever that is?

– Something like that, yes.

Helen was looking at him in a way he did not like, a sort of sizing-up-for-the-job look.

– It would be a lot easier if I had an accomplice.

– An accomp – here now, wait a minute!

– You wouldn't have to *do* anything. Just be there to distract Orloc while I get at the desk.

– But I have a train to catch!

– That's all right, it's quite near the station. We could pop in on the way.

Jake did his goldfish imitation again.

– Come on, Jake, who bought your ticket for you? Your train isn't for ages yet, and it really won't take more than a couple of minutes.

She reached out and stroked his nose again with her fingertip.

– Please?

Who could resist so eloquent an appeal?

Twenty minutes later found them surveying Orloc's shop from the café across the road. All the way there, Helen had cajoled and flattered Jake in a way that was flatly contradictory. On the one hand, she was relying on him; on the other, the task itself was nothing, she might well manage it herself, at most all Jake would need to do was enter the shop and look around to create a distraction. In the end, it was decided that Helen would go first, alone. If all went well she would return with the key and that would be that. If there was a problem, she would emerge from the shop, look at something in the window, then go back in. That would be the signal for Jake to come in and distract Orloc. It sounded simple enough when Helen described it, but Jake still had his doubts.

– Won't it look a bit funny, someone my age going into an antique shop?

– You don't have to *be* an antique to buy an antique. Lots of rich kids are collectors, it beats pop records any day. Just think yourself into the part: if you believe it, then Orloc will – he can't afford not too – he's in business to sell to whoever wants to buy. Think rich and act supercilious.

– Like you, you mean? said Jake, but only once she was out the door.

She swept haughtily out of the café and across the sunlit street. Jake watched her go with a certain admiration. She'll be back in a minute, he told himself. He visualized her emerging, smiling, the key held up triumphantly. Then I can get on to the station and we can go our separate ways. Still, it's been fun, even if she is a bit of a bossy know-it-all. He turned, by way of comparison, to his favorite object of contemplation, the delectable Claire Louise Foley. Now with her, antique buying might be fun. He was just becoming absorbed in this pleasant fantasy when Helen emerged from the shop, wearing a puzzled look. He waited, heart thudding, for her to go back in the shop, which was his cue. But instead she came back into the café. He felt greatly relieved.

– It isn't there! I looked everywhere.

– Oh well – (a carefully nursed pause). Still, you tried.

He made a move to go.

– Come on! You can't go yet, it must be in there somewhere.

– He's maybe sold it.

Helen looked aghast.

– I hardly think so. He was meant to be repairing it.

– Well, it'll be in his workshop then, and you've no chance of getting it there.

Again he made motions to leave. Helen laid a hand on his arm.

– Look, Jake, I know I've no right to ask you this, but would you just do *one* thing for me? One teeny, tiny thing? I mean so small you almost won't notice you've done it?

He looked at her warily.

– Which is?

– Just go into the shop, and hang around there for a bit – look at things – just like someone killing time waiting for a train. You could do that, couldn't you?

– Just look at things, browse about? I don't need to say anything?

– Not a word.

– How long for?

– Long enough to keep Orloc there while I go round the back to see if I can find a workshop.

– How do you know there is one?

– Well there's bound to be, if Dad put something in for repair. Lots of these places have a sort of service lane round the back.

Jake nodded. His father's restaurant was like that. Helen looked at him with pleading eyes.

– Just browse about the shop, that's all?

– Just so he'll stay there till I come out.

– Okay, but don't be too long.

Without lingering to think twice about it, Jake
propelled himself across the road and into the shop as if he
was entering a stage from the wings. The man he took to be
Mr. Orloc smiled his smooth smile and rubbed his lean
brown hands together in a way that recalled an insect. Did
the young gentleman require assistance?

– Uh, no, not right now. May I look around? Jake asked
in Italian.

– Certainly, certainly, bowed the man, still rubbing his
hands, his eyes huge and round behind the magnifying-lens
glasses.

Jake edged away, drawing a finger along the polished
inviting surface of a rosewood table. The shop was darker
than he expected, and extremely cluttered. That was
something at least: there was plenty to browse through.

Prominent among the clutter were several bronze
pieces and in these Jake feigned great interest, fingering
them and standing back to admire them in what he thought
an appropriate manner. He wondered what Helen was up
to. He peered into the gloom at the back of the shop to see
if there was any sign of a connecting door but the walls
were hung with rugs and carpets, any of which might
conceal one. He took his time with the bronzes, reckoning
that people lingered in antique shops much as they did in
second hand bookshops. All the same, with the man
hovering at his elbow, it was difficult not to feel under
pressure. He wished someone else would come in to
distract him. He wished Helen would reappear.

Then a telephone rang, an old fashioned sonorous ring
muffled by the heavy hangings. The man's head twitched,
and he looked at the right hand wall, his fingers pressed
together in an attitude of prayer. A mantis, thought Jake
irrelevantly, noting the direction of the glance; that was the
name of the insect. The phone stopped after several rings,

but whether because it had been answered or the caller had rung off Jake could not tell. Nor, it seemed, could the man – he hovered for a time undecided, head cocked to one side, as if waiting for someone to call him through.

Jake's heart raced: what was he supposed to do now? He had a vivid impression of Helen, suddenly paralyzed by the ringing of the telephone. What if the man went through now? He would be bound to catch her. The man seemed preoccupied, as if he had not quite made up his mind what to do about the phone. Then he began to make his way toward the rear of the shop. Without giving himself time to think, Jake launched into conversation. His first effort came out as a high squeak which he had to disguise as a cough, but at least it served to draw the man's attention.

– Excuse me, are you Mr. Orloc? he asked in Italian.

– At your service.

He tried desperately to frame another sentence in Italian, but found that all his vocabulary had deserted him.

– Do you speak English?

– I like to think so.

– A friend of mine told me that you do repairs.

– That is so.

It was impossible to tell what he made of this line of questioning: his spectacles concealed his eyes behind opaque discs of light.

– Is your workshop in Florence?

– Workshop?

– Where you do the repairs?

– *Ah, si – l'officina.* It is here in the back, but we only do small work. Nothing major.

Jake goggled at him: his stream of invention had run dry.

– Was there something else you wished to know? prompted Orloc, not unkindly.

– Ah, no, no thank you. That is just what I wanted to know.

He beat an embarrassed retreat to the door, pursued by Orloc with his glinting spectacles. As soon as Jake was out the door, he flipped the lock shut and hung up a sign: *chiuso*. Then he retreated into the interior, until all that could be seen were the two discs of light like monstrous eyes.

Jake scuttled across the road to the café, hoping to find Helen there, but of course she wasn't. He ordered a coffee and settled himself where they had sat before, at a table which commanded a good view of Orloc's shop and its neighbors. Helen had gone in after he had entered the shop, so he did not know what door to watch for her reappearance. He tried to work it out. To the right, the shopfronts were continuous; to the left, there were a couple of shops then a door that might have been the entrance to a house or a passageway. He tried to visualize what lay beyond: he was used to premises with little service lanes round the back, which often had entrances quite a distance from the places they served.

Then, as he watched, the door to the left opened. His heart leaped – only it was not Helen, but a man in overalls that emerged, letting the door swing to behind him. It's not a house door then, thought Jake, otherwise he would have locked it. Besides, he didn't look like someone coming out of his house. He stared at the door, willing Helen to come through it. The minutes ticked by. Where was she?

Jake reproached himself for having left the shop – but how could he have stayed, making a complete fool of himself, jabbering on about nothing? But he saw all too clearly that the very first thing Orloc would have done as soon as the shop was empty was to go through the back: he had been headed that way anyway. But Helen would have heard him coming and got clear, he told himself. So where was she then?

I didn't ask for any of this, Jake thought bitterly. Just a teeny, tiny thing, she said. Well, I've done that, and more – I *tried* to stop him. He would be perfectly within his rights to just get up and walk away, head for the station where he should have gone in the first place. No one could blame him for doing that. He had done all he could.

But it was no use: he still sat staring at the door, willing her to appear – come through, come through! The waitress began to tidy his table rather pointedly, so he committed himself to another coffee while his reason made another attempt at persuading him to leave. She's either safe or she's been caught, he told himself. If she's safe, then it doesn't matter whether I wait or not, but if she's been caught, what can I do about it? Go in and rescue her? Testify that she's my lunatic sister who's harmless really, no real danger to the public, don't worry I'll see she's well taken care of, thanks for your trouble, sorry to have bothered you? Hardly. Besides, the shop was closed now.

So that was it, then – no point in staying either way, whether she was caught or not; might as well get going –

Of course she might be trapped, some part of him that he did not particularly want to listen to observed coolly. That would fit the facts: she hears Orloc come through, but can't get away – so she hides somewhere. That would explain why she hasn't come out. So what am I meant to do? The shop's shut now. Should I go and bang on the door until he comes to open it?

You could go round the back.

Or I could just go and catch my train, he thought, rising purposefully. He went out into the street with every intention of heading for the station, but the door across the way seemed to reproach him with its blank stare. If he only went as far as the back of the building, it would at least salve his conscience. He didn't have to go any further. He pictured himself at some future date, talking to Helen: "I did not just walk away and leave you, I came looking for you!" It would be enough. Just to the back of the building.

Behind the door was a passage with a stairway leading off to one side and a door at the other end. Trying to look as if he was entitled to be there, Jake made his way to the farther door. It opened onto a narrow cobbled lane that wound between high walls, making it dark and claustrophobic. It was not an easy place to look like a casual passerby.

Turning right, he followed the lane round: the curve made it difficult to see any way ahead. He was startled by the appearance of a man in overalls coming the other way. They both stopped; Jake moved to one side to let him past, but the man moved in the same direction; then he moved back just as the man did the same. It was like some sort of comic dance. The man, a bit exasperated, reached out and took Jake by the shoulders, then almost lifted him out of the road and went on his way. Jake went on cautiously until he came to a big double door with a smaller one let into it. A tiny metal sign read *V. Orloc, Antiche.*

He hesitated in front of it, knowing that he had not yet gone far enough to salve his conscience. With his heart in his mouth, he tried the small door. It was unlocked. He pushed it open a little way, fearing to trip a bell, but none sounded. He held the door half open for a short space, reckoning that anyone inside would be prompted to call out; when no call came he opened it fully and stepped inside, heart pounding.

The workshop was brown and dim, like an old sepia photograph. The only light came from above, from a grimy skylight let into a corrugated iron roof. The place had perhaps been an open courtyard once. There was a confused clutter of furniture with a clearer space in the middle round a big sturdy workbench. On the opposite wall there was a wooden lean-to like half a garden shed: some sort of office. It had a big window giving onto the courtyard and a door at the side.

The office was in darkness, but even as he watched a light came on inside. He ducked at once behind a mass of piled-up furnishings. He realized that he had left the door to the lane open, but it was too late now to do anything but cower down and hope. After what seemed an age, the light went out again. Jake emerged slowly from his hiding place and sized up the situation. Surely he had done enough? The problem was that he could not just coolly turn around and walk away: it would be too much like abandoning Helen. If only he had ducked out the door when that light came on! Then he could have said, "I got as far as the courtyard, but someone came into the office."

But now he knew the office was empty. Besides, it was only a few steps away, and he had a clear escape route to the door. By crossing the invisible line onto someone else's property, then hiding there, he had entered a little into the excitement of the thing. It had the flavor of a childhood dare – creeping through other people's gardens in the summer twilight or daring one another up a long private driveway. How far could he go? Deep down, he had made a sort of bargain with himself; he would keep going until something turned him back. He stole across to the office and tried the door: it was unlocked. Slowly he eased it open; steeling himself, he took a deep breath and stepped inside.

He froze. In an armchair in the corner of the room a man was sitting watching him: he was swathed in dark clothes and wore a hat, from which tufts of unusual hair stuck out like straw. In the poor light his skin had the cold pallor of a corpse. Jake stood paralysed with fear. The man did not move, but he could feel his eyes watching him from under the brim of his hat. Time stretched out: there was no sound in the room save the thudding of his own heart. In the gloom before him, the unmoving face hung smooth and cold as marble.

It *was* marble, Jake realized with a sudden gush of relief – an old bust got up with a bundle of fabric, a hat and an outlandish wig. He stifled a giggle. Well that's it, he thought, that's certainly far enough.

Then something grabbed his ankle.

He looked down in fright, to see a face looking up at him from the kneehole of a desk: he had just registered it as Helen's when the light came on and Orloc stepped into the room.

The sudden light dazzled him as he looked up; on the edge of his vision he was aware of Helen drawing herself further in beneath the desk. For a moment they stood, blinking at one another. Orloc was more like an owl now than an insect, Jake thought irrelevantly; it's the way his glasses magnify his eyes. His mind raced, collecting any possible scraps of defence, of explanation. He took refuge in the role of the foreigner with limited Italian.

– You must excuse me, I wanted to see your workshop …

It was lame, but it helped him back out the door. He gesticulated helplessly, as if groping for a further explanation.

– I was in the lane. The door was open … I looked in, I saw no one …

He was in the outer yard now, and as he hoped, Orloc had followed him; he was clearly puzzled, not knowing what to make of him.

– I thought perhaps the office – but you really must

excuse me, it is unforgivable – I wondered: are all these pieces for sale, or for restoration?

It was a desperate question, but it got him within reach of the outer door. Orloc gave him a hard look. Jake felt his face had frozen in an apologetic grin

– For restoration.

– Ah! And do you do the restoration yourself?

– Yes, sometimes.

– You don't employ a workman, then?

– Yes, sometimes.

– Thank you very much. You have told me just what I wanted to know.

It was an absurd formula, but it got him out of the door. As he stepped backwards into the lane Jake had effectively become what he pretended: a nosy foreigner who had overstepped the mark out of curiosity and was retiring apologetically, hoping his foreignness would excuse his bad manners. For his part, Orloc seemed content to have seen him off the premises. He stood in the doorway looking displeased but nothing more as Jake bowed and blushed his way through a further set of apologies and took his leave, setting off briskly in the opposite direction from the one he had come, relief flooding through him. He had only gone a few paces when a shout from Orloc stopped him dead; he froze, but did not turn. The shout was repeated.

– Not that way. There is no exit. The door is this way.

– Thank you, thank you, you are too kind. Good day, thank you.

Jake walked stiffly away, aware that his knees were turning to jelly while the rest of his muscles were rigid. His bent arms were clamped to his sides, fists clenched. He tilted his head back and closed his eyes, forcing a strong hiss of breath past his teeth. Behind him, he heard the door close. Keep walking, he told himself, just keep walking.

It took him minutes to recover once he was in the passage: he had to lean against the wall with his hands on his knees; he felt he might be sick, or faint. Even after his heart rate had subsided and his breathing had returned to normal, he stayed where he was in the passage. He realized that he was afraid to go back out onto the street, because that would renew his dilemma. As long as he stayed here, he was safe: everything was in a state of suspension. To step out onto the street would be to turn one of the two possibilities into reality: either Helen had escaped, or she hadn't.

It took a great effort to force himself to walk the length of the passage, and even then he stood for a time without opening the door; he was trembling violently. Calm down, take it easy, he told himself. But all the same he had to catch himself unawares to get through the door, as if he was diving off the high board at the pool, and not stepping out into an ordinary, sunlit street.

He could not bring himself to go near Orloc's shop. Instead he set off in the opposite direction and went some way along the pavement before crossing the road and walking back in the direction of the café. As he walked he tried to calm himself by looking at shop windows and pretending to be an ordinary tourist. But bubbling up underneath it all was an insistent desperate prayer that he hadn't used since childhood: please God let her be there, please God let it be all right, please God let her have got away, please God let her be there, please God let it be all right, he implored, all the way along to the café, not so much for Helen's sake as for his own, so that there would be no more difficult decisions demanded of him. But as soon as he turned in at the door he saw at once that she in fact was not there.

He ordered a coffee and sat miserably at the window gazing across the road. He found himself wondering how

long it had been since they had both sat there. He could form
no clear idea: the encounter with Orloc seemed to have taken
longer than all that led up to it, although logic told him that
that must be an illusion. He suddenly felt completely alone.
What could he do? What more could anyone expect? Maybe
it would be better just to go, to walk away and forget about
it. It was certainly the easiest thing to do. All at once
Florence seemed the dreariest place in the world: he could
see the sunshine in the street, but there seemed to be a
shadow between it and him.

When he emerged onto the pavement, he saw that the
sign in the window had been removed: the shop was open
again. The idea that he might go in flickered briefly into life,
but he crushed it ruthlessly out. What good would it do? He
walked briskly off in the direction of the station without
looking back, feeling angrier with every stride. Well what
was I supposed to do? he snarled at an imaginary accuser. I
never asked to be involved in any of this. It's nothing to do
with me! Then someone grabbed him from behind and he
whirled round, taut with anger, ready to strike. It was
Helen, radiating excitement. She kissed him on the cheek.

– You were brilliant!

Jake found himself unable to speak, torn between
anger, relief and surprise. Helen linked her arm with his
and set off at an energetic pace. She was glowing with a
kind of fierce joy, almost crackling with electricity.

– Now that, she said, was something like being alive.

They arrived at the station in short order but missed
the train; the next one wasn't for a couple of hours, and
arrived in Naples very late.

– Never mind, said Helen airily, I'll phone your
relatives for you and explain everything. But let's get some
food first, I'm starving.

In the station café, Helen told her tale. As soon as Jake entered the shop, she slipped round the back way. She tried the door to the workshop, only to find there was someone working there. She chatted him up, to see if he would let her see the stuff in the workshop, and managed to get inside, but she couldn't see the desk.

Then she had a stroke of luck – the phone rang. The man waited to see if it would be answered, then went to answer it himself, leaving the door of the office open. She stepped across to look in, and there in front of her was the desk. She had just slipped inside for a closer look when she heard the sound of the man coming back, so she ducked into the kneehole of the desk to hide.

The man pottered about, rattling cups and switching on a kettle. Then Orloc came in, and the two of them chatted for a bit. The man, whose name was Pierluigi, kept asking about holidays that were due to him. Orloc kept putting him off, saying there was a lot of work to be done. She had nearly died when Pierluigi said he could do the inlay on that desk. By the sound of his voice, he must have been standing right over it. But Orloc insisted he was going to do that himself – it was for a special client, he said. Pierluigi had said he could suit himself. She got the impression they didn't much like one another.

Then after what seemed ages the break was over, and Orloc said he was going back to the shop. Pierluigi had gone out to the yard, where she could hear him whistling and moving things about. She reckoned it was safe enough to operate the spring for the hidden compartment and she had got the key out and the silver threepenny bit – there was no sign of the barley sugar though. After a bit Pierluigi had come back, gathered up some things, and gone out, closing the office door behind him. She was almost certain he had gone out of the yard, but she waited a bit before she looked out: the yard was empty, and the door was shut, but just as she looked it opened just a bit, then about halfway. (That must have been me, interjected Jake.)

She had ducked back down under the desk again, which was just as well, because Orloc came in and switched on the light. She was mortally afraid that he was going to lock up the office door and the yard before he went, but after pottering around for a bit he had gone out again. She had been just about to leave, when the door opened and Jake came in. She couldn't understand why he just stood there so still: so eventually she reached out and grabbed him, but just then the light had come on.

– It was great the way you drew Orloc away into the yard. I managed to scamper across the floor on my hands and knees but when I slipped through the door I wasn't in the shop at all, I was in a kind of narrow hallway. I nearly panicked, but I found the way out just in time, though I was still in the shop when Orloc came out again.

– What did he say?

– He took me for a customer, and was full of apologies for keeping me waiting. So I said I had been in earlier, and had decided to come back to buy a piece I fancied; then he recognised my name on my cheque card, and we ended up having a conversation about my Dad.

– Did he know where he was?

– I got the impression he was pretty keen to find out, so I just said that he was probably in England, but that I hadn't been in touch with him for a while. You know, after the first fright I really quite enjoyed it.

– Well I didn't. I thought I was going to be sick after I left.

– Oh Jake! you're so *dull*! I bet you wear slippers and smoke a pipe when you get older. Look!

She danced the key in front of him, like a mother trying

to amuse a fretful baby.

– Fancy a trip to Venice?

– Since when was Venice anywhere near Naples?

– Don't be such a bore! You can go to Naples tomorrow. We can stay at my cousin Laura's tonight.

– No.

She looked at him crossly, clearly surprised by such a flat refusal; then she shrugged.

– Suit yourself.

A carefully calculated pause, then:

– I expect you still want me to phone your cousin, though?

This was clearly meant to make Jake feel small and mean, and largely succeeded.

– You don't have to, he mumbled.

– It's all right. I did say I'd do it. Perhaps you could get me a map of Venice from the shop? If it's not too much trouble, that is.

Withered by this icy sarcasm, he sloped off. He took some time to find a decent map of Venice, not wanting to risk any further adverse comment. When he emerged from the shop, Helen was waiting for him. He steeled himself for a further assault but instead she smiled.

– He's a nice man, your cousin Gianni. Sensible, too.

– Oh, really?

– Yes. He agreed with me that it would be daft to go to Naples so late tonight when you could just as easily come tomorrow. He thought it most kind of cousin Laura to put you up, and said it was very good of me to look after you like this.

Jake goggled, speechless. Helen studied his face intently, her head to one side.

– No, don't tell me, let me guess – a goldfish?

*****

A sinister interlude

One of Mr. Pounce's elegant ladies of a certain age is disappointed to find his shop has shut for the day when it is only just four o'clock; she could have sworn it was open only a short while earlier when she passed. As indeed it was; but since then Pounce has received a telephone call from Mr. Orloc, which both excites and disturbs him.

– His daughter, you say – are you quite sure?

Orloc is quite sure.

– And the boy? Describe him again.

Orloc describes Jake faithfully, but is sure that he has nothing to do with it – just another tourist with deficient manners.

– Thank you Victor: I will look into this.

Pounce is rather less sure than Orloc about Jake. He does not believe in coincidence; and once the two are connected, the matter becomes puzzling, perhaps even sinister: both visit the shop separately, then the boy is found on the premises at the back while the girl is unattended in the premises at the front. But what are they up to?

On that matter, he feels he needs some assistance; which is what has brought him to this darkened room, where he sits at a table covered with a black velvet cloth, on which is placed a silver basin flanked by two candlesticks, with a crystal jug of clear liquid to one side. On the table in front of the basin is an envelope. He lights the candles, closes the remaining leaf of the shutters completely, then returns to settle himself in the solitary chair. He pours the contents of the jug into the basin, speaking all the while rapidly under his breath. With his hands, he makes passes over the basin of liquid, calling out an invocation in an unknown tongue; there is a blast of wind and the candles gutter and grow dim. When their flames steady again, they are blue and feeble.

The darkness on the other side of the table has thickened: there is something in the room with Pounce that was not there before. He takes the envelope and extracts from it a lock of dark hair, stroking the curl of it with finger and thumb. He smiles, thin lipped. With more muttered words, he casts the lock into the basin. A portion of the darkness across the table detaches itself, and hovers over the surface of the liquid like heavy smoke; then it seems to go down into it. The contents of the basin alter in character, becoming opaque and highly reflective, yet somehow still dark: like black mercury.

Pounce leans eagerly over the surface, studying it intently. He sees a girl's face, dark, good looking: her lips are moving, forming a word – Pounce strains to make it out. Next there is the same girl, accompanied by a boy who answers the description furnished by Orloc. They are in a railway station, looking at a destination board – he peers hard at the names that appear there. Now he sees them at a table, studying a map with a great deal of blue on it; as he watches, the girl folds it up, and the name on the outside confirms what he already thought: *Venezia*.

So what takes them there? he wonders. Perhaps he should go and find out; but not alone. With his hands he makes delicate, fluttering movements over the surface of the bowl, chanting rhythmically in an undertone. When he draws his hands aside, a face is looking up at him, lean and long jawed, almost skull like in its emaciation: its eyes have a black, dead stare.

Pounce contemplates the face for a time, then once more passes his hands across the surface of the bowl, now drawing them upward, fingers spread. The darkness that was in the liquid comes dragging after them like inky smoke to form a column that hovers between his hands, stretching upward to the ceiling. Then it moves away a little, to the other side of the table, where it seems to condense and grow solid. After a second or two it begins to take on definite form, and in a short time a man is standing there, unusually tall and skeletally thin. His face is the face that was in the bowl.

With evident satisfaction, Pounce looks him up and down, then turns, signalling him to follow. The door closes behind them, and the candle flames burn tall and bright, lightening the darkness; the room seems empty, but it is not. Over by the shuttered window a nimbus of light hangs in the air like luminous fog; it stretches out and grows more solid, until it, too, takes the form of a man. The man turns and opens the shutters, flooding the room with light. He stoops over each candle in turn, cupping his hand behind the flame and blowing it out; then he too, softly and quietly, leaves the room.

7

The empty city

– Please stop sulking and come over here, said Helen. I'll
show you where we're going.

Jake was deeply but quietly enraged, largely at his own
impotence. How he would have loved to turn on his heel
and say "goodbye, then" and walk away! But Helen knew
very well that he was not about to do that – he had already
made clear how much he feared being alone in Italy. He
also resented her blithe disregard of his feelings on the
matter, as if he was not entitled to have a point of view. As
the youngest of a large family he was not unused to that,
but it didn't mean he liked it.

There was more to it than that, though, some quality in
Helen herself which angered him all the more because he
deeply envied it: her total lack of self doubt. He could never
have imposed his will on anyone in that way. He would have
worried about being thought high handed, insensitive,
selfish. But Helen just swept all that away, on the strength of
one fundamental conviction: it's what *I* want that matters;
what *you* want is of no account. How did people get to be
like that? Perhaps having an awful lot of money for a very
long time had something to do with it.

However, he voiced none of these thoughts and was
careful to keep his rage at the level of silent fuming, because
deeper than his anger at himself for being unable to
abandon her was the fear that if he provoked her, *she* might

abandon *him*. So when she bade him come and sit beside her, he dutifully obeyed; he also thought it wise to turn down his level of sulking just a little.

They were on the train to Venice. Helen spread the map out on the table, indicating their ultimate destination: Murano, a small island just North of Venice itself.

– We'll have to go into Venice, then get a boat across.

She had been to Venice before, though she did not know it as well as she knew Florence. In another mood, Jake might have been interested in what she had to say, but he was still resentful, and in the face of his monosyllabic responses, Helen soon gave up. She had no sooner stopped than he regretted it: now he was left alone with his boredom.

– I don't suppose you've got anything to read, he asked in a grudging tone.

– Try looking in my bag, yawned Helen. I'm going to sleep.

She hunched herself up against the window, using her rolled up jacket as a pillow. Jake fished in the bag, coming up with a substantial volume: it was the catalogue her father had sent with the note, listing the works of art in the various houses Helen seemed to inhabit at one time or another. Lifestyle of the rich and famous, Jake thought to himself, leafing through the pages. He had expected pictures, but it was mainly text, numbered entries on each item in the collection. There certainly seemed to be a lot of them. Everywhere his eye lit, he saw something that reinforced just how different Helen's world was from his:

N° 7 : Cartoon of the Virgin and Child, with St Anne. Attributed to Leonardo da Vinci.

Although the attribution is not proven, it is well attested both by internal evidence and historical tradition ...

Hmm. He knew who Leonardo was; didn't know he

drew cartoons, though. Perhaps it meant something else.
Here was another:

*Nº 57 : Bronze Mogul Elephant in Panoply of War – Indian,
c. 16th Century.*

*This splendid specimen, which is half life size, was originally
in the collection of Sir Greville Rowley, who brought it from India
in 1761 ...*

A half size elephant, cast in bronze. How much would a
thing like that weigh? He had to remind himself that these
things were in private houses, where people lived, what
was it Helen call them? Mausoleums, but museums was
more like it! Then there was this one: he found himself
staring at the entry as you do when, half asleep, you read
the same line over and over without being able to make
sense of it. Then all at once he saw what had been puzzling
him, and he read on with mounting excitement, all his anger
forgotten:

*The subject of this portrait is an Englishman, one Roger
Anscombe, said to be of Bristol, more widely known as the Alchemist
Ruggiero da Montefeltro. The circumstances of his removal to Italy are
obscure; he ended his days in France, having amassed, it is said, a vast
fortune. The date and authorship of the portrait are matter for
conjecture, but it is generally supposed to be from the first half of the
sixteenth century.*

*The eye is drawn at once by the fantastic headgear of the
Alchemist, who stands at a bench in the foreground, his head
swathed in an elaborate and enormous scarlet turban. He gazes
directly at the viewer, as if he has just looked up from his work,
turning toward us as he does so. To the right and left, on the
extreme edge of the picture and effectively framing it, are two ivory
tusks set in heavy gold bases, inlaid with precious stones and
intricately worked. In striking contrast with the pale ivory and its
opulent setting, the Alchemist is plainly clad in a robe of dark stuff,
relieved at the neck with a collar of fur. The index finger of his right*

hand points to a large book that is open on the bench in front of him; his left hand invites us to consider a complex arrangement of phials on a tray. The phials contain liquids of different colors: red, blue, amber, green and purple, doubtless of alchemical significance. Between the tray of phials and the book reposes a splendid crystal, in size and shape like a small hen's egg.

So dominant is the figure of the Alchemist, and so well lit compared to the murky background, that it is some time before we remark the second figure of the picture, in the middle ground over the Alchemist's left shoulder: an apprentice or page-boy, whose actions seem a deliberate mockery of his master. He stands on one leg, his right, and holds the other extended, to balance his outstretched right arm, with which he too indicates a book on the shelf at some distance from him. His left arm also bears a tray, not laden with phials but what look like lots of little cakes. The expression on his face is of scarcely contained mirth: we feel he will burst out laughing at any moment, so that his master will turn and rebuke him.

The presence of the page-boy lends the painting a great immediacy, for it is as if he had just that moment come into his master's study while the artist is painting him and been unable to resist the temptation to disrupt the scene by taking off his master behind his back for the artist's benefit. We can imagine the artist, too, suddenly distracted by this humorous irruption; but closer study shows that there is no need to, for at the very back of the picture there is a mirror in which the artist himself appears, albeit minutely and in no great detail.

The mirror is not the more usual convex article that shows the whole room in distorted miniature; instead it is a large flat mirror of unusual design, occupying most of the rear wall. The frame is of dark material and bears an unusual motif of miniature hunting horns. In addition, one of the life size articles hangs on each side, with a third above. Perhaps this is a visual pun, intended to suggest that the frame itself is made of horn. There are curious inlays of the same material on its surface, as if perhaps it was not

one single sheet of mirror glass but many, so that the manufacturer,
unable to conceal the joins, had chosen instead to make a feature of
them. In the mirror we see the artist, partly obscured by his easel,
and the reflection of the page-boy, but there is no reflection of the
Alchemist, although whether that is from some trick of the angle or
intended as a comment on his diabolical associations is open to
conjecture.

Despite the presence of the artist's reflection in the mirror,
there is a persistent story – contemporary in origin with the picture
– that it was not painted by human hand.

So *that* was it! He composed himself, quelling the
excitement bubbling inside him by an effort of will. He
nudged Helen.

– Have you actually seen this picture?

– What picture? said Helen, sleepily.

–This one with the Alchemist, that's not supposed to
have been painted by human hand.

–It's an old friend, said Helen, still drowsy. I've known
it as long as I can remember. I used to make up stories
about it when I was little. I always liked the page-boy best.
Funny you should ask about that –

– What's the secret?

– What secret?

– The Secret of the Alchemist. It's what the painting's
called.

– Is it really? I only ever thought of it as "The
Alchemist." Are you sure?

– Well that's what it's called in your Dad's catalogue.

– You know, it's really funny you should ask about that
painting, because –

– It's what your dad asked your aunts about?

– How did you know that?

By way of answer, Jake slid the catalogue across, his

finger beside the heading for the entry:

N° 59 : *The Secret of the Alchemist, by an unknown hand.*

She stared at it stupidly, not yet fully awake.

– Don't you see? It's not a house at all, it's a painting! N° 59!

That woke her up all right. She seized the catalogue, as if looking at it herself would somehow make it more certain.

– Brilliant, Jake! Aren't you glad I persuaded you to came?

Persuaded? Forced was more like it. But he didn't say so, because now he was glad he had come, and that he had done something useful. Absurdly, now that Helen was paying him compliments, he felt embarrassed.

– Sounds like some painting, he said, to change the subject. What's that bit about "diabolical associations"?

– Well, it's because he doesn't have any reflection, you see. People who have sold their souls to the devil are supposed not to show up in mirrors.

– Cool! Like vampires? Hey, maybe that's his secret –

– What?

– That he's sold his soul to the devil – that's what the picture tells you!

Helen looked thoughtful, as if trying to recall the actual picture.

– The picture shows you one thing – the Alchemist – but the mirror tells you the truth about him: he has no reflection. Yes, it's just the sort of hidden meaning they put in these old pictures. You know, I've looked at that picture for years and you've never even seen it, but you've spotted something I missed. I'm impressed.

She smiled; Jake basked. He sat back, well contented. It was more than just the compliments and having solved the puzzles: the future, vague and threatening before, was now clear and predictable. For as long as N° 59 might have meant

a house, he had dreaded a repetition of this afternoon's
episode of semi-burglary. Now that it turned out to be a
painting, things were much simpler: to Venice, then Murano,
to open the locker or safety deposit or whatever it was; back
to Florence, to Helen's cousin's; then tomorrow, on to
Naples, where he would have a tale to tell. The events of the
afternoon, now safely in the past and woven into a narrative
that was almost over, became matter for pleasurable rather
than fearful recollection.

After a while immersed in these thoughts, Jake became
aware of a weight pressed against him and a soft grunting
noise: Helen had resumed her sleep, using his shoulder as a
pillow. His own eyelids felt heavy; more than once he
jerked awake as his head nodded toward the table.
Eventually he gave in, after reassuring himself that Venice
was indeed the end of the line. In a short time he too was
asleep.

He came to consciousness gradually, with the train still
under way, thinking of the last thing that was in his mind
before he fell asleep.

– Here, did you know that you snore?

All at once he was wide awake. Two men were sitting
across the table from him, watching him intently. One was
remarkably thin and gaunt with strange, dead eyes that did
not blink. The other wore a cream colored suit and a wide
brimmed hat of the same color; at his throat was a peacock
blue silk neckerchief. He was so broad that he filled most of
the seat. His dark eyes glittered in the shadow of his hat.
On the table in front of him was a curious object, like a clear
glass paperweight. His hands moved continuously above it,
weaving patterns in the air.

Jake nudged Helen with his elbow; he felt her stir
against him, then she sat bolt upright.

– You! she snarled. What are you doing here?

– And now the little lady is awake too, said the broad man, ignoring her. I don't think I've had the pleasure of your acquaintance, young man.

The voice was surpisingly high pitched, but pleasant and melodious. His hands continued to weave in and out, as if they had a separate existence of their own. Jake felt his eyes drawn toward the stone.

– My name is Aurelian Pounce. I am a business associate of this young lady's father.

– He's never mentioned you, said Helen truculently.

– Doubtless he had his reasons. But why so grim, my dear? Still sulking over that lock of hair?

Helen scowled. The man smiled. His hands moved. Something seemed to flicker in the stone.

– I'm very sorry to have to tell you that your father has disappointed me, my dear, in a matter of business. I would be most interested to know of his whereabouts.

– You're the last person I'd tell even if I did know, said Helen.

Her words seemed thick and slurred, as if she was drunk; they seemed to come to Jake from far away, as if down a long tunnel.

– Your loyalty does you credit – if only it had a worthier object! I fear that your father is no better than a swindler and a common thief. But I shall catch up with him, one way or another. If you wish to spare him – (the fluttering hands ceased a moment, then one reached out, as if to pluck the appropriate word from the air) – trouble, you really would be far wiser to tell me what you know. Like where you are going now, for instance?

Helen scowled some more, but said nothing.

– What? Cat got your tongue, my dear? (He shot a glance at Jake.) What a peculiar expression that is! Venice is such an interesting city, don't you think? But so easy to get lost in! All those little streets, and never any signposts! A tricky place for the unwary traveller ... a little frightening, too, at this time of evening, just as the light begins to fail and the shadows increase. Not wise to venture out without a guide!

The hands moved above the flickering glass.

– A guide, yes, said Jake thickly. That's a good idea.

Somewhere inside his head a voice contradicted him, telling him it was not a good idea at all. But that voice came from too far away, it couldn't be that important, what mattered was the strange, elusive flicker in the glass – he almost had it then. He tried to concentrate on it as the pleasant voice across the table went on talking:

– A place as old as that ... so full of ghosts! "Steeped in history:" that's what they say, isn't it? Well, with stones as old as these, you could quite believe that they must have absorbed something of all that crowded past, and what a past! The Serene Republic! Pearl of the Adriatic! Such things have happened there, the stones could never forget. That is why Venice is never entirely in the present, don't you know? Always liable to slip into the past, especially at night ...

He had it now! The flicker held steady, like a glowing flame, and the voice seemed to draw him toward it, like a swirling current in a pool.

– Did you know Venice was emptied once? It was during the plague: they had some idea it came from the marshes on the landward side, the lagoon was shallower then, much marshier. And in a panic the entire population cleared out, stood out to sea in boats. Just think of it: the entire city empty of life, abandoned in the moonlight, only the braziers and the torches left burning to light the empty streets and landing stages. That's the sort of past you might slip into, in a haunted city like Venice ...

Jake felt as if he was drowning: a heavy drowsiness had come over all his limbs so that it was a huge effort even to move his little finger; his body must weigh tons and tons, and he was sinking, sinking ... He wanted to breathe in, but he had forgotten how –

– Tickets please! *Signore e Signori,* your tickets please!

A big man in railway uniform hovered over their table.

– Have you got your ticket, Sir?

Pounce gave a stifled curse and fumbled in his pockets; Jake felt as if he had come to the surface after a long time under water. He breathed in a great lungful of air and with a huge effort of will forced himself to his feet, grabbing Helen by the wrist and dragging her up with him.

– Come on, he said thickly.

His tongue felt too big for his mouth and he had forgotten the proper shape of the words he wanted to say. The railway man eyed him suspiciously.

– All our stuff's in the next carriage, baggage, tickets, all that.

He made a sweeping gesture with his arm in the direction of the next carriage as the half remembered Italian phrases tumbled out in any order.

– We're from Scotland, he said by way of explanation.

– Ah, Scotland! said the guard, with a smile.

He turned his attention to the thin man.

– And your ticket, Sir?

Jake stumbled along the passageway, pulling Helen after him. Behind him he heard the clash of contending voices: it seemed the thin man had no ticket. Looking back, Jake saw Pounce rise and try to shoulder his way past the guard, but the guard was a big man too, and for a moment they were wedged together in the passage while Jake gazed stupidly on. Then a voice spoke close to his ear:

– Keep going! Go right to the end of the train!

The urgency of the tone stirred Jake from his stupor and he hurried on. As he did so, he was aware of a man rising from a table beside him – he did not see his face – and standing in the passageway to unload a quantity of baggage from the overhead rack, effectively blocking any pursuit.

Propelling Helen ahead of him, Jake stumbled the length of several carriages until, passing through a sliding door, he came to a space beside the exit doors and found he could go no farther. The train was slowing, running across a causeway with dark water on either side. He propped Helen against the wall: her eyes were glazed and unfocused and her mouth hung open. As he watched, she began to slide down the wall and ended up squatting on the floor.

Jake had no clear idea except that they must get away; his head seemed to be full of fog. He was dimly aware that some sort of shift had taken place in the way things were: something was fundamentally wrong with reality itself. If he only had five minutes' peace to think about it, he felt sure he could work out what it was, but there was some danger behind them, and they must get away, off the train. But Helen kept sitting down, she didn't seem to understand about the danger at all. It made him want to cry with frustration.

– Come on, come on, you've got to get up! You can't stay there, we must get away from here!

Sobbing and cursing he pulled her to her feet: she was a dead weight.

– Stand up, Helen, you've got to stand up!

It was no use; she slumped against him, pinning him to the wall, then began to slither back down to the floor. He clung onto her with one hand and reached across with the other and managed to open the window. The fog inside his brain seemed to have got outside too: wisps of it came into the carriage through the open window. The train jolted to a halt, lurching him forward so that Helen sprawled back against the other wall. He bent down desperately and, grabbing her under the armpits, he lugged her to her feet. He managed to get a hand free to manipulate the door handle and they both fell out onto the platform into thick fog.

He stumbled forward blindly, one hand holding Helen's arm across the back of his neck, the other round her waist. Her legs were moving, but they didn't seem to be working properly and kept getting tangled up with his own; her breath now came in loud racking gasps. He swore as a wall suddenly materialized out of the fog and dealt him a numbing crack on the elbow. He swung Helen round against the wall where she remained upright, eyes closed and head tilted back, panting harshly with her mouth wide open, as if she had been running hard for a long distance.

– Oh God, Oh God, my head is so sore!

She doubled up suddenly, retching, and remained for a good while bent over with her hands on her knees, Jake patting her back rather helplessly. At last she raised her head.

– Dear God! Sorry about that. Have you got a hanky or something? What just happened to me?

– I don't exactly know. There was this man on the train. He said he knew your father.

– God, yes! Pounce! I remember that. Then it's all muddled.

– You were great. You wouldn't let him get away with anything. Then he started talking about Venice in this sort of sing-song voice, and everything seemed to drift away. I nearly passed out. Oh, shit!

– What is it?

– The map, the bags! I've left everything on the train!

Helen scrabbled in her pocket, producing the key with some relief.

– At least we've still got this. Anyway, this is the terminus. The train must still be here.

– Then all we have to do is wait till the coast is clear and find our way back to it.

That was no easy matter: the fog curled around them as thick as ever. It was unnervingly quiet.

– Look, said Helen, if we follow this wall it should lead somewhere, and there's bound to be someone about. It is a station, after all.

Suddenly, Jake was not at all sure that it was: the feeling that had troubled him earlier, that something had gone fundamentally wrong with reality, came back with increased force. But he said nothing and they groped along the wall, Helen leading. Not being able to see any distance was bad enough, but hearing nothing was worse: Jake found himself scuffing his feet just to be sure he hadn't gone deaf.

– It is quiet, said Helen. Where have all the people gone?

– I don't suppose anyone would want to come out on a night like this, Jake reasoned, but his heart misgave him.

– Look, there's a light up ahead. And I'm sure the fog is thinner.

There was a light, showing up like a golden patch in the grey. Something about it worried Jake even more. When they were closer, he knew what it was.

– It's a torch, said Helen, an old fashioned burning torch.

The torch was fixed to an iron bracket on the wall. It burned with a steady flame, making a little pocket of golden light in the fog and giving out a soft hiss. This is impossible, thought Jake; but you'd better believe it, a voice inside him said, because it's what's happening. As they watched, the flame wavered in a breath of wind.

– Fog's lifting, said Helen, now we'll be able to see.

But what shall we see? wondered Jake. The fog was indeed clearing; he felt a breeze fan his cheek. Magically, buildings began to appear in the rents torn in the mist. It was like a partly completed jigsaw: great chunks of buildings, silvered by moonlight, hung disembodied in the air, with swathes of mist between.

They were standing at the corner of a building; almost directly in front of them a bridge sprang across a wide canal, only to vanish halfway. To their right a broad open space was similarly cut off by a wall of mist. To their left, some freak of the wind had opened up a tunnel through which a wide street ran away into the distance, lit at intervals by flaring torches. On the landing stage beside the canal, a huge brazier burned. Nowhere was there any sign of life.

– Where are all the people? said Helen.

– This is what Pounce was talking about – slipping into the past, and Venice being empty.

– Empty? said Helen, but not challenging him.

She shook her head, holding the bridge of her nose, as if she was trying to clear her recollection.

– Wasn't there something about the plague, and marshes?

– If it's a bad dream, then we're both having it. I don't think we should stay here.

The clearing fog, welcome at first, now made him feel exposed and vulnerable.

– But where can we go? The map's on the train, wherever that is.

The fog was still banked up thick behind them, and

peering back into it Jake felt again the strong sense of impending danger that had driven him from the train.

– I don't know what's going on, but I'd feel safer if we were somewhere less exposed.

He tried to recollect the map in his head: the station was right beside one end of the Grand Canal, which snaked through Venice in a giant s-bend, cutting the city in two; that must be it in front of them. If they went right, they would get cut off by the Canal, he reckoned; besides, the mist was still thick there. They could cross the half visible bridge, but there was no guessing where it might lead. The mist seemed to be clearer to the left, and the broad street looked like a main thoroughfare; if they stuck to that, they might get somewhere.

His pondering was intruded on by Helen tugging his arm.

– Listen! she hissed. Footsteps!

The natural thing would have been to wait to see who it might be, but neither of them felt the least inclination to do so. They sprinted off down the tunnel of mist to their left, keeping close in to the side, their soft soled shoes making little sound. A good distance along they ducked into a doorway and peered back. Silhouetted against the mist, they could see two figures: one unusually tall and thin, the other unmistakably broad. They kept to the middle of the road and walked at a steady pace, with no sense of hurry but a terrible air of purpose. They seemed so certain in their proceeding, their advance so implacable, that Jake felt an overwhelming urge to give himself up, to walk back toward them and surrender. Flight was useless; it would only delay the inevitable. He had already taken a step back in the direction they had come when Helen seized him violently by the arm.

– Jake! What on earth are you doing? We've got to run!

Something in her voice and her tugging his arm woke Jake from his stupor; without thinking too hard about it, he sprinted after Helen in a diagonal line across the street. Behind them he heard the footsteps quicken.

Breathless, they dashed over a bridge then turned sharp right down the quay, only to be forced left again by a dead wall; hurrying on, another right took them to a dead end by the canal. *Such an easy place to get lost in,* Jake heard Pounce's voice say inside his head. *All those little streets and never a signpost.*

Heading back in the opposite direction brought them to the main thoroughfare once more, but their pointless detour had cost them dear. Their pursuers were almost on them; again Jake felt the heaviness invade his limbs, the urge to surrender to the inevitable. Then a flaw of wind conjured a patch of mist from a sidestreet, cutting them off from sight, and once more they ran headlong, twisting and turning down the strangely empty streets, between the pools of torchlight that flared on silent buildings.

At length they paused in an area where the lights were widely spaced and the streets were great gulfs of darkness. Whether or not they had lost their pursuers, there was now no question that they were utterly lost themselves. The general sense of the shape of Venice that Jake had gathered from the map was now wholly disoriented: he had no idea now whether they were heading in the direction they had set out in, at right angles to it, or had even doubled back. His only hope lay in the fact that he could no longer hear the sounds of pursuit. Perhaps if they could slip unseen down a side alley, they could somehow lose themselves in the tangle of Venice for long enough, at least until –

At least until what? Jake caught himself asking, and immediately pushed the thought away before the sense of being in a much larger trap closed in on him.

– Let's walk close to the wall, and look for a turn-off.

– This can't last forever, Helen said, voicing his own hope. It'll have to change by morning, surely.

– I hope so.

Gingerly, they picked their way along, hugging the side of the street, ears straining for following footsteps.

The street curved so that the view ahead was lost, but glancing back Jake could see only an empty moonlit expanse. Once they stopped, the only sound was their own hearts; the stillness was utter.

– I think we've lost them, Jake breathed.

Taking Helen's hand he moved on round the curve of the street only to find himself staring directly at two figures: one short and broad, the other very tall and thin. They were farther along the street, coming toward them, but without the same purposeful air; they seemed to have lost the scent. Jake was aware of a slit-like entrance beside them, lit overhead by a sputtering torch.

– This way, there's a light at the far end.

Jake pulled Helen by the sleeve into the narrow alley mouth and they ran as hard as they could to the other end, only to find themselves skidding to a halt at the water's edge. They were on a narrow landing stage, lit by two big braziers. They peered along it: on their right, the black waters of the canal lapped the bank, less than a foot below. On their left, a dead wall soared up into the darkness, windowless and doorless. Beyond the flaring braziers the far end was lost in gloom. A glance back along the alley told Jake that they had lingered too long: against the faint light of the street he could see the outline of two figures advancing.

They came on steadily, not bothering to hurry now, and Jake guessed that there was no other way out: they were trapped. He let Helen drag him as far as the braziers, but their blazing heat could not dispel the icy chill that gathered in his stomach. Their pursuers were close enough now for their footsteps to be heard, echoing in the alleyway. Jake looked at the dark waters of the canal lapping against the stone edge of the landing stage.

– The water, he said. Can you swim?

The two figures stepped out onto the far end of the landing stage.

Jake turned to Helen with the desperate idea that they might plunge into the canal together, but as he did he felt a hand laid on the nape of his neck. All desire and ability to move deserted him. From the darkness at their backs a tall figure emerged and inserted itself between them. Its face was shadowed by a cowl: only the tip of the nose and the point of the chin emerged, with a glitter of eyes in the firelight. They were helpless in his grasp: all hope of flight was gone.

Pounce and his companion seemed now to advance with dreamlike slowness. Jake was able to take in every detail of their appearance. Pounce was holding back a smile: his sleek face wore a look of satisfaction. The other's countenance was grim and terrifying: his thin cruel mouth was set in a hard line. His dead eyes stared. Now Jake could see that his clothes were of another age; he had a long dagger thrust into a broad leather belt. His fingers twitched and worked constantly, as if he was barely containing some murderous rage.

When they were a few paces away, Pounce stopped, halting his companion with his arm. The expression on his face was a mixture of satisfaction and curiosity.

– Well, this is service indeed! I thought I had summoned only one, but here is another to do my bidding!

– You will find you always get more than you bargain for, said the cowled figure, when you meddle with what you do not understand.

His voice was deep and harsh. A spasm of anger passed across Pounce's face.

– You have done what was required of you. I will take them now.

He took a step forward. The cowled figure raised its arm, palm outwards, in a forbidding gesture.

– Come no further.

Pounce came to a jarring halt, as if he had walked into a wall. A look of surprise and anger crossed his face.

– What is this? he demanded.

– They are not for you, said the cowled one, gathering Jake and Helen to his side.

– Do you defy me? raged Pounce. You think to cheat me, who summoned you from Hell to do my bidding?

– You summoned me, certainly, rejoined the other coolly, but not from Hell, and not to do your bidding. Come no further.

Pounce wove his hands in the air in an elaborate pattern; his voice when he spoke had the ring of authority:

– Know your place, spirit! You may not baulk me! I am an adept of the left hand path and master of the secret art, a true disciple of Hermes Trismegistus. I bid you stand aside, by that power we both call master!

He raised his arm in a threatening gesture. The figure tilted back its head.

– The power that *you* call master, it sneered. *Egli è bugiardo e padre di menzogna!*

Jake heard Helen give a gasp of surprise. Her eyes were now fixed on the figure: she wore an expression of amazement. The figure shook its head and the cowl fell away. The face revealed was gaunt, lantern-jawed: a long aquiline nose, stern mouth, and jutting pugnacious chin. Pounce spluttered, at a loss for words.

– Messire Dante Alighieri, breathed Helen in an awestruck whisper.

– Truly he, smiled the gaunt figure.

– What is this nonsense? demanded Pounce harshly. Avaunt thee, demon! The dead may not impede me!

He thrust his arm out at his adversary, fingers spread. Something seemed to crackle in the air beyond his fingertips. Dante, however, stood his ground. When he spoke, his clear simplicity made all that had gone before sound mere empty brag:

– I am no ghost, but a living man.

For a moment, Pounce's mask of confidence seemed to slip: before he mastered himself, his face wore a look of incredulity and doubt.

– Impossible! he snarled.

– Yet you see it. I say again : a living man, as you are – now. Ask that Lost One at your side: he knows well enough the difference between us. What I have, he has lost forever.

At this, the face of Pounce's companion lost its terrifying look and was wrung with agony and despair. Helen had never seen a look of such anguish, such utter loss. Jake wanted to avert his eyes, but found he could not.

– You lie! gritted Pounce

– You deceive yourself. Look to your scriptures, wizard: "I am the God of Abraham, of Isaac, and of Jacob. The God of living men, not of the dead."

Pounce was now beside himself with rage.

– This is some trickery! Whatever master you serve, tell him from me: beware! He will not defy me for long! I will have what I seek!

– Tell him yourself, fool.

At this, Pounce's head looked as if it would burst. His face was dark, suffused with blood, and the veins on his neck stood out. Yet he came no nearer than the spot where Dante had halted him with a wave of his hand. Out of the darkness a boat bumped against the landing stage. Dante ushered Jake and Helen aboard, before turning to the sorcerer.

– You still think me no more than a shade? Watch carefully, fool, and know that your masters have deceived you. See how the boat goes down!

He stepped deftly in. The heel of the gondola, driven down by the additional weight, sank in the water before bobbing back.

– A trick! A lie! screamed Pounce, as Dante poled away from the bank.

By way of reply, the austere Florentine held up his fist a little way in front of his hooked nose, thrusting his thumb out between his fore and index finger.

– *Fico!* he flung back, contemptuously.

On the receding bank, the contrast could not have been greater between the two figures. The thwarted Pounce danced with rage, moving from foot to foot and shaking his fists, while from his mouth came a stream of foul invective; behind him his shadow thrown by the flaring braziers seemed to mock him, capering on the wall. His companion stood as still as if he had been cast in bronze, his face set in a look of inexpressible sadness and loss. He cast no shadow.

– It is a bitter thing for a damned soul to be reminded of what he has lost forever, said Dante, as if in answer to their unspoken thought, and for a sorcerer to find that the power he bought so dear is not quite what he was promised.

The poet smiled grimly:

– "Command the very spirits of hell," indeed!

He gave a harsh chuckle, shaking his head.

– Fool! he added, digging the pole in with a force that sped them suddenly forward.

8

Dante explains

A little way out from the landing stage, they glided into a thick bank of fog. Ahead, Jake could just see the characteristic prow of the gondola reared up like the head of some strange animal. Across from him, Helen sat rapt, gazing towards the stern. He could see the fog condense on her hair in little beads: she looked so much in a trance that he feared to disturb her. The figure that stood at the stern oar was no more than an ominous looming shadow, and Jake could not make out any distinguishing feature.

The abrupt removal of Venice from sight was disorienting: it was as if it had vanished, and all that had happened there along with it. Now there was only the white, curling fog: they could as easily have been sailing through the air as on the water. The strangest thought came to Jake, that they had died, and this was the ferryman – Charon – carrying them across the Styx. After all, he thought, no one knows what it's like to die: you only see other people do it. He thought of stories he had read where it dawned gradually on people that they had in fact died. Because of course if you did have a soul, and it did survive death, then there wouldn't be any interruption: you would just keep on existing.

Perhaps all you might be aware of would be some subtle change in the way things felt. A chill spread through him as he recalled what had happened on the train. The recollection seemed vivid, yet somehow distant, as if he viewed it from the wrong end of a telescope; but more than anything he recalled his strong sense that there was something fundamentally wrong, that reality had altered in some way. He tried to pinpoint the start of it: he had woken up, he recalled, and Pounce had been there, and the other man. But what if it had not been sleep they had wakened from, but death? A feeling of awe descended on him. He was dead! He looked across to where Helen sat, as if in a dream. She's dead too, he thought. Perhaps she hasn't realised yet. With a twinge of fear, he turned his attention to the figure at the stern, still only a dim shape in the damp whiteness. Who was that? Or what?

As he watched, the mist eddied away, revealing the figure's lower half, swathed in a long robe and cut off at the waist, like a graveyard statue that had been vandalised. Then the gap in the mist shifted and the legs disappeared, but now a face hung in the air, a forbidding countenance, hook-nosed and lantern-jawed, the eyes deep-sunk and glittering, the mouth set in a grim line.

Then all at once they were through the band of fog and into an open stretch of water like a broad lake bounded with mist. The figure, fully visible now, seemed to become aware of Jake's gaze, and looking down at him, it smiled. The face was transformed: Jake felt a flood of warmth flow over him. All his fears of a moment before fell away, but his curiosity remained.

– Are you really Dante Alighieri? he whispered.
– Truly he, as I said before.
– But – aren't you – dead?
– Do I look dead?
– No you don't – but I thought you died in 1320.
– Not a bit of it!
– You didn't die?

– Well, I died all right, but not till 1321.

– But you're not dead now?

– Dying and being dead are not the same, you know.

He gave a mysterious smile: Jake had the impression he was enjoying himself.

– Are we dead, then?

Dante threw back his head and gave a great roar of laughter.

– Do you feel dead?

– Well, no. But I think – that is, I wondered if perhaps I had died. You know, passed into the next world.

– The next world? There is no next world.

This was not what Jake had expected to hear.

– But, but surely, he stammered.

– There is only one world, said Dante.

– This one?

– Ah, but what do you mean by that? To the child the garden round his house is all the world he knows; it expands as he grows older. Who knows where its bounds may not reach in time?

Jake stayed quiet for a time, digesting this.

– So where in the world are we now? Jake asked at last.

– Where you have been all along: in Venice, in the twenty-first century.

– But the city was empty! It was the time of the plague!

– Was it indeed? Do you know, I am not at all sure that Venice was ever evacuated for the plague.

– But we saw –

– Ah, you saw! But are you confident that you always see things as they are?

He made a flourish with his hand; the distant rim of fog dwindled and on the water they saw long streaks of reflected light: electric light. Before their eyes, the city bustled with nightlife. Floodlights played on buildings; the sound of voices came across the water; the modern world made itself heard in buzzing motorboats and the distant sound of traffic.

– Has it – I mean, was it like that all the time?

– Truly: the sorcerer can manipulate appearance only; reality is beyond his power. He cannot touch the truth; the only power that the Father of Lies grants is to lie.

– The Father of Lies? said Jake.

– The devil, said Helen. *"Egli è bugiardo e padre di menzogna"*, she quoted, "He is a liar and the father of lies."

– Ah, you know my work, said Dante, with unconcealed delight.

– So has Pounce really sold his soul to the Devil, in exchange for special powers? asked Jake sceptically.

– Well, he thinks he has, said Dante, but in this, as in so much else, he is deceived. The price he has paid is real enough, but not the powers he thinks he got in exchange.

– They seemed real enough to me, said Helen with a shiver.

– Oh, they are real powers all right, but they do not belong to him.

– I'm afraid you've lost me again, said Jake.

– Have you seen a young child that has just learned his first words? asked Dante. He shouts for his mother, and his mother appears; he shouts for food or drink and she gives it to him. He thinks he is really making these things happen himself, by the power of his words, when in fact he is quite helpless, entirely dependent on his mother's good will. He could shout all he liked and get nothing if she did not feel disposed to bring it. That is how it is with Pounce: he performs elaborate rituals, thinking he compels the infernal powers to obey him, but in reality they are just indulging him for their own ends.

– But back there you said that Pounce had summoned

you, said Jake.

– As he did, but only in the sense that the sight of a masked man climbing in an upper window summons the police. Sorcery is a kind of law-breaking, you see: when you practice it, you draw the attention of the authorities. The Law cannot be broken with impunity: if you seek to gain an unfair advantage, justice will step in to redress the balance. So Pounce unleashed a higher power, thinking it would give him an advantage over you. What he does not know is that for every power of that sort that is released, another comes to counter it.

– So the forces are always balanced?

– Not at all. Our side is always the stronger. It is by no means an equal contest. That is the part that is not written in any of Pounce's books of magic.

– But then we will always win, said Jake doubtfully. It sounds too easy.

– In reality it is not easy at all, just as magic is illusion yet can do real harm. A war cannot be won without fighting, and though the ultimate victory is certain, for the individual soldier defeat is always possible. You must not forget that people are able to choose what they will do. Although one side is always stronger, not everyone chooses that side. Look at Pounce.

– But why? It doesn't make sense.

– Why indeed? It is one of the central mysteries, why people choose wrong instead of right. But perhaps the choice is not always as straightforward as you might think. For instance, which would you choose: life or death?

– Why, life, of course!

– Ah, but which is which? If the choice lay between certain death and saving yourself by abandoning your friends, then which is life and which is death?

He gave Jake a quizzical look.

– Not so easy, is it?

– I don't know ... Jake hesitated. I mean, if you knew for certain that you'd be, well, looked after, provided you did the right thing. I mean, if you knew that it wasn't just a trick, a story people had made up to encourage you to do the right thing, if there really was something, if you could be certain –

– But what would it be, to be certain in a case like that?

– If you knew beforehand that it would turn out all right –

– Ah, but you cannot always wait for certainty. Sometimes you can only act in hope.

– But what if you're wrong? pleaded Jake

– Ah! "There's the respect that makes calamity of so long life," if I may quote a fellow poet. The whole thing turns on trust, you see. It is a matter of faith, not knowledge. In the end, you always have to take someone's word for it. Concerning the future, even God can give you no more than a promise.

– But – but you're here, said Helen. Dante Alighieri, born in the thirteenth century, died in the fourteenth, and talking to us as large as life in the twenty-first.

– So I am. But what does that guarantee you any more than you know already? You saw Venice empty and lit by torches. Was that true? You have only my word for it and your own judgement whether anything I tell you is true.

– But isn't it? asked Jake doubtfully.

It seemed to him that he had been on the verge of discovering something amazing, only to have it snatched away. Dante gave a perplexing smile and cocked his head, turning his palms outward.

– What do you think?

Helen frowned, considering.

– Well you've helped us against Pounce, she said

decisively. I don't know about the rest, but that's good enough for me.

Yawning, she pulled her coat about her and curled up in the prow of the boat.

Jake sat wondering at the tall figure plying the stern oar. His face, so forbidding earlier, now struck Jake as extraordinarily beautiful – it remained the same face, yet subtly transformed, as if lit from within. Overhead, the sky had cleared into a glorious night of stars. Presently, Dante lifted his head and began to sing. His voice had a rich, golden quality, and the song too was beautiful, joyous and uplifting, though not in any language Jake could understand. When the song ended, Jake plucked up enough courage to ask a question that had been troubling him:

– Where did you come from?

– Why, from Florence of course. Do they teach you nothing these days?

– He means where did you come from just now, said Helen sleepily, before you appeared to us?

– I came here on the train, just as you did. I was the man with the luggage, remember?

– You know very well I don't mean that, said Jake, exasperated. I meant where do you come from?

By way of answer, Dante burst into another snatch of incomprehensible song, delivered, Jake thought, with just a touch of theatricality. Then he beamed at him, as if all should now be clear.

– No?

He put on a sad face.

– I thought not. For me, inexpressible; to you, incomprehensible. It cannot be said in terms you understand, and you cannot understand the terms in which it can be expressed. You must just wait and see for yourself.

– But didn't you write a book about it? said Helen from

the bottom of the boat. I thought you had a guided tour, she chided.

Dante smiled ruefully.

– All that was very wide of the mark, I'm afraid. St. Paul was on safer ground: "The eye has not seen, nor the ear heard, nor has it entered into the heart of man." Very chastening, to learn that your major artistic endeavor is just so much straw. Still, humility is endless.

Again he plied the oar, and raised his voice in song. Jake stayed awake a while longer, wondering at the silhouette that stood at the stern and seemed crowned with stars. Then after a time he too fell asleep.

Dawn found them on the Lido: across the glittering lagoon Venice rose majestic out of the early morning mists. Jake gazed across at the enchanted city, trying to decide what of his recollection was memory and what was dream. He remembered being on the train and falling asleep; but what had happened then? He was aware of a huge mass of thought that he was holding at arm's length as if he was afraid to look at it too closely. Then he looked in the direction of Helen's voice, and it all became clear again.

She was sitting on a bollard, talking to a tall man who stooped over her. His dress was modern, but the face was unmistakable.

– Ah, you are awake, my young friend. As you see, there are marvels still in the broad light of day. It was no dream, although parts of it were not what they seemed. But now I must be getting on.

– Won't you be coming with us?

– Not at present.

Jake's face fell.

– Do not be downhearted. Help is always at hand, in some form or another. Go forward in confidence, do what is right, and all will be well.

– But we can't beat Pounce on our own!

– Only have faith! You have done very well so far. Persevere. There are some things which only you can do, choices only you can make, but you are never truly on your own, though it may seem so at the time. For now, farewell!

Jake started up as if to prevent his going, but somehow the sun got in his eyes and a patch of dazzle seemed to come between him and Dante. When it cleared, he was gone.

Jake felt strangely bereft. He sometimes had dreams in which he came by something marvellous, and was just bringing it home when he somehow mislaid it – always carelessly, leaving it on a bus, or on the table in a café. The acute sense of loss he felt in the dream would persist after he woke, leaving him as sad throughout the day as if the loss were real. So Dante seemed to have let him glimpse something wonderful, only to snatch it back, as if he had snapped shut a marvellous picture book. And now that Dante himself was gone, it already began to feel as if he had never really been there at all.

– Come on, said Helen, let's see if we can get something to eat. I'm starving. By the way, did you know that you snore?

Jake, unable to think of a suitable rejoinder, followed in silence; Helen, avid for breakfast, led the way. As he passed the bollard where Helen had sat talking to Dante, the glint of metal caught his eye. Stooping, he picked up a small bronze medal on a fine chain, but slipped it in his pocket unexamined at Helen's impatient call.

9
The Kingdom of Heaven

Only when breakfast had restored him did Jake think to look at what he had found. He fished it from his pocket, catching Helen's attention at once.

– What's that?

– I found it down on the quayside.

– Let me see!

He held it out in his palm over the table so they both could see it. It was an oval medal of no great size. On one side was the head of a man, shown full face. It was done in a strange, primitive style which suggested it was very old: the face was almost flat, the features somewhat stylised. Nevertheless, the artist had captured some sense of individual character: the face was not handsome, but forceful and intelligent, with keen eyes looking out beneath a formidable brow and a set to the mouth and jaw which suggested strength and determination; not a man to be trifled with, you felt. Round the edge in raised letters were the two words "Doctor Angelicus"

– Is there anything on the back?

– Looks like more writing.

Peering close at the minute script, Helen read

Io fui degli agni della santa greggia
che Domenico mena per cammino
u'ben s'impingua, se non si vaneggia

– Sounds like Dante, though I don't think it's the *Inferno*.

– Can you translate it?

– I think so: "I was of the sacred flock of lambs that Dominic leads on the way where well they fatten if they do not stray." I wonder who it is?

– I know, said Jake smugly.

Helen looked at him with surprise and what he hoped might be respect, though the more objective part of him reckoned it was scepticism.

– It's Thomas Aquinas, the Angelic Doctor.

Helen shot him a look that was definitely sceptical this time.

– And?

– And he was born in 1225, went to the University of Naples at the age of 10, studied in Paris under Albert the Great, where he was known as "the dumb ox" –

– The dumb ox?!

– Because he was big and silent, and his fellow students thought he was stupid. But really he was thinking all the time, and Albert said "this dumb ox will one day fill the world with his bellowing". Which was true because he became the greatest philosopher and theologian of the Middle Ages, taking Aristotle's thought and applying it –

– How do you know all this? asked Helen suspiciously, interrupting Jake's machine-gun delivery of facts.

– Oh, just something I picked up by the way, said Jake airily.

– I'll bet!

– Well, all right then. I chose Thomas for my confirmation name –

– Confirmation name?

– It's a thing you do when you're a Catholic. When you're a bit older you renew your baptismal vows:

renouncing Satan and all his works, the glamor of evil and all that. You pick a new name to mark the event, so I picked St. Thomas Aquinas. And to make sure we all took it seriously we had to find out about the saint behind the name and do a talk.

– The glamor of evil, said Helen thoughtfully. That's an interesting expression.

– That bit about "fattening" is a bit below the belt, because old Tom was not the world's slimmest. In fact the story goes they had to cut a big bit out of the dining table to make room for his belly!

– What it is to have a catholic education!

– You a protestant then? said Jake, with the Glasgow Catholic's simple analysis of the world.

– I don't think I'm anything really. I used to be an agnostic, but now I'm not so sure, she smiled.

Jake laughed.

– Hey, did you hear about the insomniac dyslexic agnostic? He used to lie awake all night wondering if there really was a dog!

Helen laughed. They looked around them in the bright morning air. The daylight marvels of Venice, rising majestically from the shimmering waters, displaced the strangeness of the night before, making it more than ever like a dream.

– Come on, we've got a painting to fetch.

The vaporetto for Murano was crowded with tourists. And even after they had landed, they found themselves part of a colorful, noisy throng; but a couple of turns separated them, and all at once they were alone in empty cobbled streets. The quarter they were in seemed very ancient: the houses leaned together conspiratorially; their shuttered windows gave them a closed, secret look. The brightness of the morning sun made stark shadows in the narrow streets and narrower alleys that wound off them, zigzagged with rows of washing between the upper storeys.

It took some time to find the Calle delle Chiavi – they walked past its narrow entrance several times. A lounger with a newspaper looked at them curiously as they passed and repassed the same spot, before stepping into the narrow slit and disappearing from view as suddenly as if the shadowed stones had simply absorbed them.

The alleyway was cool and dark: Jake wondered if the sun ever came there. Helen confidently took the lead down the winding lane, which gave no impression of leading anywhere. Its twists and turns were such that you could never see very far ahead, and it was not long before Jake felt completely disoriented. Helen, however, pressed on, and found at last the little half-width door with the grimy, ancient sign: *Vetreria Regno del Cielo — Luigi Sanpietro, proprietario.*

If Signor Sanpietro was at all surprised to find one of his keys brought to him by a young girl, he did not show it. He simply grunted, took the key, squinted at the number, and disappeared into the corridor of cabinets, from where he returned a minute or two later carrying a large canvas bag. He produced from under the table a large and ancient ledger, and Helen expected to be asked to sign something; but the little man simply took a ruler, drew a line through an entry, and resumed his seat without looking at them again.

When they emerged onto the street, the same lounger was still there; but soon after they passed him, he folded his newspaper and strolled after them. They wandered through Murano for a bit, searching for somewhere suitably secluded to take a look at the picture. Eventually they found a spacious public garden, and selected a sheltered spot.

Helen withdrew the painting from the bag: it was wrapped in brown paper. It was smaller than Jake had expected, and when they unwrapped the brown paper, he saw that it was smaller still: the frame was disproportionately large and ornate; the picture itself was about the size of a sheet of copy paper. However, what it lacked in size, it made up for in brilliance: it had a quality that beguiled the eye.

Jake had not looked long at it before he developed the curious feeling that it *was* a much larger painting that he was somehow viewing from far away. It reminded him of a childhood game – looking through his mother's opera glasses turned the wrong way round. Then things assumed the same quality that the painting had now: miniaturized versions of themselves, preserving all the fantastic detail that only a larger object could have.

The Alchemist seemed like a real person, looking out at him through a window framed by two great ivory tusks. Behind him, the murky room seemed to go back with real depth: there the page-boy capered, tray of sweets or cakes in one hand, the other pointing – at what? Jake was almost surprised not to see himself reflected in the distant mirror.

The quality of the light and detail was astonishing: Jake wondered if it had been painted with the aid of a magnifying lens. Then he recalled the bit about "not being painted by human hand" and a little shiver crept over him. He returned his gaze to the Alchemist's face, grave and secretive, his dark liquid eyes looking directly at him. What did he know? What was the secret?

– Beautiful, isn't it? said Helen.

The eyes still held Jake, drawing him in, deeper and deeper. He heard Helen's question, but as if from a great distance; he felt on the verge of discovering something important. All at once things which he had kept at the bottom of his thoughts came rushing upwards to ambush him: the face in front of him changed momentarily to that of Pounce, as he had first seen it when he woke on the train. He recoiled suddenly, almost dropping the picture.

– Careful! cried Helen.

– This is what he's after – Pounce. He wants the painting.

One glance at Helen told him that she believed it too.

– What do we do? said Jake. As long as we have it, it'll draw him like a magnet!

He looked around the garden, wide-eyed, as if he expected Pounce to materialize out of the bushes. But there was no one, save a solitary man a good distance off, reading a newspaper.

– Calm down, Jake. He doesn't know we have it. How could he?

– How did he know to find us on the train? He seems to have ways of finding things out!

– Well, anyway, there's no need to panic. We could have it back in Switzerland this afternoon, and The Aunts can put it in a bank vault somewhere. I doubt if even Pounce can magic his way into a Swiss bank.

– But I'm meant to be going to Naples!

– Look, Jake, I'm sorry I tricked you into coming to Venice, but you wouldn't give up on me now, would you? I'd feel a lot happier if I didn't have to do this on my own.

Jake looked at her, and did not doubt that she would do it alone if she had to. It was that, more than anything, that persuaded him to agree.

– All right, but what about cousin Gianni?

Helen looked thoughtful.

– When's the funeral to be?

– Next Monday, they reckoned. Certainly not sooner.

– This is Tuesday. Look, Jake, are you really desperate to see your Neapolitan cousins? What I mean is that it wouldn't make sense for you to come all the way to Switzerland only to turn around and go away again. If the funeral's not till next week, maybe you could stay on a day or two. I'm sure I could persuade your cousin. We're terribly respectable people, you know.

She looked at him with a smile, but in her eyes there was something more: a pleading, almost. She's lonely, thought Jake, with a moment of insight. She'd make the trip on her own if she had to, Pounce and all. It's being on her own at home that she really can't face.

– Okay, I think I'd like that. Thanks for asking me. The smile broadened, and spread to her eyes.

– Take me to a telephone! she commanded.

The arrangements proved much more straight-forward than Jake had hoped. He spoke to cousin Gianni himself, after Helen had explained things, and formed the impression that his relative had quite enough on his hands with the arrangements for the funeral and multitudes of guests; one fewer would not distress him. His parents were not due to arrive until the Saturday, so it was agreed that Jake would appear at the same time. He rang off, feeling curiously liberated.

– We should be able to get a direct train from Venice, said Helen.

They sauntered in the direction of the landing stage where they had arrived. A man passed close to them, a newspaper under his arm, walking briskly until he was a little way ahead. Then he seemed to lose his sense of urgency, and slowed to an easier pace. A little farther on, the road forked, with a coffee bar on the corner between the two branches. The man with the newspaper now felt so little urgency that he stopped for an espresso. However, as soon as Jake and Helen had passed, taking the right hand fork, he finished and hurried after them.

– I think we're being followed, said Jake.

– Are you sure?

– I don't know. Do you remember the man who was there when we were looking for the Calle delle Chiavi? The one with the newspaper, who was still there when we came out?

– I think so.

– Well I keep seeing him. I'm nearly sure he was in the park. And he passed us just now then stopped off at the café, but now he's behind us again.

– Let's go into this shop and see what he does.

The shop was a regular tourist trap, crammed with glass ornaments, many of them uniquely hideous.

– Who buys this stuff? asked Helen.

– People's aunties.

– Not mine!

A salesgirl, misreading the signs, closed for a sale and had to be waved away.

– What's he doing?

– He's across the road, leaning against the wall with his paper. See?

– It's the same man all right, said Helen. I remember him now.

– What do we do?

– Is there a back way out, do you think?

Helen turned to the salesgirl.

– Excuse me, there is a man outside who has been bothering us. Is there another way out of the shop?

The girl sized them up. Helen gave her a smile of complicity.

– He actually works for my father. Papa doesn't approve of my boyfriend.

Jake smiled and looked boyish. The girl wagged a finger and smiled knowingly. She gestured them to follow her. There was a little courtyard at the back of the shop, with a gate to a lane.

– Go that way. It rejoins the road after a hundred metres or so.

– Thank you!

Exchanging conspiratorial smiles with their new-found accomplice, they stole off, hand in hand. They emerged not far from the landing stage, where there was something of a commotion.

– We're in luck, said Helen. They won't try much with them around.

Jake looked and saw that the cause of the commotion was the arrival of a police launch. There were a number of uniformed officers aboard, and an older man in plain clothes.

– Let's stick close to them until the *vaporetto* comes in, said Helen.

They sidled over to the launch, where the men were now disembarking. They lined up on the quayside with the air of waiting for someone. The plain-clothes man stayed on board, barking instructions.

– Think our man's still watching the shop?

– No such luck, said Helen. Here he comes now.

He was hurrying through the crowd, to the extent of jostling people, who gave him angry looks. As he neared the landing stage he caught sight of them and slowed down. Jake and Helen backed instinctively toward the police launch and the line of uniformed officers. The man came on, in no hurry now, casually striking his newspaper against his leg.

– What do we do? Try to bluff him into going on the
vaporetto first, then give him the slip? asked Jake.

– He's a cool customer, I'll give him that, said Helen.

The man did not seem at all put out by the police
presence; he exchanged a smile and a nod with one of the
men on the quayside. Then he strolled with purpose across
to where Jake and Helen were standing, and pointed his
rolled up newspaper in their direction.

– These are the ones, he said to the man in the boat.

10

Collared!

Two tall policemen suddenly appeared, one either side of Jake and Helen, and took their arms in a firm grip.

– What is the meaning of this? demanded Helen. I am a Swiss citizen.

– I beg your pardon, Signorina, but I must ask you to show us the contents of that bag.

– With pleasure, but not in this public place.

– If you would come on board the launch?

– Gladly. Tell your man to take his hand off my arm. I'm not about to run away.

Jake, who generally felt guilty as soon as a policeman looked at him, was full of admiration for her spirited stand. He followed meekly after her, still in the grip of his escort, feeling very much a desperate criminal.

As soon as they were on board, the launch pulled away and headed back toward Venice. Helen, with a haughty air, surrendered the bag to the man in plain clothes. She gave her name and address to one of the policemen, and then, with an improvisation worthy of her father, identified Jake as her cousin from Finland who spoke very little Italian, although he understood some English. She produced her passport, but said that her cousin had left his bag with all his papers on the train last night, and they would have to see if it had been handed in at the station. Jake, reduced to a spectator by this deft bit of invention, was able to marvel once more at Helen's natural authority. The policemen deferred to her as if she had been an adult, and a well connected one at that. Even the plainclothes man, who was clearly in charge, was notably polite.

The painting, when it was revealed, caused a minor sensation among the policemen. They all crowded round to peer at it, and had to be shooed away by the man in charge. One, a rather handsome fellow with a big mustache, lingered even after that and had to be told again, somewhat curtly, to remove himself. He seemed not at all put out, and retired to the stern of the boat where he lounged on the gunwale, chatting to someone on his mobile phone. In fact, the general behavior of the policemen struck Jake as remarkably relaxed: several of them were smoking. The man in charge turned to Helen.

– If you please, Signorina, I would be grateful to know the provenance of this painting, and how it comes to be in your possession.

– Certainly. It is part of my aunts' collection in Switzerland. My father, who catalogued the collection and organizes exhibitions of it, was concerned that a man named Aurelian Pounce intended to steal the painting. He deposited it at Murano for safekeeping and then asked me to retrieve it for him.

– That is an admirably clear account, Signorina, and I am most grateful to you for it. However you will appreciate that in cases of this sort we must take some steps to verify the facts. If you and your cousin will accompany us to the Prefecture, I will endeavor to ensure that the matter is dealt with as speedily as possible.

– That is most kind of you. My cousin and I will be delighted to accompany you. At least in the Prefecture we can be sure that there will be no further attempts on the painting.

She gave the policeman a winning smile, which he returned. Settling back beside Jake she gave him an account of all that had happened, speaking in very slow, clear English. Jake looked daggers at her, but she only smiled the more.

Only when they were inside the prefecture, sitting in a corner of the foyer amid a jungle of rubber plants, did they have a chance to chat unobserved. A bored-looking desk sergeant sat doodling behind a high counter; Jake and Helen shrank back among the leaves.

– Why Finnish, for God's sake? Jake whispered.

– I had to think of a language that no one was likely to speak. You don't exactly look like you're from Uzbekistan, you know.

– Why not just tell them the truth?

– You really want them phoning your parents in Glasgow to say you've been arrested?

– And what happens when they try to phone my parents in Finland?

– No point. They've just been killed in a car crash, and now you're staying with me in Switzerland. Tragic story, really.

– I'll say.

A tanned woman entered from outside and went to speak to the desk sergeant. She wore a pale blue pullover across her shoulders, tied at the throat, and had sunglasses propped in her hair – which was of a reddish hue not found in nature. The desk sergeant seemed to know her, although his expression did not suggest he liked her. He shouted something over his shoulder into the back office. One of the policemen who had been on the boat appeared, the handsome one with the big mustache. He greeted the woman with great familiarity, then nodded across to where

Jake and Helen sat. She was about to come over to them when two other officers appeared from the interior.

One, a tall, older man, asked Helen – again very politely and deferentially – to accompany him. The other, a young man with a very blue chin and dark curly hair, sat himself across from Jake, but made no attempt to engage him in conversation. His presence seemed to deter the redhead, who retired to the counter for a brief whispered conversation with the mustached officer before departing the way she had come.

It seemed to Jake that the desk sergeant shot her a dirty look as she left. It was twenty minutes before Helen returned, in the company of a rather florid-looking man in an expensive suit. Helen was in full Aunt mode.

– I accept that it is necessary, Signor Patta, but that does not make it any less tiresome. And I do not at all see why it has to be in Milan.

Patta, at her elbow, had the air of a man recently bitten, who fears he may be again.

– I am most terribly sorry, Signora De Havilland, but I regret the matter is out of my control. All the operations of the fine art section of the Questura have recently been relocated to Milan. I will endeavor to ensure that the matter is dealt with expeditiously and that there is no unnecessary delay. I will see to it personally.

– Thank you, Signor Patta, Helen replied caustically. I am sure you will do your best to see that I get my property back quickly.

He escorted them to the door of the prefecture, where Helen disdained his offer of a lift.

As soon as they were alone, Helen could hardly speak for laughing.

– That poor man! I had a hard job to keep my face

straight. I established early on that The Aunts were on *extremely* good terms with someone *very* high up in the Ministry of Justice and that they would not be at all pleased to hear of how I had been maliciously inconvenienced. From then on he practically apologized for breathing. Every step of the procedure he outlined, he looked as if I might bite his head off, so I made sure to keep snarling. But listen to this: *they* will look after the painting, which saves us the bother. There will be a court hearing in Milan to establish the title, which should put paid to Pounce – that's at two tomorrow by the way – after which we will be free to take the painting back to Switzerland. They'll probably even offer us a police escort to the border. Each new thing he said I thought, "Even better!" But all the time I kept looking more and more displeased. The poor man!

– So are we staying with your cousin in Florence tonight then?

– Not at all. We'll stay with my cousin in Milan.

Is there any European city where she doesn't have a cousin? wondered Jake. At the station, they discovered their baggage had been handed in intact. Feeling wonderfully unencumbered, they set off on a farewell stroll round Venice, to kill time before catching the train to Milan.

*****

A diabolical interlude in a Venetian café

From across the way you would take the two of them for old friends: the dark, lean-faced cleric in the old-fashioned broad-brimmed hat and the very broad man in the light-colored suit, mopping his brow with a colorful handkerchief. A high-ranking priest and a wealthy landowner perhaps, meeting over coffee to agree about the degenerate state of the modern world and regret the passing of the old values. But come a little closer, and their conversation seems at odds with their appearance.

– Your idea of a joke, I suppose, rasps Pounce, indicating his companion's priestly garb. The other smiles.

– "Go, and return an old Franciscan friar; that holy shape becomes a devil best."

He looks down at his clerical garb, which is rather well cut, and elegantly piped with red.

– Not exactly a friar, I grant you, but in keeping with the – ah – spirit of Marlowe's line – do you know the play, by the way? *Dr. Faustus?*

Pounce seems ill disposed to his companion's banter.

– No.

– Pity! You'd find it most instructive.

– What I want to know is where their assistance came from. That damned poet! If I'd known I had to do with fellow adepts, I'd have gone about things an entirely different way.

The companion makes soothing noises.

– My dear fellow, I assure you these are mere children. There can be no question that they are themselves practitioners of magic.

– Well someone at the back of them is!

– It is just one of those unfortunate things that happen from time to time. The ... ah ... Other Powers are somewhat capricious about when they choose to intervene. Very unpredictable, and not at all satisfactory I agree, but there you are.

– This is not the service that was promised me.

– My dear fellow, what we cannot gain by one means we will surely win by another. I am able to tell you that the children have recovered the painting, but have been compelled to turn it over to the authorities. There is to be a court hearing to establish their title.

He falls to examining his fingernails, which are beautifully manicured. Pounce, clearly expecting him to continue, is eventually driven by exasperation to prompt him.

– Well?

– I should have thought a man with all your connections could manage to fix a court case.

Greed and the urge to snub his companion vie with one another in Pounce's truculent face. The companion gazes blandly into the middle distance. In time, he dispenses another morsel:

– And of course the court appointment fixes the daughter to a particular place and time. What is the saying? "Assignation and Ambush have the same beginning."

That is a point, thinks Pounce. If I have the daughter, the father will come out of the woodwork soon enough. The daughter could have other uses besides, and the boy too, come to that. Time to plan a little ambush. Time to swallow his pride.

– I shall need assistance.

– On the usual terms?

– By all means, on the usual terms – someone for the painting, someone for the children. Only don't mess up this time!

He strikes the table with the flat of his hand, making the coffee cups jump. A brief glint of fire comes into the companion's eye, but his response is smooth and urbane.

– I can assure you of the most formidable assistance. When it comes to the legal profession, we have a remarkable range of talent at our disposal.

Pounce creases his brow in thought and stares ferociously in front of him. At length he comes to a decision, which he marks by striking the table a second time, rather less fiercely.

– I'll get Buonconte to handle my side.

Buonconte, handily located here in Venice, is just the man for the job: he knows art, is keen to advance his standing in the occult world, and has recently given clear evidence of his loyalty. Pounce turns to explain all this to his companion, but finds he has gone, leaving him to pay the bill.

*****

Fragments of a Venetian afternoon

In an upper room Baldassare Buonconte ensures the doors are locked before he takes from a cabinet – also locked – a large and ancient book. This he sets on an ornate reading stand, while on the table he prepares various instruments and ingredients. The table is a curious piece of furniture: in the middle of it a large circular hole has been cut out.

While Buonconte prepares there is a knock on the door, and he unlocks it to receive from a servant (who remains beyond the threshold) a large silver basin with, in it, a brimming silver ewer. He dismisses the servant and takes the basin to the table, where he sets it in the circular hole, removes the ewer and puts it on the table. Then he returns to the door which he closes and relocks.

*

Aurelian Pounce, waiting in the private library of a wealthy client, recalls the conversation of his lunchtime companion and is sufficiently curious to search the shelves for Marlowe's play, Dr. Faustus. Here it is. He takes it down, flicks through the pages. Perhaps, as happens in the

play, an invisible demon stands at his elbow, to turn the
pages and to lead his eye: however it is, in skimming
through his eye is caught only by scenes like this, where
Faustus (also in a library) takes down a book of magic:

> *Magicians and necromantic books are heavenly ...*
> *O what a world of profit and delight,*
> *Of power, of honor, of omnipotence*
> *Is promis'd to the studious artisan!*
> *All things that move between the quiet poles*
> *Shall be at my command ...*
> *A sound magician is a mighty god*

Hmm! It is, as his companion said, most instructive. He
is grateful to him for drawing attention to it. A scene he
fails to see (perhaps his eye is led away from it?) is that
where the demon Mephistophilis promises Faustus:

> *I will be thy slave and wait on thee,*
> *And give thee more than thou hast wit to ask*

But then remarks aside to the audience (as Faustus
signs a contract in his own blood):

> *O what will not I do to obtain his soul!*

Pounce does see, and agrees with, Faustus' utterance:

> *Come, I think hell's a fable*

But somehow his eye skips over Mephistopheles'
chilling reply:

> *Ay, think so still, till experience change thy mind.*

He puts the book back on the shelf. What was that line again? *A sound magician is a mighty god.* Yes indeed, really most instructive. He must read the rest of it some time.

*

Baldassare Buonconte, nearing the completion of his preparations, feels exhilarated but also (he is willing to admit) a little frightened. To have been chosen by Aurelian Pounce to perform this task is a great honor, but also a heavy responsibility. He arranges the ivory finger bowls painstakingly around the basin in the required pattern.

He has been scrupulous in his measurement and mixture of the various ingredients which each contains. A fastidious man in daily life, in this he takes particular care: these are formidable powers he is dealing with, and any lapse or weakness in controlling them will be harshly punished. Still, that is what he likes about magic – the sense of danger, of terrible forces contained and harnessed in a fine net of ritual.

There! The final item is in place. Each object on the table represents a person with a part to play in his carefully thought-out scheme: the relation between them is crucial. This is himself, in a position of importance near to the basin, the center of power – this little bowl with three dark drops of his own blood. These others are the various men and women who will act as his instruments, each bound to him by some thread of obligation, each represented by something that was once a living part of them: hair, skin, nail clippings, spittle, blood.

He thinks of them as he touches each of the bowls in turn, these people he shall shortly bind to his service: ordinary people mostly, not especially wicked, but apt to evil if the circumstances are right. People who, left alone, lead unexceptional lives, but in the presence of some stronger influence align themselves to it like iron filings round a magnet. Some stronger influence, that is to say, such as the one he is about to summon.

Baldassare Buonconte takes the ewer and pours its blood-dark contents into the silver basin. He stirs the liquid anticlockwise, casting in the contents of each bowl in turn, starting from the outside and finishing with his own, reading all the time in an undertone from the great book. He removes the stirrer, but the liquid continues to whirl around, faster and faster, until a vortex appears in the middle of it and widens steadily accompanied by a deep humming sound like the throb of a dynamo. The vortex widens until it is a dark tunnel stretching downward, through the table, through the floor, through the earth itself to some dark underworld. And as Baldassare Buonconte, still reading, watches in fascination and horror, far down something stirs and slowly begins to rise towards him.

*

Giacomo Girolamo Thomas Giacometti, known as Jake, delves in his pocket for his handkerchief and pulling it out brings with it some small thing which falls unnoticed to the pavement with a ringing sound: a coin perhaps? No, that medal – forgotten since this morning in the excitements of the day. Jake walks on. The medal lies glinting in the sun.

*

Baldassare Buonconte sees rising through the vortex toward him the outline of a man, viewed from above. The shoulders and chest are massive; so too is the head. He trembles with fear and excitement – any moment now it will raise its head and he will see the face ...

*

Helen De Havilland, her eye caught by something glinting on the pavement, stoops to pick it up.

– Here, you'd best put this on if you don't want to lose it.

She fastens it about Jake's neck.

– To ward off the glamor of evil, she smiles.

*

The face tilts towards him. Baldassare Buonconte reels back, appalled.

II

Disorder in Court

Jake's first encounter with one of Helen's relatives did not leave him with a favorable impression. Her cousin Isidora was a strikingly good-looking woman, tall, slender and beautifully dressed, but she had all the warmth of a marble slab. Her handshake was cool, her long elegant fingers with their sparkling array of rings barely brushing his proffered hand; her appraising glance was cool, her ice-blue eyes flicking over him in a second; and her attitude to him thereafter was distinctly cool, to the point of refrigeration.

Nor was she notably warmer toward Helen: a peck on the cheek, and an embrace that somehow contrived to hold her at arm's length was all she gave in the way of affection. After that it seemed Helen's role was to be a sounding board for her cousin's ideas about fashion, modern life, the political situation – she was an ardent advocate of the notion that the North of Italy should sever itself from what she called the deeply corrupt and irredeemably workshy South.

Indeed she was happy to discuss any topic under the sun, provided it was of her choosing. A brief attempt by Helen to raise the subject of her father was swiftly squashed, and even the matter that had brought them to Milan seemed of no interest to her whatever. Her interest in Helen as a person was minimal, confined to advice on her posture and her looks: she could really be quite presentable if only she didn't frown so, and did something with that hair, and of course a really good dressmaker was an absolute must. She could take her to one or two if she wished, a project for which Helen showed no enthusiasm.

Jake, who more than once had found himself envying Helen's self possession (the product, he presumed, of her wealthy background), now wondered if it was not purchased at too high a price. If all her relatives were like this then all the wealth in the world was poor compensation. He could only admire the way she took her cousin on, not giving an inch, countering icy politeness with icy politeness, in a strange sort of ritual fencing match.

Watching her now, he understood better the great interest she had shown in his crowded family, and the pleading for company he had glimpsed in her eyes in the garden at Murano. He wondered if cousin Isidora had ever been like Helen; and whether Helen, as she grew older, would become like cousin Isidora. He hoped she might be spared that fate.

The evening dragged but came at last to an end, and they were glad to escape to the haven of their beds.

Breakfast next morning, from which cousin Isidora was absent, was a much more cheerful affair. Jake came down to find Helen already well established in the spacious, stylish kitchen, surrounded by numerous varieties of food.

– Come on! I thought you were never getting up. If you're quick we can clear out and do a bit of Milan before it's time to go to court.

– Give us a chance at breakfast! I just got here.

Milan, to Jake's mind, was a much more modern city than any he had yet seen in Italy. Unlike Venice, which in some ways was almost like a museum, or Florence, where you were always conscious of the past, it seemed to live much more in the present. But for all that, it was unmistakably

Italian, the pavements thronged with wonderfully elegant people, the shops and cafés radiating style. Jake, who liked big cities anyway, thought it marvellous; it was certainly enough to keep his mind off the afternoon, but eventually Helen looked at her watch and said:

– I suppose we should be making tracks.

They paused a moment in the street, to consult the map and find the address that was on the slip Helen had been given in the Prefecture in Venice. Just as she had unfolded it, a passerby jostled her arm and seemed to twitch it from her grasp. She gave a little cry of dismay as it fluttered away from her, but a man coming in the other direction stooped in his stride and caught it neatly somewhere near the pavement, then surfaced near them, holding it out to her.

– This should be yours, I think.

– Thank you, said Helen, taking it from his hand.

When she looked she saw that the stranger had given her not one piece of paper but two: the other was a thin strip with some odd writing on it, picked out in red and black. Thinking it something of his own he had given her by mistake, she turned to call after him, but he was lost in the crowd. Then a sudden hot breath of air that might have come up from a grating in the pavement caught the thin strip and whirled it out of her grasp and away into the traffic.

– Damn! said Helen.

– Never mind, said Jake, we've still got the one that matters.

He studied the map intently, but was a long time finding the right place.

– That's funny, he said, I'd kind of looked for it before when we were on the train, and made sure it was somewhere in this bit here, but now it's like, miles away.

– You probably had the map upside down, said Helen testily. Come on then, we'd better move.

But they had not gone far when they came on a sign pointing up a sidestreet: *Palazzo di Giustizia*. Angled across the far end, they could see a section of colonnade, suggesting a large public building.

– See, said Jake, I told you it was around here.

– But it's not the address on the slip of paper.

– But it's a courthouse, at any rate – how many of them can there be?

The street was short and opened onto a broad piazza, one side of which was taken up with an impressive building proclaiming itself to be the *Palazzo di Giustizia*.

As they mounted the steps leading up to the towering colonnade, their eye was drawn to a remarkable figure near the top. In a country noted for the variety and flamboyance of its uniforms, this man's still contrived to be outstanding. He wore a long coat that was a most arresting shade of deep rose pink faced with navy blue; epaulettes and ropes of gold adorned the shoulders; the legs were clad in shiny leather kneeboots and an outlandish hat, with plume, completed the ensemble. He had an air of waiting to be of service; he drew them like a magnet.

– Excuse me, said Helen.

– Young Miss! Young Sir! he saluted them.

– Are we in the right place?

– If justice is what you seek, undoubtedly.

– It's just that we have a court appointment, but the address on the slip is quite different.

The man in the gorgeous uniform took the slip and studied it with care.

– May I ask, young Miss and Sir, if this would be a matter at all concerned with art?

– It would, as a matter of fact.

– In which case all is explained. The courts that deal with matters of art have only recently been relocated to this our fine city and are housed, temporarily, at the address you have here. Your best way is by that street you came down, then turn left. But I see you have a map! When you get there you may find the arrangements a little surprising but do not doubt that you are in the right place.

– Thank you.

They made their way back down the steps, smiling to one another at the man's flamboyant manner and strange way of speaking. But when they turned back from the edge of the piazza for a last look, they saw that he was no longer there.

The streets they followed seemed to take them away from the bustling, modern heart of the city into a less frequented district, altogether older and more rundown. The people here seemed shabby and ill dressed; they cast sidelong glances at Jake and Helen as they passed, obvious tourists with their smart clothes and their streetmap.

– I get the impression we've left the fashionable district, said Jake.

He was beginning to feel distinctly uncomfortable. He remembered once when he was small and his brother, newly qualified to drive, had taken a wrong turning and somehow ended up in one of Glasgow's bleaker districts: there had been the same sidelong looks then. He had been painfully conscious of the shiny newness of their car, and suddenly fearful lest it should break down in this desert of boarded-up tenements and grass plots gone to seed, with rusting cars and grimy children in oversize clothes pushing ancient prams. Then his brother stalled at a junction and he had dived in terror into the footwell, an action which his siblings still delighted to recall.

He felt the same sense of latent hostility now as they made their way though the dusty cobbled streets with young men on street corners staring at them as if they had invaded their territory, old men in brown suits and hats, and old women all in black eyeing them suspiciously as they passed. He glanced sidelong at Helen, envying her cool composure as she walked, head erect, with an air of being as entitled to be there as anyone else. She even broke away from Jake and went to speak to a group of rough-looking men lounging round the door of a garage workshop. Oh God, thought Jake, what are you *doing*! They'll probably kidnap you. Don't leave me here!

They stood serious and unsmiling as she addressed them; looked at one another, shook their heads, shrugged. Helen seemed at a loss for a moment, then tried some other tack. All at once the sullen men were smiling and nodding, giving elaborate directions with much waving of arms and pointing. And Helen was swapping some banter with them over her shoulder as she walked back to Jake.

– It's just round the corner, but what threw them off at first was when I asked for a courthouse. They say it's only a shop.

– It is the address on the paper though?

– Definitely. They were quite sure of that.

– Best go and take a look, I suppose.

Sure enough, the name of the next street – painted high up on the brick wall – corresponded to that on the slip of paper; but it looked a most unlikely situation for a courthouse or a public building of any sort. For a start, only half the street was there: the other side had been demolished, leaving bare sites overrun with a riotous growth of weeds and grass. The street itself was remarkably short and seemed to go nowhere, ending after about seventy metres in an expanse of waste ground: a forlorn streetlamp marked the boundary. The side of the street that was standing consisted of a grimy tenement block, much of which was derelict, with windows boarded up or dark and curtainless. In the very center was a shop, with a weathered headboard which proclaimed it to be:

Macelleria, Pasticceria e Drogheria
(Butcher, Confectioner and Grocer)

but when they looked closer they saw that a handpainted sign underneath – it looked as if the paint was still wet – said :

Palazzo di Giustizia

Jake and Helen eyed one another doubtfully. Surely it was not possible? Had the man in the gorgeous uniform not forewarned them to expect something "a little surprising" they would have turned back. As it was, they approached most uncertainly.

As they neared it, the door swung open, as if someone behind it had been observing them as they pondered outside. The shop inside was dark and smelled of blood. All manner of hams and sausages hung from the ceiling. The floor was bare wood.

Once they were in, they found that the shop was crowded with people and indeed was much larger than it had appeared from the outside. The people were doing their shopping, with a great deal of noise and bustle, but when Jake and Helen entered they quickly fell silent, all except one woman who suddenly found herself talking alone in a voice still pitched to be heard above the hubbub; she faltered into embarrassed silence.

Someone laughed.

A small dark shifty man with a hooked nose and pockmarked cheeks emerged from behind the counter. The

crowd squeezed aside to make way for him. He wore a
butcher's apron, on which he wiped his hands.

– Yes?

Helen, sooner than embark on what seemed an absurd
explanation in this place, handed him the slip of paper. He
took it, held it at arm's length, inserted a hand in a pocket
in his apron and took out a pair of half-moon spectacles
which he donned, tilted his head back, and again studied
the paper, now at a distance, now holding it close too. Then
he turned it over and studied the back, although there was
nothing on it. Finally he handed it to an assistant, a big,
simple-looking boy, who stared at it vacantly.

– That seems to be in order, said the hook-nosed man.

He opened a door behind the counter and hung up his
butcher's apron on the back of it; then he delved in the
cupboard and produced a set of dark robes. These he held
above his head and began to burrow into them, but he
became entangled and had to be freed by the boy. When he
was attired, the boy handed him a little wooden hammer,
then produced a small hand mirror for him to complete his
toilet. Once he was satisfied with his appearance, he turned
to Jake and Helen.

– The usher will take you down.

They looked around, and by a process of elimination,
established that the usher must be the boy. He now held up
his hand, bidding them stay where they were. Then he
reached down to the floor and laid hold of a metal ring set
into it. By pulling on this, he raised a large section of the
floorboards to reveal a staircase running down at a steep
angle.

He came round and went ahead of them down into the
dark. At the foot of the steps he operated a light switch,
and the darkness ahead of them was transformed into a
long brick tunnel with an arched roof and flagged floor,

dimly lit at intervals by bare electric bulbs and curving away to the left.

They were some way along this tunnel when they heard a noise and chattering behind them; looking back, they saw the customers of the shop filing down the steps to follow them. However, the boy pressed on with such speed that the followers were soon lost to sight beyond the curve of the tunnel.

All at once the boy stopped, and began to work at something in the wall. Coming up behind him, they saw that it was a small metal door, quite high up. The boy opened it, lifted out a set of steps, and climbed up them through the opening. Jake and Helen, exchanging incredulous looks, went after him.

Inside the door a short vertical ladder took them to a concrete platform and another door, made of bare metal studded with large rivets. The boy opened it out of the way, and they saw that on the other side it had the appearance of an ordinary wooden house door. The passage they stepped into was very much like the hall of someone's house, although the doors along the side were unusually small.

The boy now seemed a little uncertain of himself: he was counting the doors under his breath, until he came to one where he hesitated a long time. At last he decided to open it, and Jake and Helen, standing behind him, were surprised to find themselves looking down into a room (the door seemed to open halfway up a wall) where a family was sitting round a table eating their dinner. They looked up with more annoyance than surprise and the boy hastily pulled the door shut again.

He went on a little farther and found a door much more to his liking: this he opened without hesitation, and ushered them through. They found themselves in a short tunnel panelled with dark wood. When they emerged and looked back, they saw that they had passed under a gallery with tiers of seats. Into these, people were already filing: many of them still clutched plastic bags bulging with shopping. A thin, mournful man in black robes took charge of Jake and Helen, directing them to a low table in the corner.

In front of them, on a raised stand, was a desk – the judge's bench, which was empty. Up to the left were several levels of what looked like polished counters, with people seated behind them. Beside these was a double door, from which steps led down to the floor of the court. When they sat down, they seemed to be in the lowest part of the room, with everyone else towering over them and gazing down at them. It was not a comfortable position.

Jake scanned the faces in the body of the court hopefully, but found them uniformly hostile. They were a mixture of men and women, mostly middle-aged or older. All were clad in dark old-fashioned clothes. Some were remarkably ugly; each had a similar look of grim intent.

The benches high up to the left now began to fill with people who entered through the body of the court and climbed up to them. The big double door at the back remained shut. The people on the benches contrasted strongly with those in the body of the court. Their clothes were modern, well-cut and costly; they had the sleek well-groomed look that goes with wealth. Where the spectators sat grim, tense and upright, conscious of the formality of the occasion, these sprawled, complacent and relaxed, across the seats, leaning back to share a joke with someone on the level above or forward to pass down a paper with some scribbled message. The recipient would read the words with a smile before scribbling a reply, which he crumpled into a ball and tossed nonchalantly over his shoulder.

They were all very much at ease, but not for that any more attractive: there was a hard edge to their faces, and a cruel sharpness to their smiles, which showed a lot of wolfish teeth. Together they combined to convey an air of arrogant power and control. Jake was reminded of a set of prefects he had seen once, when they were visiting a posh school. These had the same air of studied indifference to their surroundings, which said as plainly as any words: "Watch us, we are the masters here."

The arrival of the judge, from a door behind the bench, did little to change their manner. True, they came to attention and stopped their chatter, but in such a lounging way that it seemed more insolent than respectful. The judge, perched high above the court, looked even smaller and shiftier than he had done in the butcher's shop. His face too had a hard-edged cut, clever-looking but not at all honest, with something particularly cruel about the set of the mouth. It was not a face you would look to for mercy. He gave a smart rap with his little hammer and fixed Jake and Helen with a piercing stare.

– Who appears for these children? he rasped.

He looked in turn at the thin, mournful usher and the benches to his right. The usher shrugged and turned his palms outward. On the benches, a more elaborate pantomime was taking place, as each turned to the other in mock consternation. Don't you know? I thought *you* knew – but I thought *you* – surely *someone* must know? All the while scarcely able to contain their mirth, as if the judge had actually said something tremendously funny without realizing it.

– I'm afraid, blurted one, I'm afraid we simply cannot –

But here his mirth proved too much for him, and he had to sit down, burying his head in his hands, quaking with silent laughter. The judge did not look at all pleased and brought his gavel down with a sharp crack on the bench.

– Signor Buonconte, explain yourself. I will not have this court mocked.

A large bald man with a florid complexion and baby-blue eyes rose to his feet, banishing a smirk.

– *Signor Giudice*, what my learned friend meant to say was that none of us has any idea who appears for these children.

– Then perhaps we could get on.

– *Signor Giudice*, may it please the court, we are waiting for our leading counsel to arrive. Might I beg a few minutes' indulgence? He is sure to be here soon.

– Very well. Perhaps in the meantime the clerk of the court will read out the charges.

Helen and Jake looked at one another in consternation.

– What do they mean "charges"? whispered Jake.

The melancholy usher had now seated himself in a little box affair in front of the judge's bench. He produced a sheaf of papers and began to read.

– Proceedings of the special court for the hearing of matters relating to works of art, the honorable judge Ernesto Mantalini presiding. The defendants are charged with being in possession of a work of art, namely a painting, knowing it to be stolen. They are further charged with assisting in the theft of the said painting from its rightful owners.

Helen shot up from her seat like a rocket.

– What is the meaning of this?

Mantalini gavelled furiously.

– Control yourself, Miss, or I will have you removed!

Helen was not so easily subdued.

– This is outrageous! These charges are pure invention!

– Young woman, you would be well advised to wait for the appearance of your counsel to make the case for

your defence. Acting in this headstrong manner will only
serve to damage your case. Now sit down!

Jake pulled Helen down to her seat.

– This is some sort of mistake, he whispered. I'm sure
it'll be cleared up soon.

– I doubt it very much, hissed Helen. The whole thing's
a set-up.

Mantalini   was   looking   around   with   evident
impatience.

– I cannot wait forever, he said. If counsel for neither
side has the courtesy to arrive on time then we will start
without them.

– I really would advise against that, said Buonconte.

Mantalini turned on him savagely.

– You would advise me, would you? In my own court?

– In your own interests, said Buonconte smoothly. The
person we are waiting for is not someone you would want
to get on the wrong side of.

He shot Mantalini a meaningful glance. The little judge
squirmed.

– But I must get on, he said a little pathetically. I have
business to attend to.

– I am confident that this matter will not detain you
long, said Buonconte, smirking at Jake and Helen.

Baldassare Buonconte was trembling with excitement,
mainly pleasurable, but with a substantial admixture of fear.
He could not recall the face he had seen in the vortex without
a twinge of terror. And that had been only a vision: today, it
would manifest itself.

He looked across the court to where the children sat,
imagining the fear they were soon to experience, relishing it.
It was the girl that Pounce wanted: the boy was surplus to
requirements. Which was handy, because that which he had
summoned would not depart empty handed.

All at once there was a loud hammering at the double doors behind him. Someone was trying to open them, but with more force than skill. They shook violently, as if being wrenched off their hinges, then burst wide open. Jake's heart sank. Framed by the doorway and seeming to fill every inch of it was an enormous figure.

The entire court fell silent at the sight of him, everyone straining forward in an attitude of concentrated attention. Only the party on the benches paid no heed, prevented from seeing the newcomer by the angle of their seats; instead they smirked down on the corner of the court where Jake and Helen sat awestruck. Their leading counsel had evidently arrived.

He had the chest and shoulders of an ox, and his massive head and neck were ox-like too, though the truculent set of the jaw put you more in mind of a bulldog. But for all that bulk, there was nothing slow about him: the eyes that looked out under the heavy brow had a fearsome intelligence.

As he raked the court with his penetrating glare Jake could see people quail and avert their eyes; not even the judge was exempt. With nothing more than a slight swivel of his head, he had secured the full attention of everyone, save the inhabitants of the benches, who sat gloating.

Then the man advanced down the stairs towards the floor of the court, with a powerful springing step. His black advocate's gown billowed about him like great dark wings. Neither Jake nor Helen could look away: their eyes were fixed on the advancing figure.

The big man stopped in the middle of the court and slowly scanned the spectators in deliberate challenge: they shrank, cowed. Then he turned to the benches. The loungers there turned to Buonconte for their lead, clearly expecting some gleeful acclamation in which they could join. But instead Buonconte faltered, as if suddenly uncertain: his face took on a puzzled look. There was a moment of tense silence as they gazed at one another.

Then with a swirl of his gown the big man turned to face Jake and Helen. He stalked toward them across the courtroom floor, his thumbs hitched in the lapels of his gown, his face stern and set. When he was right up against their table, he leaned to them, as if there was something he wished to share with them alone. Jake felt his mouth go dry. The big man held them both with a steady, sombre gaze.

Then he winked.

A brief smile transformed his face, like a blink of sunshine on a gloomy day, gone almost before there was time to register it. He resumed his grave expression and turned away. It was so quick that Jake and Helen were not sure they had seen it at all, and turned to one another for reassurance and confirmation.

– Did you see –?

– Didn't he just –?

– I thought he was on their side, breathed Jake.

– Apparently not, said Helen, wondering.

Their eyes followed the bulky figure, who now presented himself before the judge's bench.

– Who are you, Sir? enquired Mantalini, tetchily.

– Who am I, Sir? More to the point, who are you? No longer a practising judge in the courts of this country, that is for sure!

The judge looked as if he had been slapped. He seemed about to frame a suitable rebuke when the big man turned his gaze upon him, and he stumbled, halting, as if he spoke against his will:

– I am Ernesto Mantalini, a qualified judge. It is true that I no longer practice, but I have never been disbarred. The allegations against me were never proved. This is a legally constituted hearing. If you are to speak for these children, then we have only to wait for Signor Buonconte's leading counsel to arrive.

This seemed to revive the party on the benches; they smiled and nodded to one another; Buonconte looked confident once more, even smug. But the big man shook his great head, and fell to examining his fist, as a boxer might, checking for damaged knuckles.

– I have news for the court on that matter. The person you speak of will not be coming today.

Seeming to find his fist in satisfactory condition, he ceased his examination and returned it to his side.

– He was compelled to return whence he came.

As he said this, he looked up at the group on the benches to see how they took it. Not at all well, to judge by the expression on Buonconte's face, thought Jake. And there's more to come, he guessed, from the way the big man hovered, like a comedian about to deliver the punch line of a joke. Sure enough, just as he was about to turn away, he added, with grim relish:

– However, I must inform my learned colleagues that he still requires his fee.

At this, Buonconte made a choking noise, and slumped back in his seat, his face completely drained of color. Jake had the impression that this last sentence meant a great deal more than it said. Mantalini looked nervously about, as if for advice. At length he said:

– Er, if the leading counsel for the prosecution cannot come, perhaps the court should adjourn.

He looked to Buonconte for some response, but he sat ashen faced and did not seem to hear. The big man turned a ferocious glare upon him.

– Mark me, *Dottore*, it is a grave and solemn thing to sit in judgement on your fellows. "Judge not, that ye be not judged." None will be judged more harshly than he who judges unjustly. You did not seem to think an adjournment necessary a short time ago when these children had no advocate.

– Er, em, it is just that the complexity of the case –

– Complexity? The big man spluttered. I see no complexity. Establishing the matter of ownership will overturn the preposterous claim that these children stole the painting. You cannot steal your own property.

Mantalini let out a yelp as if he had been stabbed with a pin.

– Em, the ownership is disputed. The matter is, er, more complex than at first appeared.

– Disputed? Disputed! Who dares dispute it?

– I, er, these gentlemen … they have a witness.

The big man turned to the court and rolled his eyes heavenward, which drew a laugh or two; then he turned to the melancholy usher

– You had better call him then, he bellowed, like a hungry man calling for his dinner.

The usher swallowed nervously.

– The court calls Signor Di Luca to the stand, he croaked.

There was a stir in the main body of the court: a little bantam-like fellow, very sharply dressed, stood up and strutted down from the gallery, exchanging humorous remarks with the spectators as he passed. Once on the stand he looked around with an air of impudent swagger, although he was careful to avoid the big man's eye. Jake noticed the people in the body of the court exchanging nods and grim, wolfish smiles, as if looking forward to what the man was going to say and do.

– Why are you here, Signor Di Luca? asked Mantalini.

– To testify to the ownership of the painting, said the little man jauntily.

– What painting is that, asked the big man in mock surprise. I see no painting in this court.

– It, is – er, in safe keeping, said Mantalini.

– I insist that it be produced, retorted the big man.

The judge looked about him uncomfortably, as if imploring someone to come to his aid.

– Produced, nothin', said Di Luca. No need. I know that paintin' without havin' to see it.

– Do you even know what it's called, I wonder? asked the big man silkily. So far he had not troubled to look at the witness; he addressed his words to the court.

– Sure I do, said Di Luca.

– Well?

There was a pause, then the big man cupped a hand to his ear, as if the witness might have said something that he missed. Di Luca looked sidelong at the judge.

– I do not think the dispute is about the name of the painting, interrupted Mantalini. It is The Secret of the Alchemist. We are agreed on that.

– Sure we are, said Di Luca. The Secret of the Old Chemist!

There was a burst of laughter. The big man cocked a sceptical eyebrow.

– And could you describe this painting for us, do you think?

– Sure I could, said the man with a grin. It's a picture of an old chemist and – er – of his secret, he added as an afterthought, smirking at his friends in the court, and making a gesture as of wiping sweat from his brow.

– Again there is no dispute as to what the painting shows, said Mantalini, merely as to its ownership.

– Sure, echoed Di Luca. Merely its ownership is what I'm here to talk about. Nothin' else.

– I do feel that the witness' claim might be a little more

credible if he showed the least familiarity with the painting in question, said the big man, with a hint of weariness.

– The witness is a man of character, in good standing with this court, said Mantalini.

– Yeah, sure in good standing, said Di Luca. Besides, why should I not know what the painting is about when I painted it myself?

There were gasps; even Mantalini seemed a little taken aback by the brazenness of this claim. The big man rolled his eyes.

– Perhaps we can have a chair for the witness? he asked the usher with sudden concern.

– I do not see the need for that, said Mantalini.

– Me neither, said Di Luca. Why would I want a chair? Do I look weak or somethin'?

– I merely thought that a man of your years must find it tiring to stand for so long, the big man replied.

– A man of my years? asked Di Luca suspiciously.

– Why, yes. Given that the painting in question is popularly supposed to have been painted in the early sixteenth century, you must be well on the way to your five hundredth birthday.

There was a ripple of laughter at this. Jake saw that although most people in the court tutted and shook their heads at the big man's sallies, there were a few who could not keep a straight face, even though the others glowered at them.

– Which your "popularly supposed" means nothin'. What do people know? I tell you I painted that thing myself, a few years back.

– Do I take it you claim to be a forger of some sort, Signor Di Luca?

– Aw, these are harsh words! A skilled imitator, no more.

– And you claim that this painting, "The Secret of the Alchemist"–

– That's the one! interjected Di Luca chirpily, to laughter.

– Is one of your skilful imitations?

– For sure it is.

– No possibility of a mistake, I suppose?

– Not a bit of one. I'd swear it on my mother's grave, only she ain't dead yet, God bless her. I'd swear it on my father's, only I don't know who he is!

A more general ripple of laughter went round the court; Di Luca was playing his audience like a skilled comic. Jake felt the whole thing was descending into farce; he looked across at Helen, who was staring in front of her, tense and whitefaced.

– I swear it by my own name, continued Di Luca jauntily, by my own name I swear that I painted that painting, the – whatever it's called – a few years back. By my own name.

He repeated the words emphatically, looking solemn now, his hands held out to the court in token of his openness and honesty.

– By your own name? said the big man, with a stifled laugh. You swear it by your own name, do you?

He smiled at the little man, the first time he had troubled to look at him directly, Jake noted.

– By your own name, he repeated with a chuckle, as if Di Luca had made a very good joke indeed.

Di Luca smirked back, nodding and laughing. You poor fool, thought Jake, you're for it now. There was something in the big man's sudden affability much more menacing than any anger would have been; Jake was glad it was not directed at him. The big man, still smiling and shaking his head slightly, strolled across to the witness box and leaned on it companionably, his elbow on the rail, as if he and Di Luca were drinking in a bar together.

– Have you ever noticed, he said, addressing the court in an easy, conversational tone, how a dishonest fellow will always be swearing? A simple "Yes" or "No" is never good enough for him; it must always be something big and impressive sounding like "as Heaven is my witness" or "by the soul of my dead grandmother." Of course he's careful never to choose anything that might turn up to contradict him. What a shock he'd get if he looked up and there was his dead grandmother, shaking her head at him!

He laughed lightly, as did a few in the court, and Di Luca joined in, but rather uneasily. Jake could see him trying to work out where this might be leading.

– This fellow, now, swears by his own name. Names, of course, are of great significance –

– Is this leading anywhere? enquired Mantalini, tetchily.

– Most assuredly, said the big man suavely. Even today, among primitive peoples, you will find that their true names are secret, known only to few. They appreciate that names are potent things, and not to be taken lightly.

Di Luca now looked distinctly uneasy. The big man turned to him genially.

– Your own name, now, what would that be? Would it be … Paolo?

He spoke teasingly, as if playing a guessing game with a child.

– No, said Di Luca sullenly. A lot of the jauntiness had gone out of him.

– Or Giacomo, perhaps? It must surely be Giacomo!

– It's Thomas, mumbled Di Luca.

– Thomas? said the big man with relish, as if the name was something to savor. Tomaso Di Luca! That's a *fine* name! After your uncle, I suppose? he added, casually.

Di Luca shook his head.

– Your *grandfather*, then?

– No, said Di Luca indistinctly, it was for a saint.

– Saint Thomas? I beg your pardon! That would be Thomas the Apostle, I suppose, he added with a laugh. Doubting Thomas, given your doubtful nature?

The little man bridled at this, and seemed to recover some of his spark.

– Doubtin' Thomas nothin', he said, this was a proper Italian saint, a Neapolitan saint: Tomaso d'Aq – d'Aq –

The big man had swung suddenly round, his face inches from Di Luca's own. He said something quickly that Jake could not make out at all, but which Helen with her sharper ear guessed was some sort of Neapolitan dialect. The effect on the little man was startling: his jaw dropped and his hands clutched the rail of the witness box as if he was having difficulty standing up.

– But – that's impossible, he mumbled, you can't be!

His eyes bulged; he seemed to have shrunk to half his size. Helen shot a puzzled look at Jake, but Jake's face was staring incredulously, an expression of rapt wonderment on his face. His hand went up to his throat; there was something warm and pulsing there.

– It's him, Jake said, fumbling with his shirt buttons, it's him!

He drew out something like a coin that seemed to glow with a throbbing light. Helen recognized it as the medal they had picked up on the quayside at the Lido.

– It's him, breathed Jake, Thomas Aquinas!

By now, Di Luca was on his knees in the witness box, babbling wildly:

– San Tomaso, forgive me, forgive me! I never meant it. They, he gave me money to say so (he gestured wildly at the benches, now in uproar) They paid me but I never saw the painting. Forgive me, it was wrong, I did not mean it!

With that, he crawled out of the stand on all fours, and started to get up just as the usher stooped to seize him, with the result that both of them went sprawling on the floor. There was pandaemonium in the body of the court: some of Di Luca's associates leaped over the barriers to assist him. Beyond the mêlée on the floor, Jake saw the people on the benches opposite moving in concert, as if to some prearranged signal; then the lights went out. There were wild cries and the crashing of furniture, but the darkness lasted only a moment. Then the room was lit by a soft golden effulgence that seemed to come from the person of Thomas Aquinas himself. He turned to Jake and Helen:

– Quick! You must get away – over there!

He pointed to where Mantalini was ducking out the little door behind his bench. They scrambled over the table and began to clamber their way up the front of the judge's bench. One of the opposition lunged at them, but Aquinas swung a mighty fist and felled him with a single blow. As they scrambled across the bench to the door another man blocked their path, but Helen hit him with a heavy glass inkstand and Jake used the door to shove him aside. Glancing back, the last thing he saw was Aquinas brandishing a huge table to bulldoze a mob of spectators in the well of the court. Jake pulled the door shut and they sprinted off down a narrow passageway.

They ran headlong down the echoing corridor, Helen some way ahead. She vanished round a bend, but her voice came back,

– Quick Jake, there's daylight this way!

They scrambled out onto a piece of waste ground. On the far side of it, like a mirage, they saw the everyday bustle of the city: cars moving up and down a road, people crowding the pavements. Without needing to confer, they ran full tilt towards it, and did not stop until they had reached the street, gasping for breath. It did not feel safe enough to linger and they did not have the breath to talk, so they walked on briskly, taking great gulps of air. Only when they had put several streets behind them did Helen voice what they were both thinking.

– That was more sorcery, I suppose, just like in Venice.

Jake looked around him at the crowded street, the modern buildings, the passing cars. They should have made the very idea of sorcery ridiculous, but somehow it didn't work: the chill feeling stayed in his stomach. He felt uncomfortably like a fly walking on a spider's web. How far did these people's influence extend?

– Do you think the whole thing was a set-up from the start? Even the police in Venice? he asked.

– I don't think so. If they could get hold of the painting there, why bother with the court case?

– So there really was a court case?

Helen's jaw dropped as the realization hit her.

– And we've missed it!

A swift consultation of the map sent them pelting through the streets.

They arrived at the real courthouse nearly two hours late, and entered it with little hope. A grey haired woman at a big desk went off to attend to their enquiry, but before she had returned a voice hailed them in a rasping whisper:

– You're too late, kids. They got the picture.

The voice had an American twang. Turning, they saw the woman with the distinctive red hair who had turned up in the Prefecture in Venice.

– Best not hang around, guys – they're on the lookout for you here.

– What do you mean?

– Tell you later. Come on.

By this time she had shepherded them to the door, all the while looking nervously about.

– Step on it! she hissed. The grey haired dame is coming back with two guys that look a lot like cops!

She shoved them through the swing door.

– Quick! Duck down there.

Too startled to do anything else, Jake and Helen took refuge behind a screen of potted plants. Shortly after, they heard the click of heels and the sound of a collision, then an American voice raised in protest.

– Hey! What's the rush? Can't a woman come through a goddam door without getting knocked over?

Muttered Italian apologies and other speech came indistinctly from the corridor beyond.

– Two kids? Na, not this way, said the redhead loudly.

Footsteps clicked past: two men, walking briskly. Another door swung and they moved out of earshot.

– Coast's clear, kids, but make it snappy.

They emerged from behind the foliage and she hustled them out a side entrance into the street, where she walked briskly to the corner and hailed a taxi.

12

An unexpected ally

They all squeezed into the back seat of the taxi, the redhead panting somewhat.

– Guess I'm getting a bit old for this cloak-and-dagger stuff. I should introduce myself – I already know who you are. My name's Roberta Tardelli. I'm a freelance journalist. My speciality is art: if it's changing hands, being faked, being stolen, I want to know about it.

– You were in the police station in Venice, said Jake.

The woman patted her hair a touch ruefully.

– Guess it's this, huh? How come it never looks like it does on the package?

– Where exactly are we going? asked Helen.

– To my hotel.

– Why?

– Because since roughly two-ten this afternoon, you two guys, if not exactly Milan's most wanted, are certainly up there on the list.

– How come? said Jake.

– Because after waiting five minutes, another five was all it took for this suave character who did turn up to persuade the court that the painting was the rightful property of Aurelian Pounce, and that you two kids had stolen it.

– Oh, no! groaned Jake.

– What's your connection with all this? asked Helen.

– Like I just said, honey, I'm a journalist, and my specialty is art. A friend of mine in the Venice police tips me the wink that two kids have turned up with a rather unusual painting that it happens I am interested in, and then mentions the name of a Mr. Aurelian Pounce, that it also happens I am interested in.

Jake had a vivid recollection of the boat at Murano, and the painting unveiled. The big policeman with the mustache staying to study it, even at the cost of his boss' disapproval; then, once he was sure, using his mobile. After that, the redhead at the Prefecture: she had been going to approach him, but had backed off when another officer appeared.

– How come you're interested in this painting? asked Jake.

– Cute Finnish accent you've got there, buster. Any chance your ancestors came from Scotland?

– Any chance you're trying to dodge the question? said Helen.

– Hell no, honey. When it comes to paintings, I'm happy to say that The Secret of the Alchemist is high on my list of all-time favorites.

– Which still doesn't answer the question *why* you're interested in it.

– I think what your Scotch friend said was "how come," but let that pass. How I came to be interested in it is quite a long story, which I thought we might discuss privately.

– Why? said Helen.

– Heck, honey, I worked for editors who were pussycats compared to you – talk about direct! Okay, I'll level with you. Thanks to my friend in the Venice police I got a few shots of the Alchemist while he was in their custody, but even so I guess I might have problems using them. I gather your family's not so keen on their collection being photographed.

– You could say that.

– Well what I thought was this: suppose I was able to get that picture back, you figure your family'd grant me some kind of exclusive on the collection? Not just the Alchemist, I mean, but the whole lot?

– What makes you think you can get the picture back?

– What makes me think I can get the picture back is that I got what Mr. Pounce really wants – and don't say "which is?"

– Which is? said Helen.

– Which is what we'll talk about when we get up to my room, said Roberta Tardelli, in a conspiratorial whisper, as the taxi drew up outside the hotel.

It was an impressive building: fountains played outside; there was an unusual amount of activity around the door. Large vans with satellite dishes were parked everywhere. Once inside, they saw that the foyer was swarming with television crews.

– Must have known we were coming, said Jake.

– *I vont to be alone,* said Helen, shielding her face Greta Garbo style.

– Probably some celeb, said Roberta Tardelli. Film star, or maybe a footballer. This is the place to stay in Milan.

She pressed ahead to the lift.

– Any chance she'll offer us dinner, do you think? whispered Jake.

– We can work on it.

Her room turned out to be a corner suite with a balcony; Miss Roberta Tardelli was clearly used to living in some style.

– Journalism must pay pretty well, muttered Jake.

– Or something does, said Helen.

Their hostess was busy in the next room on the telephone.

– What do you make of this? said Jake.

– I don't know. Let's hear what she's got to say.

Roberta reentered the room: on the tall side, thought Helen, so she can just about get away with that extra weight she's carrying. Not bad looking, thought Jake, but she should stop pretending to be younger than she is – she must be at *least* thirty.

– Okay, guys. Can I trust you?

– To do what? said Helen.

– To stay here and wait for me? I have to go out.

– Why should we wait for you?

– It's a fair question, honey, and I'll give you a fair answer: you don't have to wait for me, not at all. You can take your chances on your own if you like, but it'd make a helluva difference to me. And of cou˞˞ ˞ ˞ might just come back with the painting.

– What can *you* offer Pounce that would make him give up the painting?

Roberta smiled a lazy smile, easing her jacket off her shoulder in a parody of a vamp.

– You think I got nothing to offer that Mr. Pounce might want? she drawled.

– Well, not that, anyway, said Helen.

The redhead laughed.

– When did young people get so old all of a sudden? Okay, I'll level with you. It's not the painting Pounce wants, it's the secret.

– That the Alchemist has sold his soul to the devil? said Jake, hoping to be smart.

Roberta snorted.

– Hell no, that's about as secret as the fact I dye my hair. No one took you seriously as an alchemist if you *hadn't* sold your soul to the devil. It was kind of a professional entrance fee, you might say.

– So what is the secret? asked Helen.

– I'm about to tell you for nothing, having spent five years working my butt off to find out? I don't think so!

– Fine then. So what is there for us to wait for?

– Okay honey, fair point: but you'll appreciate if I don't fill in the details. What do you know about alchemists?

– That they wanted to turn base metal into gold, said Jake. A kind of get-very-rich-very-quick scheme, using a thing they called the Philosopher's Stone.

– And what do you know about our man, Roger Anscombe, called Ruggiero da Montefeltro?

– Born in Bristol, lived in Italy, died in France, said Jake.

– Not quite the full story –

– Oh, and he amassed a fortune, said Helen.

– Indeed, amassed a fortune, and didn't so much die as disappear off the face of the earth. In fact, after having spent some twenty years in Italy hawking himself from court to court, from one great man to the next, Ruggiero da Montefeltro one day ups stakes and moves to France, where he has a villa built for him by an architect, and for a short time leads the life of an *extremely* wealthy man –

– Meaning?

– Well, meaning that either he discovered the Philosopher's Stone, or something next door to it that did exactly the same thing.

– So what was it? asked Jake.

Roberta Tardelli smiled but said nothing.

– *That's* the secret of the painting?

– Got it in one, give that boy a coconut! Now listen kids, I really have to go, but stick around. If you want any food, just order it. I'll leave word at the desk it's to be put on my bill. I'll try to be back as quick as I can.

With that, she whirlwinded out of the room, leaving Jake and Helen staring.

*****

A deductive interlude

Aurelian Pounce puts down the telephone, his irritation further increased, and intertwined with it a growing suspicion. First Buonconte, and now this. No: first *Venice*, then Buonconte, and now this.

True, he had the painting; a week ago that was all he would have wished for. But then he thought he would have leisure to study it, to win the secret from it by slow degrees. Now it seems that someone else has knowledge of the secret: Gerald De Havilland. Why else would he have gone back on a deal that was as good as done? The price was more than generous: what else could have tempted him to such a risky course, except some ken of the far greater prize that the painting could reveal?

So now having the painting is no longer enough – he must have De Havilland too, both to wring the secret from him and to prevent his passing it on to someone else. Finding De Havilland will take time, time which he cannot afford to waste; but De Havilland will come running if he knows Pounce has his daughter.

And he would have her, had not Buonconte failed this afternoon. Of course Pounce upbraided him as a fool, a bungling blunderer, because the error cost him dear; but not as dear as it will cost Buonconte. Almost he could feel sorry for him, so wretched he looked: already the shadow has fallen between him and the world. At the table, how little he ate – Baldassare, always so fond of his food. And how often he looked over his shoulder, as if he sensed some presence there! It will go hard with him, as the days stretch out, and that feeling of always being watched grows on him.

But of more concern to Aurelian Pounce than the ultimate fate of Baldassare Buonconte is the question of how he came to be defeated. If it were an isolated incident, Pounce would incline to think he had made an error of judgement: that in Buonconte his trust had been misplaced. But it is not isolated. It is the second time in three days that he has been thwarted. He has no doubt that whoever was responsible for defying him in Venice is also responsible for the defeat of Buonconte. The question is, who that can be?

A fellow adept, undoubtedly.

His chief rival for the secret of the picture, certainly.

One of very few, to be able to defy *him*.

One of only two, he is inclined to think.

Salazar or the Romanian.

But Salazar is an old man: he has lost his passion for this kind of thing.

So the Romanian then.

And now this journalist: Roberta Tardelli. Bad news, as journalists always are. But in this case, probably something more: Venice, Buonconte, then this journalist phoning to arrange a meeting and throwing out vague hints, as her sort always does.

Too much of a coincidence.

A cat's paw.

She, the paw; the cat, the Romanian.

That is the likeliest explanation by far.

Better see to this.

13
A hasty exit

– Well, said Helen at last, what do you make of her?
– I really don't know. Is she for real?

Helen was up and roaming about the room, full of restless movement, picking things up and examining them, punching cushions, clearly in the throes of trying to decide a course of action. Finally she said:

– I vote we make the most of our opportunity. You order food. I'm going to have a bath. If there's one thing I love, it's luxury hotel bathrooms.

Strange tastes people have, thought Jake, but he was flattered that Helen had left the decisions about food to him. Once he had ordered he went and lay on the bed, guessing that Helen's love affair with the bathroom was unlikely to be a brief one. He felt physically very tired, and as sometimes happens in that state, his mind was working in a curious, detached way, taking its own course undirected.

He seemed to look down on himself. Why am I lying there? he wondered. Because a woman who happened to be waiting in the real Palazzo di Giustizia – and why was she still there if the case had taken only ten minutes? – said the police were after them, hurried them into hiding– so that they did not actually see the men she said were pursuing them – then hustled them into a taxi and brought them to her hotel room. Hustled: that was a good word for it. There was a little too much of the hustle about Roberta Tardelli. He thought how Dante, instead of trying to convince him, invited him to pause and consider how much he was taking on trust; but this woman whirled on from one stage to the next, as if unwilling to dwell too long on anything. The police are after you – duck behind these plants – jump into this taxi – stay in this hotel room. *But what if the police were not after them?*

Then the whole thing began to unravel: they had been brought here, and persuaded to stay, under false pretences. Meanwhile, Roberta was away – doing what? Was it not just as likely that she would return with Pounce as with the painting? The more he thought about it, the less it seemed a good idea for them to stay here until she came back. He jumped up from the bed and banged on the bathroom door.

– Is that the food already? came Helen's voice from within.

– I need to speak to you!

– You *are* speaking to me.

– I think we should go!

– We can't. I'm not nearly finished yet.

A knock at the door interrupted them.

– Who is it? asked Jake without opening the door.

– Room service.

He hesitated, then opened up. A waiter appeared with a trolley well laden with food. There was a moment of awkwardness before the waiter, realizing that all he would get from Jake was thanks, withdrew. Jake turned to see Helen issuing from the bathroom in a cloud of steam, fetchingly attired in a bathrobe. For a moment they looked at one another, Helen becoming aware of the effect she was creating, Jake of how plainly he was showing it in his face.

– Mm, food –

– The food's here, they said simultaneously, and laughed.

Helen arranged herself on the bed with a plate.

– Now, what were you saying?

– That I didn't think we should stay here, said Jake, slowly and with great reluctance, trying not to stare.

– Why ever not? said Helen, plainly amused by his discomfiture.

– It was just an idea I had, that maybe Roberta wasn't telling us the truth.

– What makes you think that?

Under this cross examination, Jake began to wonder himself: it had seemed very clear at the time. He tried to recollect his straying thoughts.

– Well, for a start, why was she still at the court when we arrived? She said the case only lasted ten minutes, and we were two hours late. And another thing. Did you actually see the men who were supposed to be after us?

– No, but that doesn't mean they weren't.

– How do we know the court case even took place? Wouldn't they just postpone it if we didn't appear? We never got the chance to find out, because she hustled us away before the woman came back.

Helen frowned, beginning to take it seriously.

– And she hustled us in here in the same sort of way, said Jake.

– She was very anxious for us to stay till she came back.

Helen pondered, then made up her mind.

– All right. Suppose we finish our food then move downstairs? We should be safe enough with all those cameras crawling all over the place, and even if the police are after us, there's no reason for them to look for us here.

– Brilliant, said Jake.

– And now we've settled that, perhaps you can give your attention to your food, and not whether my bathrobe is going to fall open.

Jake ate.

Helen was getting dressed when there was a second knock at the door. Probably the waiter for the trolley, thought Jake. He was surprised instead to find a man with a slide projector and a screen.

– You want it where, please?

Jake gestured vaguely in the direction of the other room, where the man busied himself about setting it up. There was the same awkward pantomime at the end before he too departed unrewarded. Helen reappeared, drying her hair, just as someone else knocked.

– Your turn, said Jake.

– Who is it? called Helen.

– Package for Signora Tardelli.

She opened the door on a boy of about their own age, in a messenger's uniform. He proffered an oblong package, which Helen took, then offered a clipboard for her to sign. Helen signed with great coolness in an unintelligible scribble, and tipped the boy enough to make him grin. Jake gave her a look of mingled admiration and reproach as she tore open the package.

– Well, she did expect us to be here, so it's probably something she was going to show us anyway.

It was a box of slides.

– Shall we take a look? said Helen. Better double lock the door so we're not disturbed.

They went next door to where the projector was set up; Jake switched it on while Helen opened the slides. She held the first one up to the light and squinted at it.

– I can't make this out at all.

– Here, put it in, we'll see better.

It was an odd picture indeed: it showed a book open at the title page, which was in very old-fashioned print, but still clear enough to read: *Architectura, by Theophilus Bullen, London, MDXXXII.* It had a curious grainy quality.

– Try another one.

The next one was upside down, but there was something about it that they both recognised; as soon as Jake righted it, they saw what it was.

– That's the page-boy's tray out of the painting!

Helen was scrabbling through the remaining slides, holding each up in turn then discarding it.

– Here it is!

Jake set the slide in the projector, and there on the screen they saw the Alchemist, as large as life. It was a beautifully clear, sharp picture, with all the detail Jake recalled from that moment in the garden in Murano, but magnified.

– These must be the ones her friend in the police let her take. So at least that part of her story's true. As far as I know, there aren't any photos of the painting – The Aunts won't allow it.

– There's the book that's in the first slide!

It was indeed; it stood open on the shelf that the page-boy was pointing at; in fact, it was the very thing he was pointing at.

– Put the rest of them in the carousel, said Helen.

All the slides showed some part of the picture: the Alchemist's tray with its phials, each with a tiny label bearing some writing or a symbol; the book he was indicating, which, viewed close up, was written in some strange script that might have been Hebrew; the shelves where the other book stood; the mirror with the artist's reflection; the page-boy, with separate shots of his head, his hands, his doublet; a similar treatment of the Alchemist himself.

– What's she up to? asked Jake.

– I think I'm beginning to get an idea. Remember on the train when I was puzzled by the title, "The Secret of the Alchemist"? I'd only ever thought of it as "The Alchemist" – just a straightforward portrait. But if Roberta's right, then some clue to Ruggiero's secret – the Philosopher's Stone or whatever it was – is in this picture.

– How?

– Do you know what a rebus is? It's a kind of visual pun – people used it in their coat-of-arms. Like if your name was Lockhart, you'd have a heart and lock as your emblem.

– So you think there are puns in the picture?

Helen nodded. Together they stared at the slide of the full picture. The Alchemist stared back with, it seemed to Jake, a touch of mockery.

– How about the page-boy? he said suddenly. You know, page as in servant, page as in book.

– He's certainly pointing at a book, said Helen, but what page is it?

– One? There's only one page, not likely though. Wait a minute – count the things on his tray!

– Twenty-three, no, twenty-four.

– How about page 24 of that book then?

– Could be, said Helen, tapping her teeth. It does give a reason for the page-boy being in the picture. He's not really necessary otherwise.

Jake felt a rising excitement.

– Do you think it's true, about the Philosopher's Stone, I mean?

– Well, it might explain why Pounce is so keen to get the painting.

He found Helen's coolness maddening: the more he thought about it, the surer he felt.

– Look, this could be one of the great discoveries of the world: it could make us a fortune! The least you could do is show some excitement!

– If it *is* the solution to the puzzle. There's so much else in the picture. Could it really be that simple?

She jumped up.

– I'll give my dad a ring in London. I'll have to tell him about the picture anyway. I'm sure Roberta can bear the expense.

They went through to the next room. Helen picked up the phone and asked the switchboard to put a call through to London.

– Of course he might not be there – it's ringing now – what's the matter?

Jake was pointing urgently behind her, a finger to his lips. Without any knock or attempt to try a key, someone was turning the handle of the door. The stealthy manner of it, and the fact that no knock or shout followed the discovery that the door was locked, suggested that it was no ordinary visitor. Helen signed to Jake to go to the next room, and they tiptoed through. From the projector screen, the Alchemist gazed at them enigmatically.

– Is there a fire escape on that balcony? whispered Helen.

Jake went to check, and nodded that there was. Helen moved the slide carousel out from its place and removed the picture of the Alchemist. In the next room, the furtive activity at the door was continuing. Now it seemed that someone was trying discreetly to force the lock.

The fire escape was an affair of sliding ladders and made a dreadful clatter, but fortunately it was not attached to any alarms. They scrambled down to the street where Helen hailed a taxi, giving cousin Isidora's address.

When they arrived, however, there was no one in.

– There's a café round the corner, said Helen. We can

wait there for a bit.

On their way they came on a main arterial road: two blue-and-white police Alfa Romeos were attempting to storm a path through the early evening traffic for an ambulance behind them. The sirens of the police cars and the ambulance were of different pitches, and with growing orchestral support from the full range of motor horns, the din was truly hellish.

– It's like something from the Inferno, said Jake, as they made their way into the café.

*

In his darkened London flat Gerald De Havilland sat slumped in an armchair, looking very much the worse for wear. Since his panic flight from Florence he had scarcely slept, fearful of what might come to him if he did. In normal circumstances he would have had recourse to alcohol, but now he dreaded anything that might further reduce his already shaky self control. In the past few days his regular diet had consisted mainly of cigarettes and black coffee. His horror at what he had got himself into was increased by the fear that he might also have involved Helen in it. What had seemed such a good idea at the time – having her retrieve the picture – now struck him as a stupidly selfish act which had endangered his daughter.

He had been desperate for her to call, but when the phone had rung at last, earlier that afternoon, he found himself unable to answer, for fear of who it might be. After that he decided to use the ansaphone, setting it to cut in after the first few rings. He did not want to leave the house but a craving for tobacco drove him out and he returned in the early evening with a parcel of fish and chips and a renewed supply of cigarettes. The light on the answering machine was flashing. With a trembling hand, he switched it on. An unfamiliar male voice, light and caressing, spoke to him out of the dark:

– Mr. De Havilland, this is Aurelian Pounce. I thought you would like to know that despite your efforts I have the picture in my possession. I shortly expect to have something else as well, much dearer to your heart. It would be in your best interests to contact me as soon as possible. It would be a serious mistake to contact anyone else. That would only bring harm to yourself and those that are dear to you. I look forward to hearing from you.

The machine clicked off. De Havilland stared at it in horror. The cold feeling began to grow on him that this was more than just a matter of money, that Pounce had not wanted the picture for a client at all but for himself, and that now Helen was in serious danger. As these thoughts came crowding in on him, the phone rang.

– Hello Dad, this is Helen. If you're there, please pick up the phone –

He snatched it from the cradle.

– Helen, are you all right? I mean, where are you? Are you free to speak?

– I'm fine, Dad, but you sound really shaky. What's the matter?

– Just tell me exactly where you are!

– What? I'm in Milan, in a café just round the corner from cousin Isidora's. Dad, are you all right?

Her voice sounded normal enough. The vision he had of her with Pounce at her side holding a knife to her throat faded.

– You're really all right then? No trouble or anything like that?

– Well, I wouldn't exactly say that. We did manage to get the picture back, but I'm afraid we lost it again. And we might be in some trouble with the police as a result. But it's all a misunderstanding, so I'm sure it'll soon get sorted out.

The calm way she says these things!

– Listen, Helen, I don't think you should stay in Italy.

– We were planning to go to Switzerland.

The spectre of Pounce reappeared.

– We? Are you not on your own?

– I have a friend with me.

– Another girl?

– What is this, Dad? Twenty questions? No, the friend is male.

– What age is he?

– Dad! What are you on about? Worried that I might be travelling with an unsuitable male companion, some older man?

– He's not, is he?

God, he sounds really shocked. What's brought this on?

– Would that be so terrible?

– Just tell me he's not!

– Keep your hair on. He's just a boy – the same age as I am only a lot younger. I don't even fancy him. It's a perfectly chaste relationship.

The audible sigh of relief at the other end caused Helen some amusement. Was he really so concerned about that?

– It's all right Dad, I do know about these things. I'm not about to get into trouble and bring disgrace on myself and the noble house of De Havilland. I'm sure you're not ready for grandchildren yet anyway.

What is she on about? O, I see – still, at least Pounce is not in the picture, not yet at any rate.

– Look, Helen, I'm serious. You really should get out of Italy. Perhaps it would be better if you came here. I, I've got a bit of explaining to do, I think.

Well, well – remorse of conscience! This is new.

– You can bring your friend too, if you want. What's his name?

– Jake. I suppose I'd better. I said I'd look after him.

– Good girl. Get right on a train and give me a ring just as soon as you get to London.

– Okay, Dad. You can buy me that lunch you promised.

– Sure. See you, then.

– Bye.

Helen put down the phone, her horizons much brightened. A missed lunch in Florence was well worth the prospect of a stay in London. The last time she'd been there she'd been too young to enjoy it. She supposed she'd better take Jake along, if he wanted to come. He could always make some arrangement with his parents from there. She went back to the café bar where Jake was watching the television.

– Jake, you hadn't really set your heart on Switzerland, had you? It's just that –

He held up a hand to quiet her, then pointed at the screen. The volume was turned down, but it was evidently a news item of some sort. The newscaster's face cut to the scene of a hotel foyer, with shots of limousines arriving outside. A couple that Helen recognised but could not put a name to emerged to a barrage of flashing cameras.

– Hey, that's the hotel we've just come from!

Jake nodded, but still held up his hand. His face was tense and anxious: he did not take his eyes from the screen. The scenes of the star couple being mobbed in the foyer cut suddenly to the outside again. Blue lights, in a parody of the earlier flashguns, flickered rhythmically across the outside of the building. Two police cars and an ambulance stood by an area roped off with black and yellow tape. A police officer was doing his best to deflect the camera crew. Over his shoulder they could see an ominous hump in the road, covered with a white sheet. The camera swung suddenly upwards to show a balcony on the corner of the hotel.

– Jake, is that – ?

He nodded, eyes still fixed on the screen. The picture that came up next had the look of a passport photograph or an identity card. The face was younger, the hair not quite so wildly red, but it was unmistakably Roberta Tardelli.

– Oh God, no! said Helen.

She felt sick in the pit of her stomach. Jake turned to her, his face white.

– What are we going to do?

Helen thought quickly.

– What my Dad just suggested: we'll go to London.

Jake looked astonished at this proposal.

– Don't worry, we can sort it all out there. Right now we'd better get moving.

They thought it better to shun the most direct route. They were bound to have been seen at the hotel by the various people who had come to the journalist's room. But they had no idea whether the police would connect them with the two teenagers who should have turned up for a court case about a painting; nor could they be certain whether Tardelli's account was to be trusted, although her death lent her a grim sort of credence. If the police were after them because of the painting, then they knew Helen's real identity, and could connect her with both Switzerland and London. They even knew her father lived there. It seemed wiser to avoid making either a direct destination, so they boarded a coach to Genoa where after an uncomfortable night spent huddled in the bus station, they took the early morning express to Nice, caught the TGV to Paris and then, after a short taxi ride from the Gare de Lyon to the Gare du Nord, took the Eurostar on to London Waterloo.

14

Silk House

After Helen's call her father felt considerably better than he had done for days. For a start, he had allowed himself to sleep, with no adverse consequences. On rising, he had thought it better – out of deference to his daughter – to shave and shower and dress in fresh clothes. He had even gone for a walk through Camden Town, stopping for breakfast at a pavement café then enjoying a pleasant stroll in the sun through Regent's Park before returning to the flat, where he now sat, cigarette in hand, in a somewhat philosophical and reflective mood.

Although he had long since abandoned the religion of his boyhood, he still retained some sense of sin and forgiveness. It seemed to him now that he had repented, and been forgiven: his own foolishness had put his daughter in danger, but now she was to be restored to him. In a life so much composed of misfortune, here was a stroke of luck, a moment of grace.

It seemed a suitable point to start thinking of fresh starts and clean slates. Perhaps he could start over: it would not be the first time. Indeed Helen, now he came to think of it, was the fruit of his first fresh start. When he had met her mother in Switzerland, he had been playing the role of an international playboy, part of a complex and highly organised art fraud. He had taken the name De Havilland (borrowed from a famous aircraft manufacturer of his youth) as more suited to the part he was playing than his own name, which was Boyle.

It was as Gerald De Havilland that he had been introduced at a party to Romaigne Gellert, a rather wild young woman rumored to be fabulously rich. What had begun (for his part) as a game, the creation of an additional bit of cover, had soon deepened into something more serious. The conspiracy eventually collapsed and the gang dispersed, but he had retained his new identity and, after a few brief months, had clandestinely married Miss Gellert. When she announced the fact, her family, enraged, had tried to buy him off. He was tempted by the offer and felt obliged to reveal to his new bride that he was not the wealthy man he had represented himself to be.

Far from being disgusted by his deception, she had been delighted. Nothing gave her greater pleasure, it seemed, than disappointing the expectations of her family. They had fled to London where they lived a wild and bohemian life on rapidly-dwindling resources until the birth of Helen had brought about a grudging reconciliation. They returned to Switzerland, where for a time the charmed circle they wove about the three of them sufficed to protect them from the icy hostility of the rest of the family. But it could not last, and things had finally come very messily apart.

Still, there was no use dwelling on the past – the great thing was to make a better job of the future. Taking up his pen, he gave himself over to *The Times* crossword. The phone rang, but he let the ansaphone take it; after his own voice, he heard his daughter's telling him that they were at Waterloo Station and hoped he had something to eat, because they were both starving. He smiled at that, congratulating himself on having had the foresight to restock the fridge, and lifted the receiver. All he heard was a succession of pips as the call was cut off.

He returned to his crossword and pondered the next clue: "Confused, I draw the last letter – I could curse you! (6)." *What could that be?* He looked at the related clues and solved three in quick succession. That gave him - I -AR -. Still, he could not see it, so he pressed on with the rest.

He had almost completed the grid when the doorbell rang, in what seemed a surprisingly short time after Helen's call. *That was quick.* His mind still absorbed in the elusive clue, he perched his freshly lit cigarette on the ashtray and went to answer the door. *Of course, it's an anagram, I see it now –.* He broke off, startled. There in the doorway, almost filling it with his breadth, was a man in an ivory colored suit and a blue silk waistcoat.

"Wizard," that was it.

When Jake and Helen arrived about fifteen minutes later, the door of the flat was ajar, but the flat itself was empty. A cigarette in the ashtray had transformed its length into ash; the newspaper with the almost complete crossword lay on the table with a pen beside it.

– Probably just stepped out, said Helen, but left the door open because he knew we'd be here any minute.

Even as she said it, she realized that she had begun the process of warding off disaster. They headed for the kitchen and made substantial inroads on the contents of the fridge. Still her father did not appear.

– Maybe he got a phone call, said Jake, something urgent.

He felt as if he was conspiring with Helen to avert the truth.

– We could check the answering machine, Helen suggested.

Pounce's voice, coming into the room with them,

crystallized their apprehensions into definite fear. The message ended and they stood looking at one another, saying nothing. *Now what do we do?* thought Jake.

Helen had gone white. She's going to faint, he thought, feeling the onset of panic, seeing himself alone with her unconscious. Her breathing came in strange short gasps; she trembled, clenching and unclenching her fists, eyes tight shut. He watched in fascinated horror as she went to the edge, then slowly, slowly, came back. She opened her eyes. Her jaw was set.

– Can you make proper coffee?

Jake was completely thrown by this matter-of-fact request. Can I indeed make proper coffee? he wondered, stupidly.

– Of course, he said at last.

– Make some then. Dad keeps his beans in the freezer. I need to think.

Jake was absorbed in the intricacies of hand-grinding when Helen reappeared, wearing a brisk and determined air.

– We have to assume that Pounce has got Dad, because that's the worst that could happen. We can hope it's something better, but we've got to act as if it's the worst.

– Fair enough, but what do we do – go to the police?

Helen shook her head.

– No, for all sorts of reasons. We have to concentrate on what Pounce would want with Dad. It must be something to do with the painting.

– But he's already got that.

– So Roberta was right. It's not the painting, it's the secret he wants.

– And he thinks your Dad knows it?

– Or can help him find it, something like that. So if we

can get at the secret first, we might be able to use it to bargain with.

Jake received this in silence. It struck him as a pretty long shot, but he felt that now was not the time for candor. Finally, exasperated by his silence, Helen said:

– Have you got any better ideas?

– No, replied Jake truthfully.

He refrained from adding that even so, he did not think this a particularly good idea.

– So where do we start?

– With the book. If we can find that, we're getting somewhere.

Maybe, thought Jake, continuing the coffee-making operation. He no longer felt the certainty he had in Milan about that first inspired guess. He was much more inclined to see the sense of what Helen had said, that there was a great deal more in the picture that they hadn't taken into account. But when he looked at Helen, he realised this was not the time to say so.

– So where do we find the book?

– The British Museum Library? The big universities?

And we can just walk in and ask for it? He set the coffee on the stove.

– Is your Dad on the Internet, do you think? I saw a computer in the next room.

– I've really no idea, said Helen, who tended to share The Aunts' negative and conservative views about information technology.

– It's just that if he is, we might be able to find out about the book from here.

– Really? Could you do that?

– Maybe, said Jake cautiously.

At least it will give me something to do.

– I'll bring the coffee through, said Helen, somewhat

cheered. I better try to find some sort of contact address for Pounce – Dad's bound to have it somewhere.

It took Jake a little time and some guesswork to log on. His first encouragement was when he guessed the password: "Helen." He had been going to try and find the library catalogue for one of the big universities, but then another idea came to him, something he had done quite recently; if only he could remember how he had got into it.

– The Inland Revenue Service? asked Helen, looking over his shoulder as she passed by.

– Just wait, said Jake.

She lingered a while and watched him, wondering what he was up to. After some fiddling with a list of sites, he increased her puzzlement by finding his way into one that seemed all about paying tax, but he pressed on confidently, working his way through the index. Finally, with a little noise of triumph, he clicked on "Conditionally exempt works of art" and brought up another website, entitled "Register of Conditionally Exempt Works of Art."

– Did you know that if you own a work of art in this country, you can avoid paying tax on it if you agree to make it accessible to the public?

– I won't bother asking how on earth you knew that.

– I saw it on a poster in the library, as a matter of fact. This web site lists all the items that we are entitled to go and see if we want to, and tells us where to find them and how to arrange to see them.

– And you think that this book might be among them?

– It's worth a try.

After the first ten attempts turned up "no matches found", Jake began to wonder if it was worth a try after all. So far, he had stayed in the vicinity of London, as defined by his somewhat hazy notion of English geography. Helen wandered off and began to search her father's desk for an address book. Soon she had something.

– This looks promising, she said. You had any luck?

– Not so far. I'll bet the only copy is in the Outer Hebrides.

He broadened his search to Yorkshire, and there was a gratifying delay as if the computer was searching a vast database of sixteenth-century books; but in the end it came up "no matches" once more. From the noises she was making, Helen seemed to be doing rather better in her quest. Then he tried another county at random, and there it was.

Chattel Detail
Unique ID: 62598
Location: CAMBRIDGESHIRE
Primary Category: Books and manuscripts
Secondary Category: BULLEN, THEOPHILUS
Tertiary Category: 16TH CENTURY
Other Category: BOOKS
Agency Name: Mr. Stephen Langton
Agency Address: Silk House, nr Manorhampton, CAMBRIDGESHIRE
Contact or Reference at Agency: Mr. Stephen Langton
Description : Bullen (Theophilus): Architectura, first edition, title within woodcut border, numerous engravings, early seventeenth century needlework velvet binding by the Nuns of Little Gidding (rebacked and repaired), Folio, Giles Aldus, 1532.

His shout of triumph brought Helen dashing across.

– Is that it? That's brilliant. You must show me how to work these things. So who do we contact?

– This guy, Stephen Langton. Is there an atlas in the house?

– Stephen Langton? Wait a minute, said Helen, and dashed back to the desk.

A few minutes later she was back with a book.

– Found one? Great! Look up Manorhampton then.

– I *thought* I'd seen it before.

– Seen what?

By way of answer, Helen thrust the book she was holding under his nose. It was not an atlas at all: it was her father's address book. The entry at the top of the "L" page was: "Langton, Stephen — Silk House, Manorhampton, Cambridgeshire."

– What? You mean your dad actually *knows* him?

– Looks like it.

– So what do we do now, phone him up?

– Then he'll want to fix an appointment. If we just turn up, we can bluff our way in.

*

Silk House was some miles from Manorhampton station, but an enterprising Stationmaster had a sideline in cycle hire and the flat countryside made for easy cycling. It was a beautiful evening, the sky cloudless and a heat haze shimmering over the fields. After several miles of pleasant country road they found themselves running alongside a high stone wall, the boundary of some large property. Sure enough, rounding a corner, they came on a driveway marked with a discreet sign: Silk House. They turned their bikes down the elegant white gravelled drive that curved away through overhanging trees toward an unseen destination.

For Jake the sense of intruding was immediate. He felt increasingly nervous as they penetrated the grounds: big country houses were unknown territory to him, and his fertile imagination conjured up armed security guards and the full range of sinister personages associated with such places in television dramas. What on earth were they going to say? They might even be arrested for trespassing. Helen was much more at home. With a twinge of shame and envy, Jake slackened his pace to let her get ahead.

The house when they saw it surprised them: they had expected something tall, probably with pillars and steps, but it was low and elegant, single-storeyed and almost camouflaged by the overgrowth of ivy and creepers. The drive broadened out into a kind of apron at the front of the house and on it was parked a beautiful pale green motor car. Jake gave an appreciative whistle.

– That's a *Villa D'Este* Alfa Romeo.

He was glad to be able to focus on something he could feel confident about.

Much to his surprise, Helen gave a dissenting noise, wrinkling her nose, as if to say it might be, but she didn't think so herself. Classic cars were not a subject on which Jake expected to be challenged, least of all by a girl, but he knew Helen well enough by now to think twice before making any smart rejoinder.

– Too big, she said, squinting at it with her head to one side. And it's got four doors.

Jake realized that his initial identification had been based on a rather careless glance, for he now began to see the irregularities himself.

– What is it then?

– Judging by the fluting over the number plate and that medallion on the bumper, I'd say it's a Daimler.

This was delivered in such a considered way that Jake could only gape: recollections of sounding off about cars to Helen came back to him and made him blush. With a growing sense of admiration, he let his bike down onto the gravel, and trotted after her to look more closely.

Sure enough, the radiator grille was undoubtedly that of a Daimler, swept back in an arrogant curve, and topped off with the same distinctive fluting that Helen had drawn his attention to on the rear numberplate. But Alfa or Daimler, it was a beautiful piece of machinery. Their admiration was interrupted by a voice behind them.

– Just what do you think you are doing?

They turned to see a tall thin man in a light-colored suit and a panama hat looking sternly at them. Jake quailed under his stony gaze, but Helen was not in the least put out.

– We were admiring your car. My friend here thought it was an Alfa Romeo but I reckoned it was a Daimler. I seem to have been correct.

The man was clearly as nonplussed by this display of confident connoisseurship as Jake had been; his expression softened a little.

– You *are* a remarkable young lady. It is indeed a Daimler, a DQ 450 Majestic Major to be exact. Although I think your friend could be forgiven his mistake, since it carries a body by Touring of Milan, which is in fact modelled after the *Villa D'Este* Alfa which many reckon the most beautiful car of its day.

Jake surreptitiously stuck his tongue out at Helen. The man, granted an unexpected opportunity to talk about his possessions, continued in the manner of a lecturer

– I call it a DS450 Continental. Yes (he held up his hand as if begging their indulgence), I know the terminology is inexact, but the next available letter is T and I find DT has the wrong associations; whereas DS allows an exquisite French pun on her curvaceous lines: *Déesse*, goddess, if one may make such remarks before a lady in these dismal days of political correctness.

He smiled archly at Helen, who, to Jake's amazement,

actually simpered.

– And like any goddess, she is of course unique, added Langton.

More arch looks, more simpering from Helen. Then an impressive cut to business:

– I'm afraid that we are rather imposing on your time, Mr. Langton. It was not actually your car we came to see you about. We rather hoped that you might let us see your copy of Theophilus Bullen's *Architectura*.

If the man had been surprised before, it was nothing to what his face registered now: in quick succession it wore a look of astonishment, annoyance, then finally amused surrender.

– Young lady, you have me at a disadvantage. You evidently know who I am, but I cannot – forgive me – ever recall being introduced to you.

– My name is Helen De Havilland.

Langton's face clouded.

– Not Gerald De Havilland's girl? he said angrily.

– Oh dear, said Helen. Do you know Daddy at all?

– To my cost!

There was an uncomfortable silence; Jake felt that the ground they had gained was suddenly slipping away.

– It's not Helen's fault that her dad's a – well, that he's –

– Somewhat less than honest? said Langton coldly.

At this, Helen surprised them both by bursting into tears. For a second or two the Jake and Langton stood helpless, then both decided to move to comfort her, and got in each other's way, pantomime fashion; Jake thought it politic to give ground.

– My dear young lady, said Langton, I have been most terribly unfair.

Helen allowed herself to be folded to his bosom, from where she gave Jake a disconcerting wink.

– Won't you come inside?

And with his arm round Helen's shoulder, he led them into the house.

15

The Secret of the Alchemist

Fortified with tea and cakes, they sat in Mr. Langton's exquisite drawing room, looking out over a handsome expanse of lawn where peacocks moved ponderous and stately, throwing out occasional raucous cries.

– I am sorry to hear that your father is in trouble. It must be very distressing for you, although I fear it does not greatly surprise me. But tell me again about this painting, and what led you to me?

Between them, Jake and Helen recounted the whole tale, from the loss of the painting to the Inland Revenue website. At the mention of the Philosopher's Stone, Langton put on a sceptical air, but it seemed to Jake that this was a cover for his curiosity. He certainly asked Helen to repeat all the details about it, and thereafter he seemed much enlivened, although he maintained his languid exterior.

– You really are two most intrepid young people: I take my hat off to you. But what on earth you expect to find in Bullen I cannot guess. It is a rare book, certainly, but scarcely an occult or mysterious one.

– It has to be something on page twenty-four, said Helen with determination. It's got to be.

There was a hint of desperation in her insistence, Jake thought. The idea that he had hit on the solution at the first attempt now seemed a most unlikely chance. If it was that simple, wouldn't someone else have solved it long ago? On the other hand, he told himself, it is the simple solution that is often overlooked.

– Well, I see little point in speculating, said Langton. Let us go and take a look.

He rose, and went over to a section of shelves but instead of choosing a book he pressed against a hidden lever with his hand, and the whole section swung inwards like a door. Smiling, he beckoned them to follow.

The room they entered was peculiarly dim: the windows which ran along one side were hung with some sort of muslin curtain that filtered the light. There was an impression of clutter: the floor was occupied by two large museum cabinets, glass-topped, but with protective blinds drawn over them; here and there were individual stands with various objects on them. An enormous orrery stood on a low table in one corner; against another wall were all manner of time-pieces, some standing on the floor, some arranged on shelves and sideboards; a display cabinet on the wall held row upon row of pocket watches. An array of scientific instruments occupied the distant corner.

On the areas of the wall between cabinets were a great variety of mirrors, of all shapes and sizes, some very plain, others wonderfully ornate. The books were in an upright cabinet on their left, again fitted with protective blinds. Langton raised the blind, fished in his pocket for a tiny key, and took down a large rather untidy-looking book, which he laid open on a marble-topped table. Jake and Helen stood eagerly on either side as he turned the rough-edged pages with care. Despite his earlier doubts, Jake felt the excitement growing inside him like a bubble: they could be so near to the solution of the mystery.

However, page twenty-four was something of a disappointment, being a highly technical and rather dry discourse on the different methods of constructing walls.

Helen turned away almost at once, biting her lip. Jake pored over it with increasing desperation, determined to make something of it for Helen's sake. Mr. Langton, standing to one side, maintained a tactful silence.

– It must be something here, muttered Jake. It's got to be – we're just not seeing it.

He stared ferociously at the page as if he could force it to yield its secret by sheer power of gaze.

– I've got it! It's a code of some sort!

– If that is the case, then what is the key to cypher? said Langton. Does the picture give any indication of that?

– I don't know – we never looked for one.

– I think it is time we took another look at this picture of yours.

Stephen Langton set the projector up in another room which had a large blank wall and heavy curtains. With the flick of a switch the Alchemist was once more looking out at them across five centuries, his dark eyes and shrewd expression mocking them; meanwhile, behind his back, the immortal page-boy mocked him. Langton, seeing the picture for the first time, was fascinated. The scale of the projection made the tiniest detail very clear: he could easily read the title of Bullen, propped up on the shelf.

For some time he moved around in front of the picture, now diving in close to scrutinize some particular, now stepping back to consider the whole effect. From time to time he made noises, a mixture of grunts and whistles, interspersed with drumming his fingers on his fist or the table or striking them against his cheek. It was difficult to know what it meant exactly, but the general trend seemed hopeful. At length he stood still, his mouth covered with the tips of both hands, his head inclined, his eyes with an inward look, as if he was putting the final pieces of some complicated pattern of thought in place.

– We-ell, I think you are right in your basic interpretation of the picture: all the clues direct us to the page-boy as the real object of interest.

– What clues? asked Jake.

– Well, there are these tusks for a start. Look how they act as a frame for the foreground of the picture: but what are they doing there? Rather more than mere ornament, I think.

All three gazed abstractedly at the picture for a time; Jake felt completely at sea.

– I know, said Helen, suddenly brightening. I've just remembered something: it's the gate of dreams, isn't it?

– Very good, my dear, very good indeed. And they say the young have no education!

– Would someone mind letting me in on this? said Jake, querulously.

– The Greeks believed that there were two kinds of dreams, said Helen, ones that showed you the truth and ones that were lies. They said that the kingdom of sleep had two gates, one of ivory and one of horn – and the false dreams came out of the ivory gate.

– Bravo, my dear! So the artist is telling us not to believe what we see in the foreground of the picture, but to look elsewhere.

– In the mirror, said Jake, which is framed with horn!

– Precisely.

– And the Alchemist doesn't appear in the mirror, though the page-boy does. We thought that was just because he'd sold his soul to the Devil, said Jake, remembering with a shiver Pounce and the damned soul on the landing stage at Venice.

– It could mean that as well, of course, said Langton. The one interpretation does not preclude the other: but the main message is, as you correctly surmise, to pay attention to the page-boy.

– But what is he trying to tell us? asked Helen.

– Now there I think you have missed something: he indicates the book, which we have next door; and he is himself a page. But what is it that he has in his hand?

– A tray, said Jake.

– A plate, said Helen, at the same time.

– A plate, she repeated, it isn't *page* twenty-four, it's *plate* twenty-four!

– I'll fetch the book, shall I, Mr. Langton? said Jake.

– Please do. I need not ask you to be careful.

They turned on the lights, and while Jake scurried next door, Langton set up a large reading stand in front of the projected picture. The Alchemist, faded in the brilliance of the light, seemed like a captured ghost, frozen, awaiting his fate. Jake returned with the book, having somehow resisted the temptation to look at plate 24. Langton placed it on the reading stand, and found the page with due ceremony. They all stared hopefully at it for some time until Jake broke the silence:

– I don't know about you, but this doesn't tell me much more than the other one.

In the top third of the page was the drawing of a house, not a picture, but an architect's drawing: it showed the front elevation, but in section, as if the house had been sliced in half, so that you could see the arrangement of the rooms inside. The remainder of the page showed a regular pattern of shaded lines, squares and circles.

– Oh, right! said Jake at length. It's the plan view of the same house. The thick shaded lines are walls, and the squares and circles must be pillars. These breaks are doorways, and that funny lined bit is a set of steps, and those are staircases.

Helen, however, was in a world of her own; then all at once she gave a muffled yelp, and switched out the light.

The faded ghost of the Alchemist sprang to life on the wall.

– Hoy! said Jake, fumbling to switch on the little light on the reading stand, so that he could at least see the plate.

Helen had stationed herself at the right hand side of the projection. She gave an elaborate theatrical bow, fluttering her hands as if she was an impresario about to present the eighth wonder of the world. But instead of saying anything, she struck a pose not unlike that of the page-boy, stretching across with her arm, her finger pointed.

Slowly she began to trace a pattern on the picture, running her finger along a bit, then lifting it to run it along another bit. At times she simply stabbed at a single spot. Jake and Mr. Langton watched, mystified: she seemed to be tracing the outline of the mirror, running her finger along each part of the horn frame in turn.

Then Jake looked down at the book in front of him, and saw that the inexplicable framework of the mirror was an exact copy of the plan of the house in front of him. Mr. Langton, coming to the same realisation, nodded slowly.

– My God! he said. The page-boy's reflection, what is it pointing at?

Helen, still in dumb show, ran her finger along the page-boy's reflected arm until her finger and his indicated the same spot, a square of horn inlaid on the mirror.

– It's in the pillar, said Jake. Whatever it is, it's in that pillar!

– But where is that pillar, exactly? said Langton, going to open the curtains.

Daylight flooded into the room. Their host returned to the reading stand to consult the book more closely, leafing through the pages with a great deal more haste than he had shown before. At length, he clapped his hands.

– Here we are! Although many of the drawings in this

book are just that, this is the plan of an actual house, built by Bullen in the South of France. Would you like to hazard a guess who the client was?

– Ruggiero da Montefeltro? asked Helen.

– The Alchemist! said Jake.

– The very same.

A short time after, they were in the front room, Jake and Helen demolishing a mountain of ham sandwiches of their own manufacture, while Langton made a series of phone calls, starting in English, but progressing rapidly into French, Italian, German and Spanish; now he was back to French again. At length he put the phone down, strode over to the table with a satisfied look, wolfed three sandwiches and took a long pull on a bottle of beer. He seemed transformed from the rather fastidious, world-weary gentleman of an hour or so before.

– That last call was most fortunate. The young lady took me for a client's secretary, phoning to confirm arrangements on his behalf. She was so accommodating with the information she gave that I could not bear to disabuse her. The property has only recently been let, after standing empty for many years. The new tenant is going to take up residence in three days' time. His name is Aurelian Pounce.

Langton seemed well pleased with the electrifying effect this piece of news had on Jake and Helen.

– My dear young people, it appears that we must move quickly.

– We – ? said Jake and Helen simultaneously.

– You surely weren't thinking of excluding me from the adventure at this late stage? It would be too cruel entirely. Besides, I have too long denied myself the pleasure of a really good drive on the continent.

16

Travelling

At about the time that the beautiful pale green Daimler swept out of the drive at Silk House with Stephen Langton fresh and eager at the wheel and Jake and Helen snug in the luxury of green leather, polished walnut and deep pile Wilton carpet, a black Mercedes limousine with smoked glass windows pulled up in front of a handsome marble villa in the foothills of the Alps. The driver hastened to open the door to the rear compartment. A somewhat theatrical figure emerged, thickset and broadbuilt, a walking stick in his right hand, his face shaded with a broadbrimmed hat, his shoulders draped with what appeared to be an opera cloak, though it was light-colored, like the rest of his attire. The man was Aurelian Pounce.

He paused for a moment to confer with the tall driver, who inclined his head toward him as if straining to hear what he said. Then with an imperious gesture, he summoned with his stick a servant who had been hovering by the open door of the villa. The thickset man went into the house with a dainty, catlike step.

The driver reached into the front compartment of the Mercedes and operated something, so that the boot yawned slowly open like a great mouth. Then he went with the servant to the back of the car, and the two of them leaned into the gaping boot, emerging not with luggage, but what appeared at first glance to be a roll of carpet, although it was so heavy that they had trouble carrying it between them. It was, evidently, a body, wrapped in some material bound about with rope, but whether it was dead or merely unconscious was impossible to tell. They carried it with some difficulty into the house, then other servants came out to fetch in the more usual luggage.

Inside, Pounce sat at a plain deal table in the kitchen; he had not yet removed his hat or cloak. Before him, untouched, stood a glass of wine and a bowl of walnuts; beside him on the table his stick lay like a weapon; his broad hands were spread in front of him, rings glinting in the light. On the other side of the table Victor Orloc stood, distinctly nervous.

– You have secured the house?

– Yes, Sir. I confirmed the details this afternoon, although the babbling girl seemed to think she'd already told me.

Pounce gave him a sharp look, but said nothing.

– You have made no headway with the picture, I take it?

– Nothing positive, I fear. I can confirm that there are no secret compartments anywhere in the panel, and the x-rays show nothing remarkable under the surface of the picture. Dr. Angelo at the University is still working on the text in the book, and I have someone in England who is investigating the meaning of the phials – he is quite sure that the colors are significant. The problem seems to be that no one really knows what form the Philosopher's Stone took, though most reckon it to have been some sort of chemical compound. They are all at pains to stress that this sort of thing is slow, patient work.

Pounce struck the table with the flat of his hand, making the wine glass and the bowl tremble.

– Bah! What use have I got for slow, patient work? If

I'd wanted that kind of thing, I'd have become a furniture restorer! For those who are bold enough to take them, there are always shorter ways. If the picture won't tell us, then there is someone else who will.

– De Havilland?

This time Pounce struck the table with his stick, making Orloc jump.

– De Havilland knows nothing. He is a cheap confidence trickster and a fearful coward. If he had anything to tell us he would have spilled it even before we tortured him. If Ludovic at his most persuasive could get nothing from a wretch like that, then I am convinced there is nothing to get. All the same, we shall hang onto him. I may have a use for him yet.

– But if it is not De Havilland, then who?

Pounce looked up with a wolfish grin, showing all his teeth.

– Why, Ruggiero da Montefeltro, of course!

Orloc blanched.

– Losing your stomach for it, Victor? That is what the house is for – and what De Havilland is for, now.

– I'm not certain I follow you, Sir.

– Summoning spirits from the dead is not difficult, Victor, but there are certain rules that must be followed. They will not appear just anywhere, for a start. The place of death, for instance, where they made their exit from this world, is generally a propitious spot.

– Montefeltro died in that house?

– He certainly made his exit from it: whether he actually underwent the conventional formalities of dying is a matter for conjecture. The popular account has him carried living into Hell. Certainly no body was ever found.

Orloc clutched at the table.

– May I, may I sit down, Sir?

– I think you should, Victor – you don't look at all well. Of course having the right place is only part of it – there is also the question of price. Such transactions are not cheap. That is where De Havilland comes in.

Orloc made an inarticulate sound in his throat.

– A life for a life, Victor, that is the rule: if we are to summon Ruggiero da Montefeltro from beyond the grave to tell us his secret, then we must send someone back with him. At last an opportunity for Mr. De Havilland to do something useful with his life, don't you think?

Pleased to have settled his plans, Pounce dismissed the tiresome picture from his thoughts, sipped his wine, and helped himself to the walnuts.

*****

Jake and Helen had slept on the ferry from Dover to Calais, waking briefly to stumble down echoing metal gangways to the noise and glare of the car deck, then dozing off almost immediately, swathed in travelling blankets, as Stephen Langton threaded the Daimler through the dark streets of the town and out into the sleeping countryside beyond. It was full day, but still early, when they woke and breakfasted on delicious croissants and strong black coffee at a little village café. Then they were off again, powering down the long straight *routes nationales* between rows of poplars, through strangely empty landscapes. With a subdued murmur the Daimler loped along, the road slipping under its wheels at the rate of two miles a minute. At the wheel, Langton was relaxed and in excellent humor; not for ages had he enjoyed himself quite as much.

Jake's thoughts at first were all on the journey, thrilling to the strangeness of the French heartland, and the tale of incredible speed told by the big dials on the walnut dashboard, where the rev counter and speedometer needles rested for mile after mile well round to the right, with scarcely a flicker. Before him the great expanse of bonnet stretched between the curved swell of the wings, culminating in the fluted radiator from which the Daimler emblem rose like a gunsight.

However, after a time, his thoughts drifted back to the purpose of their journey. Could they really be going to find the Philosopher's Stone? The central secret of Alchemy that had made Ruggiero's fortune? He could scarcely believe that he was actually taking part in something so adventurous. He sensed that Langton beside him shared the same excitement: there was an almost boyish liveliness beneath his outer coolness.

Helen, curled up in the back seat, was thinking about her father. She would not allow herself to consider the possibility of failure. It was straightforward: they would find whatever it was that was in the pillar, they would do a deal with Pounce, and she would get her father back. How desperately she wanted that!

For all his fecklessness and neglect of her, the promises made then broken, the long periods without so much as a telephone call, Helen's dad represented something she could not do without. He was her entry into a different way of life, her escape from the stifling world of The Aunts. Whatever his faults, he had more life in his little finger than the entire congregation of her aunts and cousins. Maybe that's why Mum married him, she thought, feeling sympathy with her mother for the first time.

She could not share the excitement of Jake and Langton about what the pillar contained: to her it was a bargaining counter, nothing more. All she wanted was her father, alive and well.

*****

Gerald De Havilland was indeed alive, though he was far from well. Confined once more to the boot of the Mercedes, he was aware only that they were travelling at some speed, to judge from the noise of the tires on the road His mind swam in and out of consciousness against a background of constant pain. He was desperately thirsty and he could not recall when he had eaten last.

How long had he been tied up like this? His only gauge of time was when he was taken out of the boot, but he could no longer be sure how often that had happened. It was certainly more than twice, but was it three times or four? Even if it was four, what did that mean? They had stopped for some time on each occasion, so it might have been for the night; but then again they might have stopped four times in the space of a day.

What had happened when he was removed he did not care to think about. The driver, Ludovic, had an extensive range of methods for causing pain, and it had taken a long time to convince them that it was not heroic fortitude that kept him from talking but sheer ignorance – he had nothing of value to tell them. The squat dark man had questioned him, issuing dispassionate instructions to Ludovic when he felt that an answer was unsatisfactory, or might be amplified by inflicting a little more pain.

Always it was the same: what was the secret of the painting? How were they to obtain it? Had he communicated it to anyone else? Did he have contacts with a businessman in Romania who called himself Draganu? Sometimes the questions were direct, at other times they started in a more roundabout way, but always they led back to these things: the painting, the secret, the Romanian.

Perhaps for the first time in his life, when questioned he stuck to the truth: his interest in the painting had only ever been its monetary value. He had hung onto it because he thought Pounce was acting for a client, and he might get a better deal for himself if he cut out the middleman and did business on his own account. No, he had not succeeded in contacting anyone he thought might be that client. Yes, he had been to Bucharest, but not for a long time. No, he had not had any contacts with a man in Romania calling himself Draganu. He had only hoped to make a little money. That was all. He was sorry if he had caused any inconvenience.

In his more lucid periods, he began to consider whether they meant to kill him. They already had the painting; and he seemed to have convinced them at last that he had nothing to tell them, since they had given up asking. Yet if he was of no further use to them, why did they hang onto him? If they meant to kill him, why had they not already done it? On the other hand, why should they want to kill him? He might not be of any value to them, but he was scarcely a threat. Somewhere at the back of his mind the hope kept burning, like a tiny flame: the car would pull up, the boot would open, his bonds would be cut, and they would dump him. That was all he asked.

17
L'heure bleue

It was dusk in the valley when the Daimler slipped off the main road and began the winding ascent to the village of Forcalquier. Fireflies winked in hollows by the roadside; below them the valley unfolded in layers of blue shadow speckled with pinpoints of light. Stephen Langton, a seasoned international traveller, had negotiated accommodation for them before they left his sitting room in England, and they arrived in the little village square to find themselves expected. Jake and Helen sat in the square while Langton enjoyed a pastis on the hotel terrace overlooking them and the innkeeper's wife prepared their evening meal.

The lights were just coming on, but they shone feebly as yet, for up here in the hills it was still daylight enough for the old men across the way to finish their game of boules; over their heads an early bat dived and twisted among the insects drawn by the streetlight. From a great distance came the hollow sound of a sheepbell; in the dark of the valley below, a pig squealed. Everything was slowly merging into amethystine dusk.

– *L'heure bleue*, murmured Langton, surveying the tranquil scene.

I'd like it to stay like this forever, thought Helen, just this moment, stretched out, with no before and after. The simple perfection of everyday things struck her with peculiar force: everything, everything is beautiful, she thought. Only let me come through this all right and I'll never forget that, never take anything for granted again.

Jake was studying a map he had obtained from the innkeeper.

– Anyone fancy a walk before dinner? We should be able to see it from the end of the street.

There was no need to specify what "it" was. Helen stood up reluctantly and stretched.

– I suppose so. It's what we came for, after all.

Langton waved them on their way. The street was cobbled, with trees on either side festooned with strings of lights; those among the leaves were haloed with green. There was a rough stone trough with water running in it, and Helen dabbled her fingers in the refreshing liquid as she passed. Influenced by the magic of the evening, she slipped her arm round Jake's waist, and without saying anything, he put his arm round her shoulders.

The road sloped steadily downwards; at the foot of the hill, the trees and houses ended, and they found themselves at a junction with the main road which snaked its way in a series of hairpins up the side of the hill from the valley below. There was no sign of the house, which the map suggested should be at the end of the road. Then they crossed over and found themselves right on top of it. It backed onto the slope, some distance below them. The view they had of it was an almost perfect plan, an upside down version of that in Bullen's drawing. Jake felt he could pinpoint almost exactly where the pillar indicated by the page-boy was: it was toward the rear of the building, and over to the right.

Without saying anything, Helen tugged his arm and pointed. A little way along from them was a gate; running down from it was a haphazard wooden staircase, which clambered awkwardly down the slope then disappeared round the side of the house. As if unwilling to break the spell by speaking, she inclined her head toward it and raised her eyebrows interrogatively; Jake shrugged, turning his hands outward, as if to say that such a golden opportunity could not be ignored.

Still unspeaking, they stole down the steps, which seemed sound enough, although the paint was cracked and peeling. The hill slope was covered in rough scrub: long yellowing grass and short stunted trees and bushes. The stairs reached the house a bit below the level of the roof, then ran along the side of it on a flat gangway for a good distance.

Jake saw that there were unusually tall windows on this side, with rounded tops and colored leaded glass that reminded him of the stained glass windows in church. Although their tops were above the gangway, the lower edge was well below, and Jake pictured a pillared hall within. Helen was ahead of him, rapidly vanishing down the next flight. He hurried after her.

The steps came to an end some way short of the front of the building, leaving ten yards of white gravel path for them to scrunch along. The prospect of imminent exposure around the corner made the feeling of being in hostile territory very strong, and Jake had to resist the urge to press himself against the wall as if he were a commando raiding enemy HQ.

At the corner of the building Helen paused and looked round. She held up her hand to tell Jake to stop. Looking back at him, she signed toward the bushes, then crept stealthily across into their cover. Jake followed her.

Behind the bushes was a sort of green corridor, arched over by branches. Simply stepping into it took Jake back at once to his childhood, and games of hide-and-seek and dares played in other people's gardens in the long summer evenings. The bushes were very large and leafy, but the foliage was not dense, and it was easy to get a view of the house.

Parked in front of it was an ancient mushroom-colored Citroen van of the sort that looks like a corrugated iron pig. Between this venerable vehicle and the front door an equally venerable man in blue overalls and straw hat was shuttling to and fro, evidently readying the house for habitation. They watched him make several journeys, carrying various things into the house, seeming to get slower all the time.

Then he stopped halfway, set down the chair he was carrying, sat on it and produced a pipe from one pocket of the overalls and a much folded newspaper from another. He settled down as if to read and smoke, but it was clear within a few minutes that he would do neither for long: his head would sink gradually towards his chest, then jerk up again. At the third occurrence, he gave up, set down his paper and his pipe, folded his hands in his lap, and was soon asleep.

Helen pointed urgently to the open door, raising her eyebrows questioningly. Jake nodded, and they made their way back round to a point where a short dash across the gravel would take them to the stone steps. They tiptoed carefully across the path, ran softly up the steps and slipped in through the door.

The interior of the house was dark and cool. They were in a wide room with a grand staircase in front of them that climbed to a broad landing, where it divided into two and angled back to the upper floor. In the middle of the landing was an archway. Helen nodded toward it, and they went quietly up the wide staircase.

The arch led onto a balcony which commanded an excellent view of a great pillared hall that rose to the full height of the house; the floor was tiled in black and white in a complex pattern; along either side were the tall church-like windows they had seen from outside. About halfway up these windows, at the same height as the balcony they were on, a broad gallery ran round three sides of the hall. At the far end, opposite them, it was built out like a platform, rather in the style of a choir loft.

The pillars supported the gallery; they were all of different shapes and designs. The nearest to them on the left was like a giant bit of black twisted rope; the next to that was round, of reddish marble; the third was square – they both looked at this pillar, then at each other, eyes widening in excitement. Helen pointed down into the hall: Jake nodded his agreement.

They crept back down the stairs, doubling back at the foot through a short passageway with an open door at the far end. They padded through this door and into the great hall itself. Shafts of light from the tall windows angled through the dimness; at the far end, below the choirloft, the gloom was thick.

Everything about the place put Jake in mind of a church: it was strange to think of it as the lair of the Alchemist. Three pillars away from them lay an extraordinary secret, something that had lain hidden there for centuries, and in a very short time they were going to liberate it.

For the moment, Jake had forgotten all about Helen's father: his mind was entirely taken up with the discovery they were about to make. What would it be like? Because of the name, he imagined it as some kind of stone tablet, with inscriptions on it; or maybe it would be some kind of gemstone, like the crystal in the painting. He found that as they approached the pillar he was holding his breath.

The four sides of the pillar were clad in bronze, with

panels depicting scenes in low relief. Each panel was dominated by a figure that closely resembled Ruggiero himself, clad in long robes and wielding a staff in his left hand; the end of it was tipped with a twisting spiral, that might represent flame or light. Around him, on a much smaller scale, the panel writhed with a multitude of other figures, not all of them human, engaged in various activities.

Jake found he did not care to look too closely at the detail of these scenes, and gave his mind instead to the question of finding what was in the pillar. Squatting down at one corner, he tapped the panels to right and left: they gave out a dull, solid sound. Helen positioned herself on the other side and did the same, with the same result. The next layer up proved no different, but at the third, one of the panels Helen struck sounded hollow.

They studied it as closely as the poor light would allow, but could see no obvious fixings. The hollow-sounding portion was a square area in the center of the panel; the border around it sounded as solid as the others.

– Looks like we'll have to prize it off with something, like a chisel or a knife blade.

– Don't suppose you have one on you, said Helen.

– There might be something in the house.

– I'll have a look over here.

Jake was headed back toward the door, and Helen was half-way to the choirloft, when they heard the unmistakable sound of voices at the front of the house. Helen dashed for the darkest corner of the hall, beneath the choirloft; Jake decided to close the door first. He had just done so when he was startled by the sound of voices just a little way above his head. They must be on the balcony, he thought. He pressed himself back against the wall, but realized that he would have no cover at all if anyone came through the door. He began to edge his way along under the gallery, his back pressed against the wall, praying that he was out of sight.

The two figures were still talking, but their words were indistinct – it was not possible to tell even what language they spoke. Then one must have altered his position, and Jake heard a familiar light tenor voice say:

– This space will suit admirably. Go and give Victor a hand to bring him in.

By this time, Jake was nearly at the end of the gallery, and looking up he saw to his horror that he had a clear view of Pounce standing alone on the balcony. Fortunately he was looking the other way. With his heart thudding, Jake squeezed along the wall and took refuge behind a large crate that was stored in the space beneath the choirloft.

Of Helen he could see no sign, and he did not dare make a sound: from where he lay, he could not see the balcony, so had no idea if Pounce was still there. Cautiously, he adjusted his position so that he was looking out at the hall round the end of the crate. The overhang of the choirloft cut off his view of the balcony, but now at least he had a clear view of the door and most of the hall.

He was just wondering if he should venture farther out when the door opened and Pounce came through. He had a large gladstone bag in one hand and a heavy straight walking stick in the other – Jake was reminded at once of Ruggiero's staff in the bronze panels. Behind him came two men carrying a bundle between them. The one in front wore a chauffeur's uniform, with high polished boots up to his knee; the other was Orloc. Pounce led them through between the third and fourth pillars, but paid the square pillar no particular attention.

From the far side of the dark space under the choirloft,

Helen watched the approach of the little party. She guessed at once from the way they carried it that the wrapped bundle was a body, and reasoned that it must be her father. She held at bay the possibility that he might be dead. Why would they trouble to bring him with them if he was?

– Set him down over there.

He indicated a spot on Helen's side of the hall with his stick.

– No, farther away. We must keep a safe distance. And check that he's still breathing – he's not much use to us dead.

Helen held her breath as she watched the chauffeur kneel and bend his head low over the bundle.

– He's still with us, boss.

She breathed out again, but her relief was tempered by a dread of what Pounce was planning to do, and what part her father would play in it: the preparations looked ominous.

– Go and fetch the other things from the car. Victor, come over here.

Jake saw that Pounce had fitted something to the end of the staff, and was drawing some design on the floor with it. Orloc came to him and stood by, looking most uneasy.

– In the bag, Victor, you will find five silver bowls. Arrange them round the points of the pentacle.

Orloc delved in the bag and took out the bowls: one clattered to the ground, setting up a ringing echo that filled the hall.

– Steady, man, said Pounce. Anyone would think it was *you* we were going to sacrifice.

Orloc arranged the bowls around Pounce.

– Now, take the flask and fill each one. Don't spill any!

It was not clear whether Pounce meant his instructions strictly, or was indulging in some form of grim teasing.

Orloc certainly took them seriously, filling each bowl fearfully and with extreme caution. Meanwhile, Ludovic went back and forward, bringing first two large braziers, and then a number of sacks. When he had accumulated all that was required, Pounce directed him to the center of the hall, taking some care to get him in the position he wanted.

– There! That will do. Set up the braziers on either side and put in the coals. Have you finished there, Victor? Good. Now add a drop of this to each bowl – just a drop, mind!

He held out a little bottle, which Orloc took. He knelt by each bowl in turn and dispensed a glistening drop into it.

– The copper bowl on the stand, Ludovic – set it up in front of the braziers. No, damn you, not between them – in front – on this side! Now, take the bowl and get some of De Havilland's blood, but make sure you bind him up after. I don't want him bleeding to death before it's time: otherwise we'll have to offer them Victor here instead!

Orloc, uncertain of how seriously to take this threat, scurried across to help Ludovic. He hefted the body up by the shoulders, while the chauffeur produced a knife and opened a vein in the wrist. Blood trickled over the hand and into the bowl. After what seemed a long time, Ludovic grunted, and handed Orloc a length of white linen bandage. He lifted the bloody hand out of the bowl, which he took back and set on its stand, while Orloc bent to bind up the wound.

– Now come over here to me. Once I close the circle you must not step outside it, on peril of your lives. When I open the portal there may be certain, ah, manifestations. If you cannot look on such things without panicking, you had better close your eyes. Ludovic, you must hold my book.

They crowded together in the area Pounce had marked out: Pounce in the middle, Orloc behind him, Ludovic a little to one side holding a huge book open for Pounce to see. Pounce began a long incantation in a strange tongue, his voice rising and falling in a sing-song chant. He pointed the tip of his staff at each of the five silver bowls: as he did so, the contents of the bowl flared up in white flame, and a heavy fragrance filled the air. The air in the hall seemed to thicken and grow dark: the light in the bowls glowed brighter. Pounce raised his staff and pointed at the braziers, speaking a word of command: first one, then the other sprang into crackling life. The coals caught with amazing speed. Soon the braziers glowed fiery red, shooting up bright yellow flames and plumes of smoke that thickened the atmosphere still further.

Pounce ceased chanting, then spoke a clear pronouncement in an unknown language, after which he added:

– Let the portal appear!

He struck the ground with his staff and was answered with a deep rumble: the whole building shook as if in an earthquake. In the area between the braziers, the darkness intensified; a deep groaning, so deep it was felt as a vibration as much as heard, emanated from below; the ground itself began to heave and buckle, slowly at first, then with a fluid motion as if the floor was a blanket with bodies moving underneath it. The groaning reached an almost painful intensity, so that the whole building seemed to vibrate as if it would shake itself to pieces. Then the sound died away to a low gibbering and faded into silence.

All this time, the lights in the braziers and the bowls had continued to burn as before; around each of them a hazy halo formed as the air condensed into black fog. When the groaning ceased, the lights guttered, and the flames turned blue. A harsh whispering began: it seemed to be everywhere at once. The words were almost, but not quite intelligible; there was an occasional dry, mirthless laugh. Suddenly, the braziers flared up again, with an eerie green flame: the space between them now seemed filled with some solid object. Its outline at first was vague and rippling, like something viewed under water, but gradually it resolved into a huge arched door.

The whispering died away, and Pounce again struck his staff upon the ground.

– Let the portal be opened!

There was a sudden yammering on the other side of the door, as of many creatures clamoring to get out. A thin line of fire appeared down its center from top to bottom, and slowly broadened, spreading around the outline of the two halves of the door. It was like a furnace opening, but without the heat: the glare was blinding.

Then portions of the glare detached themselves and shot outwards, swooping over the floor and up into the smoky air. They seemed to have some bodily form, but it was inconstant, twisting and reforming all the time: there were glimpses of faces, limbs, and clutching hands. More and more of these writhing shapes issued into the hall, forming a luminous swarm in the upper air; meanwhile the glare in the doorway lessened until it was no more than a faint glow. Raising his arms, Pounce uttered a long invocation, then struck the ground a third time, saying:

– Roger Anscombe, called Ruggiero da Montefeltro, I summon you from beyond the grave.

The light in the doorway disappeared altogether: an icy breath passed into the hall. Then, from far, far back in the darkness a tiny seed of light appeared, growing as it approached until it assumed the size and proportion of a man. Slowly it condensed into definite form, and the Alchemist Ruggiero da Montefeltro stood once more in the great hall of his house. He looked much as he did in the portrait, but his face was weary and without hope. He peered about irritably. The swarm of writhing shapes above his head set up a sudden ululation. The darkness in the doorway seemed to deepen, as if something very large and dark had settled on the threshold. Now Pounce spoke again.

– Ruggiero da Montefeltro, the blood of a living man stands in that bowl. I bid you drink, and answer me.

With a movement of infinite weariness, the Alchemist approached the bowl, lifted it from its stand, and drank. He set the bowl down and stood listlessly, waiting.

– Ruggiero da Montefeltro, I charge you to reveal the secret of the picture.

The Alchemist nodded very slowly, as if to show that he had understood; he opened his mouth, but the only sounds that came were inarticulate, as if he had forgotten how to speak; then at last there were words, stammered in a hoarse, cracked voice, so slowly that there seemed an age between each one:

– It … is … in … the…p–p–p–

The final word gave him great difficulty, and he made clutching motions with his hand as if trying to pluck his meaning from the air; at last he managed to finish:

– In the pillar.

His arm fell back to his side as if the effort had greatly wearied him. Pounce wore a look of consternation. He struck the ground angrily with his staff.

– Speak again, I command you! What do you mean?

The Alchemist shook his head sadly.

– What pillar, damn you? Show me – I command you!

An angry murmur greeted this outburst; the darkness in the doorway seemed to shift, like some great creature moving on its haunches. With excruciating slowness, the Alchemist raised his arm and pointed with a trembling hand at the square pillar; then he passed his hand over his face in a gesture of weary hopelessness. All at once, some great force seized him from behind, and he was snatched bodily through the doorway as if he had been sucked into it. The swarm of shapes in the air, drawn back by the same force, swept after the Alchemist, clamoring as they went. In the heavy stillness that followed, the dark shape in the doorway began to emerge.

18

Forza, Ulisse!

Helen, crouched in the gloom in the far corner of the hall, had watched the proceedings with deepening despair and helplessness. She had guessed correctly that the burden Ludovic and Orloc carried must be her father, and though her heart rose when she heard he was still alive, it sank like a stone when Pounce said "sacrifice." She racked her brain for some solution, but with each minute that passed it was as if a layer of illusion was stripped away until at last she was alone with the knowledge that there was no way out. She had to bite her hand to stop from crying out at the bloodletting, and when the ritual got under way, she looked on in fascinated horror.

With the closing off of all hope, a settled calm overtook her. She had never been one to shrink from the consequences of her actions. It was one of her few rules in life, to accept whatever she brought on herself without complaint; but it troubled her that Jake should have to suffer too. She saw with painful clarity how she had drawn him into this; without her, he would be happy among his cousins in Naples. It now struck her as monstrously selfish, the way she had led him on, cajoled and tricked him into helping her, really for no better reason than that she was bored. And now, almost casually, she had led him to his death.

That they were going to die, she had not the least doubt: she saw now how foolish she had been to entertain notions of bargaining with Pounce. He had snuffed out Roberta Tardelli, and he would do the same to them. He would probably like people to beg for his mercy, but he would never think of giving it.

The thought of her own death did not distress her: she had often considered it. Death to her meant extinction; for all their encounters with Dante and Thomas Aquinas, she could not bring herself to believe that there was anything beyond death. Whatever happened, happened in this life; and when it was done, there was nothing. Her own life was not so joyful that she could grieve to abandon it. If her father was to die with her, she could not think that anyone else would be greatly affected by their disappearance.

But that Jake should be deprived of his life, and through her fault, distressed her. People would miss him: he had brothers and sisters, parents who loved him, a whole great family of which he was a part. His going would leave a hole in other people's lives.

Until now, despair had paralyzed her, but the thought that she had wronged Jake set her thinking again. It might be possible to do something: there was no escape where she was, but Jake was on the other side, with a clear run to the door. No one knew either of them was there: perhaps, if she chose her moment, she could create a diversion that would allow Jake to escape. Now that she had something she could try, her despair lifted. For her, it was just a matter of where she chose to stand – she would as soon die by her father as here in this corner; but for Jake, it could make all the difference in the world.

Timing was vital: if this was the last thing she was going to do in her life, she didn't want to make a mess of it.

Jake had watched Pounce's preparations with mounting fear and horror as it gradually dawned on him what he intended to do. Like Helen, he had assumed from the outset that the body was her father. When Ludovic bent over to check his breathing, he was ashamed to find himself thinking "let him be dead, let him be dead." He saw that if Helen's father was already dead, they had a better chance. No one knew they were here, and if they stayed hidden until it was all over, they could slip away unnoticed: he did not think that Pounce would stay long once he had what he came for. The main attraction of this plan for Jake was that it required no action from him. He could just stay where he was, hidden in the dark.

When Ludovic said Helen's father was still alive, Jake's heart sank. Now the situation became complicated: it was like it had been in Florence, when Helen had been in Orloc's shop. Could he simply do nothing? Was he not obliged to try and do something? When it became clear that Pounce intended to sacrifice De Havilland, Jake's horror deepened. The feeling that he must do something was countered by his clear sense that any action was hopeless: they were up against three grown men, to say nothing of whatever it was that Pounce was preparing to summon. The memory of Pounce's companion in Venice, cruel and merciless, came back to him.

Surely Helen would see that there was nothing he could do? The only sensible thing was to stay where he was: she could not reproach him for that. He had a sudden vivid image of Helen at some future date, not reproaching him, just gazing at him with a look of infinite sadness. *What am I supposed to do?* he thought angrily. Why can't Dante or Thomas Aquinas just turn up like they did before? There's nothing I can do.

You could intervene.

That's a stupid idea, he rebuked himself. What difference would that make?

You've no idea what difference it would make – but you know exactly what will happen if you do nothing.

And I know exactly what will happen if I do something: I'll just get myself killed, as well as Helen's father.

And Helen? What about her?

What about her? If she has any sense she'll see she can do nothing and stay where she is. It's up to her what she does. I can't do anything about it.

If your choice is between dying and abandoning your friends, then which is life and which is death?

That isn't fair, that's not what he meant at all. There would be no point in throwing my life away, it wouldn't do anyone any good.

He left a space in his thoughts for the answer to come, but his inner voice was silent.

What, nothing to say? No answer to that?

Silence.

No, I do not already know the answer.

I do not, I do not, I do not.

I won't think it.

As the horrors unfolded, Jake found himself unable to look away. He saw the weary figure of the Alchemist summoned and made to speak, and the darkness gather behind him in the doorway. Throughout it all, he repeated like a mantra: there would be no point, it would do no good.

The Alchemist vanished; the demons went yammering back into the dark. In the silence that followed, a still small voice within him said,

You cannot always wait for certainty – sometimes you can only act in hope.

Jake looked at the door: it was no more than thirty

yards. If he could reach that; if he could persuade them to follow –

He took off his jerkin, bundled it into a ball and stood up. A memory came back to him, of the theatre in Florence, and waiting in the wings – I'm playing Ulysses again, he thought, "putting forth upon the deep open sea with but one ship." He poised himself to run.

The dark thing came out of the portal like boiling smoke; it sent out long tendrils that whipped in the air and crawled across the floor. A foul stench came with it. The lights burned low and blue.

Helen stood calmly and walked toward her father. As she came out from under the shadow of the loft, she saw Jake dash out on the opposite side. How did he know to run? she wondered. Then she heard him shout:

– I have the secret! I have the secret!

And in that moment she understood: he was doing it for her. She felt her throat tighten and tears prick her eyes. She saw as in slow motion Pounce slew round, his face contorted with anger, and point his staff: a spurt of flame leapt from the end and travelled like a bolt at Jake. But just when it should have struck, he nimbly stepped aside with a movement of such gallant grace her heart leaped. The floor erupted in a fountain of fire.

– Run, Jake, run! *Forza Ulisse!*

At her shout, Pounce, staff poised for another stroke, jerked around, confusion on his face; the bolt miscarried, sizzling into the gallery. Jake was two strides nearer escape.

– Run, run! she yelled, *Forza, forza Ulisse!*

She saw Pounce's mouth distort in a curse as he turned angrily back on his escaping prey. His staff swung down in an arc: from its tip a jet of flame seared out.

When Jake broke cover, he had glimpsed a movement

on the far side of the hall and guessed it must be Helen; he yelled and saw Pounce turn toward him. The staff pointed like a gun: he saw the spurt of flame. At the same moment he sidestepped, and right in front of him the floor erupted in a blast of heat. He heard Helen's shout and sprang forward for the door, dodging a second time, but no shot came. He was almost level with the last pillar now, and for that instant he was Ulysses, rejoicing with his goal in sight – then it was as if he had slammed into a wall: every bone in his body jarred, and pain like fire ran up his arm. For a moment he seemed to soar, clean off the ground, then he slammed into the floor.

Helen saw the bolt of fire go wobbling through the air with what seemed painful slowness: it would surely never reach its fleet footed target. But Jake too had slowed – she saw the shift and flex of every muscle as his foot struck the ground, how his leg bent, tensed, then sent him springing forward like a deer. In mid-stride he was clean off the ground, and that was when the bolt struck him, twisting his graceful body in an ugly sprawl and dashing him to the ground.

She could not believe the injustice of it: that he should have come so close. Heedless of the blackness mounting like a wave before her, she stepped forward, straddling her father's body, and with arms outspread gave out a defiant, unbelieving yell:

– NO!

The darkness halted in front of her, a tide almost waist deep. Then slowly it began to draw together and concentrate into a column, a pillar of darkness rising above her. It began to rotate, slowly, as if there was a vortex at the heart of it.

Jake where he lay was beyond pain; he seemed disconnected from his body. He watched the darkness rise in front of Helen until it was a column towering over her that began to twist with terrible, slow power. From the main body of it, thin whip-like spirals shot out like clutching tendrils – then his sight deserted him. One moment he could still see her, arms outstretched, alone and defiant, the next his eyes were dazzled by a blaze of light and he could see nothing.

Pounce within his circle felt a powerful surge of pleasure as he smote the boy, then turned to annihilate the girl. The seething darkness was his will embodied, rushing toward her to engulf her: already its tendrils curled about her feet. He urged it upward with his hands and, as it rose, Pounce felt a foretaste of the power that would soon be his, when he knew at last the secret of the Alchemist.

Dark and serpentine, the column stood in menacing gyration before the girl, coiling its unending spiral to the ceiling: then slowly, slowly, it bent toward her.

This is death, thought Helen. It is not what I expected. She felt no fear; it was as if she floated on a sudden tide of warmth.

I have gone blind, thought Jake. But it isn't dark at all, it's dazzling, like looking at the sun. Or a range of mountains, layer on layer dissolved in light, marching back forever, rank on rank like soldiers. Or a crowd of people, a huge number impossible to count, and with such faces: so fierce, so bright, so joyous. Faces that he seemed to know: Dante, and Thomas Aquinas, and in the middle, right at the front – wasn't that Helen?

Pounce watched uncomprehending as behind the girl the walls dissolved to reveal a throng of people, a mighty host bright and terrible stretching as far as the eye could see. Before them he saw the darkness waver, suddenly baffled, like a column of smoke in the instant before it is blown away by a gust of clean air. He gave an incredulous

laugh, thinking: they lied to me, they told me there was
nothing else; and as the realization hit him, he felt an
immense surge of relief, as if even now a door he had
thought closed for ever had opened in front of him and all
he had to do was walk through it to escape unscathed. A
line from somewhere came into his mind

O, I'll leap up to my God – who pulls me down?

and he stepped out of the circle to embrace the shining
throng. But all at once the vision vanished, and the light.
Huge above him the great black column reared, and as he
knelt, imploring, at its foot, it toppled in a slow cascade, an
all-consuming avalanche of dark.

19

The Shadow in the Garden

The air was heavy with the scent of flowers. Peacocks paraded in the shimmering heat, fanning their superb tails, the blue-green of their throats jewel-like in the sun. Banked up on either side of the emerald lawn were masses of poppies, blue and yellow and red; old roses, cream and pink; blue delphiniums; irises, lupins and late-flowering clematis. The buddleia was alive with butterflies; nectar-heavy bees went their secret ways from bloom to bloom. A cat rolled intoxicated in a clump of purple-blue plants.

This is paradise, thought Helen dreamily. Paradise: a garden. The Garden of Eden. So where's the Tree? she mused. Two trees, it should be: the Tree of Knowledge and the Tree of Life, at the center of the Garden. The only tree in this garden was at the far end, an Italian Cypress. Dark and tapering, it struck an oddly somber note amid the riot of color, a monitory finger raised to warn or forbid, dense black against the flawless sapphire sky.

She turned to see a figure, clad in dazzling white: an angel. When she focused her eyes, it resolved itself into her father, carrying a silver tray with two tall drinks, each garnished with a slice of lime, ice tinkling faintly against the glass.

– You're awake, then? he said. You were dozing.

– Maybe I am still, said Helen. This is too good to be

real: it must be a dream.

She indicated the garden with a lazy sweep of her hand. Her father sipped his drink and made an appreciative face.

– Seems real enough to me, he said.

– But I might be dreaming you as well, said Helen.

He surprised her with a burst of song:

– Merrily, merrily, merrily, merrily, life is but a dream!

– You used to sing that to me when I was small.

She propped herself up on the cushions, shading her eyes with her hand.

– I used to think it was "life's a butter dream." I always wondered what that meant.

– It was your mother who told you that, said her father with a smile.

Helen sipped her drink, remembering.

– I thought I saw her, you know. I suppose I must have been dreaming. She was here in the garden, kneeling down by the flowerbed as if she was the gardener.

Her father smiled: his eyes had a faraway look, as if he was seeing her too, among the roses and delphiniums.

– Who knows what might happen? he said.

What indeed? thought Helen. It really did feel as if anything might, in this enchanted place: and so much had happened already.

She had no recollection of being taken from the house in France, and her memories of what had occurred there were so strange that she wondered if she had been given morphine or something in hospital afterward and had imagined it all.

But then they had let her see the newspaper. The photograph on the front page must have been taken from a helicopter: it showed all that was left of the villa Ruggiero.

It looked as if someone had ridden over it with a giant bicycle: there was a kind of trench that ran through it from front to back. The outline of the house was still clear: it seemed to have collapsed in on itself, imploded. The report said the building appeared to have been sucked down into the ground: it spoke of stones at the center being vitrified, fused together in a solid mass. There was some fanciful speculation about subterranean pockets of natural gas igniting, but it was evident no one had any real explanation to offer.

The destruction was so complete that it seemed impossible anyone could have survived; yet Helen and her father were virtually unscathed, though he was suffering from dehydration and bore signs of his torture at the hands of Ludovic. Only Jake, with a broken arm, had any serious injury. There was no trace of anyone else, though the black Mercedes parked near by was registered to one Aurelian Pounce, whom the authorities were anxious to locate, on account of the stolen painting found in the car.

And that was that. Jake, Helen and her father had spent a few days in a French hospital, enjoying a brief celebrity in the local press. Helen and Jake, his arm in a cast, had been pictured as "lucky English tourists," a misdescription that amused her but infuriated Jake. Her father had steered well clear of the publicity, as had Stephen Langton, who had done a lot of work behind the scenes to smooth things over, especially with Jake's parents. And now here she was in his garden, at Silk House, waiting for Jake to arrive.

Stephen Langton was fetching him from Glasgow in the Daimler Continental: they should be due any minute. It was a couple of weeks since they had seen each other. She wondered what they would talk about.

In the hospital in France, they had told everyone else

that they had no clear recollection of what had happened, which was readily accepted: the doctors nodded wisely and spoke of the effects of concussion.

But when they were alone, they had found themselves suddenly shy of discussing what they did remember. Perhaps it was because the shock was too recent; or perhaps, Helen now thought, neither of them wanted to have to believe it. As long as they made no attempt to confirm their stories with each other, they kept the possibility open that maybe, after all, it was just something they had imagined: the effect of concussion or drugs. And maybe that was the sensible thing to do: close it off, play it down, eventually forget about it.

She did feel that she had been party to something miraculous, but it had nothing to do with what happened in the house. It was the bargain she had made in the back of the car, as they drove through France – with herself? with God? – that she renounced all interest in the Alchemist's secret, if only she could have her father back, safe and sound. Her wish had been granted: her father had been restored to her, beyond all hope. Because deep down, ever since the moment she realised the flat in London was empty, she had feared he must be dead. And in exchange, the Alchemist's secret had been taken: it was lost to the world forever, melted into the rubble of Ruggiero's house.

What could it have been? It was an endless source of fantastic speculation – that was what she could discuss with Jake! Imagine if it really was the Philosopher's Stone: what might they have done with it? It was amazing to think what they had almost had in their grasp, but when she looked at her father, stretched out on the other chaise longue, hand behind his head, tall glass tilted to his lips, she could not regret its loss.

She heard a distant scrunch of gravel, the heavy clunk

of car doors, the sound of voices approaching. Jake and Langton appeared around the side of the house. She saw that Jake had discarded his sling: the heavy plaster cast had been replaced by a lightweight one, wrapped in green gauze. He smiled at her, a little bashfully, Helen thought. But after all, they had known one another barely a week, and that in a foreign country, in extraordinary circumstances. In the two weeks since, he would have been back to everyday reality, among his family and friends.

She began to wonder if theirs was a friendship that could survive ordinariness and, more to the point, separation: for what chances would they have to meet, with her in Switzerland and him in Glasgow? They would write, of course – but how often? And how long would they keep it up?

Langton was busying himself playing the host, with much old fashioned gallantry, particularly toward Helen. He's rather smitten with me, she mused. She wondered what he thought of the turn his life had taken, his comfortable old age invaded by two children dragging him into an improbable adventure. She had the impression he rather enjoyed it. He was certainly much more animated, more zestful than the languid old gentleman who had confronted them that day in the driveway.

– Champagne, I insist, Gerald. We must wean these young people from their foul addiction to sickly, sugar-laden soft drinks. One cannot celebrate life with them, no matter what the advertisers try to tell us.

He bustled away, singing disconnected snatches of *La vie en rose*.

– He's very lively, I must say, said Helen.

Her father smiled, in a knowing sort of way.

– He's an interesting man: we've been talking about things. He's very taken with you, you know.

– What's that supposed to mean?

But her father was already out of earshot, inside the house. She turned to Jake, still standing, a little bemused, looking at the garden.

– Hi!

– Hi! How are you?

– I'm fine. How's the arm?

He held it up for her inspection.

– New cast, I see.

– Yeah, it's a lot better than the other one, but it's still murder when you get an itch inside it.

– I'll bet!

They looked at the garden in silence for a time.

– Fantastic garden, said Jake.

– Isn't it?

– I love those peacocks!

Silence again. Helen strove for something to say. Then Langton returned, bearing a tray.

– Champagne, smoked salmon and caviar, he announced, setting it on the table.

He distributed the tall flutes of pale gold sparkling liquid. Helen's father emerged with silver ice buckets containing reserve supplies.

– In the shade, there, Gerald, I think. Here's your glass.

They were all standing now; beneath the surface jollity, Helen sensed a suppressed excitement. Her father and Stephen Langton were exchanging looks, like guilty schoolboys. Langton raised his glass.

– A toast! he said, exuberantly. To Life!

They raised their glasses, murmured in embarrassed response, sipped the champagne. It was deliciously dry and cool: Helen felt the bubbles filling her with exhilaration. Langton had his glass held aloft again.

– And to my new associate, curator of my collections

and general factotum.

Helen looked at her father, who was grinning broadly, but trying to seem modest and undeserving at the same time. Helen felt her own face expand in an image of his smile. Who knows what might happen, indeed? she thought. She drank her to father's health.

– Gerald, of course, will be staying here at Silk House, said Langton. Which brings me to my final toast: to you two young people, who must feel free to come and visit as often as you can. You will always be welcome here.

The glasses were raised to them: Jake and Helen toasted each other, exchanging looks and smiles. Helen was almost afraid to think how happy she was, as if it was a beautiful bubble that might vanish if she touched it. The air seemed to vibrate with possibilities, all sorts of things that she could put off thinking about now, for the pleasure of considering them later, one by one. She took in the glorious garden and the marvellous house with a sweeping gaze, then raised her glass in turn:

– And to Mr. Langton, for making all this possible!

– Hear, hear! said her father.

– Cheers! added Jake.

Langton bowed his head in acknowledgement, then beamed on them all. He turned to Helen's father and gave a slight nod.

– And now I think, Gerald, *la pièce de résistance.*

Her father slipped into the house; Langton busied himself opening another bottle of champagne.

– Drink up! Drink up! he encouraged them.

He came over and refilled their glasses. Helen wondered if he was not a little drunk: he seemed brimming with excitement; his eyes sparkled and his lips twitched as if he was trying to keep himself from laughing.

They had ended up in a semi-circle, facing the French

windows, like a reception party waiting for Gerald De Havilland to emerge.

– MEEE-YOK!

Behind them, a peacock gave its startling cry; her father stepped into the sunlight.

He was carrying a bundle wrapped in some dark material; he held it up in front of him, as if it was a solemn object, worthy of veneration. Helen felt a slow chill spread over her: dark foreboding clutched her heart.

Langton was talking; her father had set the bundle on the table and was unwrapping it.

– The pillar, you see, had split open, I suppose with its being hollow.

No, this is a nightmare, thought Helen: *I want it to stop.*

– It was the work of a moment to reach inside, in the darkness and confusion. Of course I had no idea if you, or anyone else, had already looked there.

The work of a moment. Helen had a sudden vivid recollection of where Jake had fallen, by the pillar closest to the door: had Stephen Langton passed him by in his eagerness to find the secret?

– From the remarkable condition of the wrappings, we judge the pillar to have been sealed in some way, though of course the cloth itself may have been impregnated with something.

Her father had unwrapped it now, to reveal a curious array of metal objects that glinted in the sunshine: they looked like nothing so much as the innards of an old clock.

– The metal is quite untarnished – if you look closely, many of the surfaces are finely engraved.

– Cool! said Jake, bending to see.

– It shouldn't be too difficult to reassemble: I thought that Gerald and I might make this our first project together. You too, of course, since it was you who discovered it!

– Cool! said Jake again. What d'you think, Helen?

But Helen was no longer there: she had turned her back on them, and was walking stiffly down the garden. There were tears in her eyes: she was raging inwardly. *Why did he have to do that?* It had all been so right, so perfect, until a moment ago: why could it not last? They were free, they had got clear, won through against all the odds, like a village that has miraculously escaped the plague – and then her father had come in with that dreadful bundle, like the stranger who all unwittingly brings in the fatally-infected bolt of cloth.

She could not rid herself of the conviction that she had somehow traded the Alchemist's secret for her father's life, and that if he involved himself with it again, the bargain would be rescinded. She wanted to turn and plead with them: *no, don't touch it, put it back, I made a promise, don't you see –*

She was at the end of the garden now: the Italian Cypress stood between her and the sun, ink-black and ominous. She turned around. The tree's shadow made a dark path across the brilliant lawn, almost to the edge of the terrace where the three of them sat, poring intently over what lay on the table. They were still in sunlight: the shadow had not reached them yet; but Helen knew, with a sinking of her heart, that it was only a matter of time.

The End

(for the moment)

The adventure of the magical machine continues.

Be sure to watch for Part 2 of

The Fate of the Stone:

The Stone of Sorrow,

to appear all in good time.

Excerpt from
The Stone of Sorrow

The little green car dropped into first gear to round the hairpin then labored harshly up the return slope, climbing higher and higher into the Carpathian mountains. The driver, a small man with a scrubby brown beard, was perched on the edge of his seat, the steering wheel pulled almost to his chest, head straining forward as if it was thick fog he drove through and not this bright, pleasant morning tinged with frost. On the seat beside him was a large, old-fashioned doctor's bag. Presently the road reached an ancient narrow bridge, hump-backed and ill-suited to motor traffic; the little car groaned its way over at walking pace then toiled up the short slope to the village.

The villagers would be there already, just over the rise, crowded into the cobbled space before the inn, drawn by the sound of the approaching car. He could picture them pressing forward, eager to flag the stranger down, to warn him that the road beyond was impassable – blocked by fallen trees or rocks, or else a broken bridge, or it had subsided. Maybe all of these at once, such was their anxiety to prevent further progress, to draw the stranger in to enjoy their simple hospitality, then presently send him back down the valley laden with their blessings (including plastic bottles of the fierce local spirit), puzzled but delighted by the warmth of their welcome and their concern for his well-being.

As the green car breasted the rise, he saw them move into the road, then check themselves as they recognized first the car, then its driver; he saw them draw back as one, the look on their faces changing from eager anxiety to fear. Several crossed themselves; others held their hands downwards with the middle two fingers curled into the palm, the outer two pointing to the ground, the ancient sign to ward off the evil eye. The little man sneered as he rattled past them without slackening his already modest speed. Superstitious fools!

But as the car climbed out of the deep cleft of the valley into the stony heights above he felt his own fear grow like a cancer in his stomach, spreading through his whole body. A huge feeling of oppression weighed on him, crushing him down, almost a physical force – indeed, the little car seemed to feel it too, gasping to a halt just below the brow of the final hill, where it rested for a time as if it too must gather all its small strength for the final push. The man sat, rigid and sweating, for some minutes before he felt able to continue.

The car emerged onto a flat stony plateau ringed by craggy hills. The road – now little more than a track – ran straight ahead to its end, a distinctive spur of rock rising up from the hill slope and surmounted by a squat turret. Such maps as marked it called it the Warlock's Tower, though its local names were more graphic and obscene. The little man, jaws clenched, hunched behind the wheel as if for protection, forced the car on the last couple of miles. When he killed the engine he was assailed on all sides by an immense sense of desolation: not a bird called; not so much as a blade of grass seemed alive in this stony wilderness. He took his bag and eased himself reluctantly out of the car, closing the door with exaggerated care, as if he feared to break the windy silence.

The spur of rock had long ago been burrowed into, hollowed out to make a dwelling place of sorts: a heavy wooden door was set into the foot of it. Before this the little doctor stood, bag held defensively at his chest, making a conscious effort to stand upright. Presently, the door swung open; the doctor stepped through, and it closed behind him, without human agency. The hall within was vaulted, the walls of bare stone, unadorned, the floor stone flags. The temperature was several degrees lower than outside.

The man shivered, but not from the cold. Though a frequent visitor here of late, he could not free himself from the feeling he had on entering of being stripped naked under the gaze of a pitiless scrutiny. He took refuge in his own insignificance: he knew himself to be an unimportant man, not very clever, by no means brave, protected by his abject fear from any suspicion of treachery, a mere insect in fact, but useful, for a time, so likely to be tolerated. He steeled himself for the great effort of mounting the stair that rose before him, carved from the living rock.

The turret room was in darkness, the air heavy with a fragrance that could not wholly conceal a less pleasant odor of decay. The atmosphere was close, almost stifling.

– Close the door, a voice breathed.

– I must have light, said the man pathetically. I cannot see.

– Stand still until yours eyes adjust. It is not wholly dark.

The man stood for what seemed a long time. The only sound in the room, apart from the thud of his own heart, which seemed very loud to him, was a hoarse, slow breathing, punctuated by the sputter and hiss of what he took to be an incense burner. Gradually the utter blackness gave way to a brown gloom, in which he could make out the shapes of what was in the room. Finally he could see well enough to discern the great mass of a man propped up among cushions in the middle of the floor. He advanced toward him and knelt at his side, opening his bag.

    – I need to travel, the voice breathed.

    – Far?

    – Bucharest. Istanbul, perhaps.

    – I wouldn't advise it.

    – I didn't ask you for advice. Can you make it possible?

    – At a cost.

A rumble from the seated man made him correct himself hastily.

    – To your health, I meant. Whatever I do to arrest the, ah, process will accelerate it later.

    – How long can you give me?

    – That depends. The greater the physical demands you make, the shorter the time and the severer the reaction. If you are content with a wheelchair, then I could guarantee a fortnight, maybe a month. The stress of travelling is hard to calculate.

    – So short a time, said the seated man, but as he seemed to be speaking to himself, the other made no reply.

    – This reaction – what form will it take?

    – Again, that depends. You have a choice between mind and body. The body might be sustained for an indefinite time at the expense of mental function. If you wish to keep your mind unimpaired then the body will fail more rapidly, but the mind will go too in the end, or at least your faculties will fail you – speech first, then sight. Your hearing should be last to go.

    – Could I write?

    – I doubt it: creeping paralysis will be the first symptom of reaction, with a general loss of feeling in the limbs.

– But my mind would remain clear to the last?

The man shrugged.

– I think so. This goes beyond the limits of my knowledge. All I can do is borrow time, at the expense of something else.

The seated man made a curious rasping sound that might have been laughter.

– Don't talk to me about borrowing time. I must travel, and my mind must remain clear. Do whatever is necessary for that and you will be well rewarded.

For a time the doctor busied himself with the contents of his bag, aided by a small pen flashlight. He drew out a number of syringes, made various injections; his patient sat impassive as a statue throughout. The doctor forced himself to concentrate on what he was doing, not for fear of doing it wrong, but of letting his mind wander.

Once before in doing this the thought had come to him that his monstrous patient was at his mercy, that by a simple switch of syringes he could free himself from this terrifying bondage. But no sooner had the idea formed than he found himself paralyzed, then visited by an excruciating cramp that slowly bent him double. As he writhed on the floor, a voice that seemed inside his head whispered, *I can hear what you are thinking*. Since then, he had been careful to keep his mind wholly on the task at hand.

When the round of injections was complete, the doctor stowed his gear in his bag as slowly as he could, though every nerve in his body was straining to get him out of that room, away from this accursed tower. After what seemed an age, he stood up to take his leave, backing awkwardly toward the door, his stomach in turmoil: it was all he could do to stop himself from running headlong. In the doorway he found that he was unable to move.

– Wait, whispered the voice. I did not say you could

go. Further service is required of you.

He opened his mouth to plead, but no words came. His body no longer obeyed his will: with no motivation on his part, he felt himself turn and lurch heavily back into the room.

At dusk a huge old-fashioned car, travelling at a steady and determined speed, rumbled through the village lower on in the valley, laying down behind it a blanket of blue-grey smoke. Its somber hue and curtained rear compartment gave it a more than passing resemblance to a hearse, which given its cargo it had certainly the right to claim. The beams of its enormous headlights betrayed its coming a long way off, and by the time it had reached the village all the houses were shuttered and dark: not a soul lingered outside as the big car sped by with a curious rhythmic hissing. It squeezed over the little bridge with a grating sound as its long chassis grounded briefly on the crown of the arch, sending out a shower of sparks, then lumbered on down the valley, its single red tail light glowing like a malevolent eye in the gathering night.